I0823619

OCTOBER SHADOWS

OCTOBER SHADOWS

CLASSIC GHOST STORIES FOR HALLOWEEN

SELECTED
AND ILLUSTRATED
BY
JOHN A. RICE

ABBEVILLE PRESS
New York London

CONTENTS

INTRODUCTION

Autumn has always been my favorite time of year. The air itself becomes as thin and crisp as the leaves that litter the ground. The sunlight takes on a special quality, casting everything in a golden glow—like a candle burning brightest before it gutters out, or the final flash of a falling star. These last weeks before winter make us shiver and pull our coat collars tighter, while around us, the season offers quiet meditations on life cycles, abundance, desolation, and our own mortality. Curiously, it reminds us to live.

Halloween is the moment in the year when we are invited to toe the line between this world and the next, the living and the dead, the known and the unknown, the safe and the dangerous. It is this liminal space—the place where boundaries blur—that I find compelling. Perhaps I choose to dwell there more than most. The stories in this collection emerge from that place, each one offering a glimpse under the shadowy veil of the season.

Here, I have gathered a varied collection of ghostly tales, drawing from a diverse range of authors and narrators, from nobility to housemaids to hard-laboring seamen. Spanning September to December, the stories take readers from sunlit New England forests to desolate English heaths and frigid Arctic seas. It felt essential to include works that expand our perceptions of the supernatural, such as Elizabeth Stuart Phelps's "Since I Died," which presents a surprisingly frank portrayal of same-sex love, rare for its time, and Paul Laurence Dunbar's "The Haunted Oak," a poem that offers a strikingly different perspective on mortality and nature as the anthology's coda.

The artwork in this collection was created with the same reverence for the season and its mysteries. Each piece was inspired by the natural patterns, colors, and creases of autumn leaves, using their delicate veins and textures as a foundation for the imagery. At the beginning of each story, the artwork is presented in daylight, while its counterpart at the story's end is backlit by candlelight, revealing the leaf's true colors, paper lantern style. I am fascinated by this phenomenon—the way the hidden lattice of a leaf's veins and its deepest hues are only fully visible in the glow of a flame. Sometimes, these nocturnal versions unveil more than what originally meets the eye: truth revealed in shadow.

Though the leaves may appear real, they are in fact made of a canvas-like florist's cloth. When I first shared the artwork with friends, nearly everyone asked the same question: *Are these real leaves?* Their colors, textures, and veining are remarkably lifelike, but I chose them for more than just their appearance. My mother, a lifelong florist, had kept them in her basement studio for years. When I told her about this project, she pulled them from her collection—and I knew immediately they were perfect. Not only did they carry personal significance, but they also offered the durability and longevity I needed for a body of artwork I hoped would last.

More than anything, I hope this collection conjures the feeling of walking alone on a brisk autumn night, your feet crunching over fallen leaves while jack-o'-lanterns grin at you from porch stoops. I hope it roots you in a sense of time, place, and tradition, reminding you to look at the world with wonder and curiosity as the days grow short and the shadows lengthen. Each story here explores this transitional time in nature, a reflection of our own impermanence—the thin line between life, death, and whatever lies beyond.

—J.A.R.

I

NATHANIEL HAWTHORNE

Young Goodman Brown

1835

Young Goodman Brown came forth at sunset, into the street of Salem village, but put his head back, after crossing the threshold, to exchange a parting kiss with his young wife. And Faith, as the wife was aptly named, thrust her own pretty head into the street, letting the wind play with the pink ribbons of her cap, while she called to Goodman Brown.

"Dearest heart," whispered she, softly and rather sadly, when her lips were close to his ear, "prithee, put off your journey until sunrise, and sleep in your own bed to-night. A lone woman is troubled with such dreams and such thoughts, that she's afeard of herself, sometimes. Pray, tarry with me this night, dear husband, of all nights in the year!"

"My love and my Faith," replied young Goodman Brown, "of all nights in the year, this one night must I tarry away from thee. My journey, as thou callest it, forth and back again, must needs be done 'twixt now and sunrise. What, my sweet, pretty wife, dost thou doubt me already, and we but three months married!"

"Then God bless you!" said Faith with the pink ribbons, "and may you find all well, when you come back."

"Amen!" cried Goodman Brown. "Say thy prayers, dear Faith, and go to bed at dusk, and no harm will come to thee."

So they parted; and the young man pursued his way, until, being about to turn the corner by the meeting-house, he looked back and saw the head of Faith still peeping after him, with a melancholy air, in spite of her pink ribbons.

"Poor little Faith!" thought he, for his heart smote him. "What a wretch am I, to leave her on such an errand! She talks of dreams, too. Methought, as she spoke, there was trouble in her face, as if a dream had warned her what work is to be done to-night. But no, no! 't would kill her to think it. Well; she's a blessed angel on earth; and after this one night, I'll cling to her skirts and follow her to Heaven."

With this excellent resolve for the future, Goodman Brown felt himself justified in making more haste on his present evil purpose. He had taken a dreary road, darkened by all the gloomiest trees of the forest, which barely stood aside to let the narrow path creep through, and closed immediately behind. It was all as lonely as could be; and there is this peculiarity in such a solitude, that the traveler knows not who may be concealed by the innumerable trunks and the thick boughs overhead; so that, with lonely footsteps, he may yet be passing through an unseen multitude.

"There may be a devilish Indian behind every tree," said Goodman Brown to himself; and he glanced fearfully behind him, as he added, "What if the devil himself should be at my very elbow!"

His head being turned back, he passed a crook of the road, and looking forward again, beheld the figure of a man, in grave and decent attire, seated at the foot of an old tree. He arose at Goodman Brown's approach, and walked onward, side by side with him.

"You are late, Goodman Brown," said he. "The clock of the Old South was striking, as I came through Boston; and that is full fifteen minutes agone."

"Faith kept me back awhile," replied the young man, with a tremor in his voice, caused by the sudden appearance of his companion, though not wholly unexpected.

It was now deep dusk in the forest, and deepest in that part of it where these two were journeying. As nearly as could be discerned, the second traveler was about fifty years old, apparently in the same rank of life as Goodman Brown, and bearing a considerable resemblance to him, though perhaps more in expression than features. Still, they might have been taken for father and son. And yet, though the elder person was as simply clad as the younger, and as simple in manner too, he had an indescribable air of one who knew the world, and would not have felt abashed at the governor's dinner-table, or in King William's court, were it possible that his affairs should call him thither. But the only thing about him that could be fixed upon as remarkable, was his staff, which bore the likeness of a great black snake, so curiously wrought, that it might almost be seen to twist and wriggle itself like a living serpent. This, of course, must have been an ocular deception, assisted by the uncertain light.

"Come, Goodman Brown!" cried his fellow-traveler, "this is a dull pace for the beginning of a journey. Take my staff, if you are so soon weary."

"Friend," said the other, exchanging his slow pace for a full stop, "having kept covenant by meeting thee here, it is my purpose now to return whence I came. I have scruples, touching the matter thou wot'st of."

"Sayest thou so?" replied he of the serpent, smiling apart. "Let us walk on, nevertheless, reasoning as we go, and if I convince thee not, thou shalt turn back. We are but a little way in the forest, yet."

"Too far, too far!" exclaimed the goodman, unconsciously resuming his walk. "My father never went into the woods on such an errand, nor his father before him. We have been a race of honest men and good Christians, since the days of the martyrs. And shall I be the first of the name of Brown that ever took this path and kept—— "

"Such company, thou wouldst say," observed the elder person, interrupting his pause. "Well said, Goodman Brown! I have been as well acquainted with your family as with ever a one among the Puritans; and that's no trifle to say. I helped your grandfather, the constable, when he lashed the Quaker woman so smartly through the streets of Salem. And it was I that brought your father a pitch-pine knot, kindled at my own hearth, to set fire to an Indian village, in King Philip's war. They were my good friends, both; and many a pleasant walk have we had along this path, and returned merrily after midnight. I would fain be friends with you, for their sake."

"If it be as thou sayest," replied Goodman Brown, "I marvel they never spoke of these matters. Or, verily, I marvel not, seeing that the least rumor of the sort would have driven them from New England. We are a people of prayer, and good works to boot, and abide no such wickedness."

"Wickedness or not," said the traveler with the twisted staff, "I have a very general acquaintance here in New England. The deacons of many a church have drunk the communion wine with me; the selectmen, of divers towns, make me their chairman; and a majority of the Great and General Court are firm supporters of my interest. The governor and I, too—but these are state secrets."

"Can this be so!" cried Goodman Brown, with a stare of amazement at his undisturbed companion. "Howbeit, I have nothing to do with the governor and council; they have their own ways, and are no rule for a simple husbandman like me. But, were I to go on with thee, how should I meet the eye of that good old man, our minister, at Salem village? Oh, his voice would make me tremble, both Sabbath-day and lecture-day!"

Thus far, the elder traveler had listened with due gravity, but now burst into a fit of irrepressible mirth, shaking himself so violently, that his snakelike staff actually seemed to wriggle in sympathy.

"Ha! ha! ha!" shouted he, again and again; then composing himself, "Well, go on, Goodman Brown, go on; but, prithee, don't kill me with laughing!"

"Well, then, to end the matter at once," said Goodman Brown, considerably nettled, "there is my wife, Faith. It would break her dear little heart; and I'd rather break my own!"

"Nay, if that be the case," answered the other, "e'en go thy ways, Goodman Brown. I would not, for twenty old women like the one hobbling before us, that Faith should come to any harm."

As he spoke, he pointed his staff at a female figure on the path, in whom Goodman Brown recognized a very pious and exemplary dame, who had taught him his catechism in youth, and was still his moral and spiritual adviser, jointly with the minister and Deacon Gookin.

"A marvel, truly, that Goody Cloyse should be so far in the wilderness, at nightfall!" said he. "But, with your leave, friend, I shall take a cut through the woods, until we have left this Christian woman behind. Being a stranger to you, she might ask whom I was consorting with, and whither I was going."

"Be it so," said his fellow-traveler. "Betake you to the woods, and let me keep the path."

Accordingly, the young man turned aside, but took care to watch his companion, who advanced softly along the road, until he had come within a staff's length of the old dame. She, meanwhile, was making the best of her way, with singular speed for so aged a woman, and mumbling some indistinct words, a prayer, doubtless, as she went. The traveler put forth his staff, and touched her withered neck with what seemed the serpent's tail.

"The devil!" screamed the pious old lady.

"Then Goody Cloyse knows her old friend?" observed the traveler, confronting her, and leaning on his writhing stick.

"Ah, forsooth, and is it your worship, indeed?" cried the good dame. "Yea, truly is it, and in the very image of my old gossip, Goodman Brown, the grandfather of the silly fellow that now is. But, would your worship believe it? my broomstick hath strangely disappeared, stolen, as I suspect, by that unhanged witch, Goody Cory, and that, too, when I was all anointed with the juice of smallage and cinque-foil and wolf's-bane——"

"Mingled with fine wheat and the fat of a newborn babe," said the shape of old Goodman Brown.

"Ah, your worship knows the recipe," cried the old lady, cackling aloud. "So, as I was saying, being all ready for the meeting, and no horse to ride on, I made up my mind to foot it; for they tell me there is a nice young man to be taken into communion to-night. But now your good worship will lend me your arm, and we shall be there in a twinkling."

"That can hardly be," answered her friend. "I may not spare you my arm, Goody Cloyse, but here is my staff, if you will."

So saying, he threw it down at her feet, where, perhaps, it assumed life, being one of the rods which its owner had formerly lent to the Egyptian Magi. Of this fact, however, Goodman Brown could not take cognizance. He had cast up his eyes in astonishment, and looking down again, beheld neither Goody Cloyse nor the serpentine staff, but his fellow-traveler alone, who waited for him as calmly as if nothing had happened.

"That old woman taught me my catechism!" said the young man; and there was a world of meaning in this simple comment.

They continued to walk onward, while the elder traveler exhorted his companion to make good speed and persevere in the path, discoursing so aptly, that his arguments seemed rather to spring up in the bosom of his auditor, than to be suggested by himself. As they went he plucked a branch of maple, to serve for a walking-stick, and began to strip it of the twigs and little boughs, which were wet with evening dew. The moment his fingers touched them, they became strangely withered and dried up, as with a week's sunshine. Thus the pair proceeded, at a good free pace, until suddenly, in a gloomy hollow of the road, Goodman Brown sat himself down on the stump of a tree, and refused to go any farther.

"Friend," said he, stubbornly, "my mind is made up. Not another step will I budge on this errand. What if a wretched old woman do choose to go to the devil, when I thought she was going to Heaven! Is that any reason why I should quit my dear Faith, and go after her?"

"You will think better of this by-and-by," said his acquaintance, composedly. "Sit here and rest yourself awhile; and when you feel like moving again, there is my staff to help you along."

Without more words, he threw his companion the maple stick, and was as speedily out of sight as if he had vanished into the deepening gloom. The young man sat a few moments by the roadside, applauding himself greatly, and thinking with how clear a conscience he should meet the minister, in his morning walk, nor shrink from the eye of good old Deacon Gookin. And what calm sleep would be his, that very night, which was to have been spent so wickedly, but purely and sweetly now, in the arms of Faith! Amidst these pleasant and praiseworthy meditations, Goodman Brown heard the tramp of horses along the road, and deemed it advisable to conceal himself within the verge of the forest, conscious of the guilty purpose that had brought him thither, though now so happily turned from it.

On came the hoof-tramps and the voices of the riders, two grave old voices, conversing soberly as they drew near. These mingled sounds appeared to pass along the road, within a few yards of the young man's hiding-place; but owing, doubtless, to the depth of the gloom, at that particular spot, neither the travelers nor their steeds were visible. Though their figures brushed the small boughs by the wayside, it could not be seen that they intercepted, even for a moment, the faint gleam from the strip of bright sky, athwart which they must have passed. Goodman Brown alternately crouched and stood on tiptoe, pulling aside the branches, and thrusting forth his head as far as he durst, without discerning so much as a shadow. It vexed him the more, because he could have sworn, were such a thing possible, that he recognized the voices of the minister and Deacon Gookin, jogging along quietly, as they were wont to do, when bound to some ordination or ecclesiastical council. While yet within hearing, one of the riders stopped to pluck a switch.

"Of the two, reverend Sir," said the voice like the deacon's, "I had rather miss an ordination dinner than to-night's meeting. They tell me that some of our community are to be here from Falmouth and beyond, and others from Connecticut and Rhode Island; besides several of the Indian powwows, who, after their fashion, know almost as much deviltry as the best of us. Moreover, there is a goodly young woman to be taken into communion."

"Mighty well, Deacon Gookin!" replied the solemn old tones of the minister. "Spur up, or we shall be late. Nothing can be done, you know, until I get on the ground."

The hooves clattered again, and the voices, talking so strangely in the empty air, passed on through the forest, where no church had ever been gathered, nor solitary Christian prayed. Whither, then, could these holy men be journeying, so deep into the heathen wilderness? Young Goodman Brown caught hold of a tree, for support, being ready to sink down on the ground, faint and over-burthened with the heavy sickness of his heart. He looked up to the sky, doubting whether there really was a Heaven above him. Yet, there was the blue arch, and the stars brightening in it.

"With Heaven above, and Faith below, I will yet stand firm against the devil!" cried Goodman Brown.

While he still gazed upward, into the deep arch of the firmament, and had lifted his hands to pray, a cloud, though no wind was stirring, hurried across the zenith, and hid the brightening stars. The blue sky was still visible, except directly overhead, where this black mass of cloud was sweeping swiftly northward. Aloft in the air, as if from the depths of the cloud, came a confused and doubtful sound of voices. Once, the listener fancied that he could distinguish the accents of town's-people of his own, men and women, both pious and ungodly, many of whom he had met at the communion-table, and had seen others rioting at the tavern. The next moment, so indistinct were the sounds, he doubted whether he had heard aught but the murmur of the old forest, whispering without a wind. Then came a stronger swell of those familiar tones, heard daily in the sunshine, at Salem village, but never, until now, from a cloud of night. There was one voice, of a young woman, uttering lamentations, yet with an uncertain sorrow, and entreating for some favor, which, perhaps, it would grieve her to obtain. And all the unseen multitude, both saints and sinners, seemed to encourage her onward.

"Faith!" shouted Goodman Brown, in a voice of agony and desperation; and the echoes of the forest mocked him, crying—"Faith! Faith!" as if bewildered wretches were seeking her, all through the wilderness.

The cry of grief, rage, and terror, was yet piercing the night, when the unhappy husband held his breath for a response. There was a scream, drowned immediately in a louder murmur of voices fading into far-off laughter, as the dark cloud swept away, leaving the clear and silent sky above Goodman Brown. But something fluttered lightly down through the air, and caught on the branch of a tree. The young man seized it and beheld a pink ribbon.

"My Faith is gone!" cried he, after one stupefied moment. "There is no good on earth, and sin is but a name. Come, devil! for to thee is this world given."

And maddened with despair, so that he laughed loud and long, did Goodman Brown grasp his staff and set forth again, at such a rate, that he seemed to fly along the forest path, rather than to walk or run. The road grew wilder and drearier, and more faintly traced, and vanished at length, leaving him in the heart of the dark wilderness, still rushing onward, with the instinct that guides mortal man to evil. The whole forest was peopled with frightful sounds; the creaking of the trees, the howling of wild beasts, and the yell of Indians; while, sometimes, the wind tolled like a distant church bell, and sometimes gave a broad roar around the traveler, as if all Nature were laughing him to scorn. But he was himself the chief horror of the scene, and shrank not from its other horrors.

"Ha! ha! ha!" roared Goodman Brown, when the wind laughed at him. "Let us hear which will laugh loudest! Think not to frighten me with your deviltry! Come witch, come wizard, come Indian powwow, come devil himself! and here comes Goodman Brown. You may as well fear him as he fear you!"

In truth, all through the haunted forest, there could be nothing more frightful than the figure of Goodman Brown. On he flew, among the black pines, brandishing his staff with frenzied gestures, now giving vent to an inspiration of horrid blasphemy, and now shouting forth such laughter, as set all the echoes of the forest laughing like demons around him. The fiend in his own shape is less hideous, than when he rages in the breast of man. Thus sped the demoniac on his course, until, quivering among the trees, he saw a red light before him, as when the felled trunks and branches of a clearing have been set on fire, and throw up their lurid blaze against the sky, at the hour of midnight. He paused, in a lull of the tempest that had driven him onward, and heard the swell of what seemed a hymn, rolling solemnly from a distance, with the weight of many voices. He knew the tune. It was a familiar one in the choir of the village meeting-house. The verse died heavily away, and was lengthened by a chorus, not of human voices, but of all the sounds of the benighted wilderness, pealing in awful harmony together. Goodman Brown cried out; and his cry was lost to his own ear, by its unison with the cry of the desert.

In the interval of silence, he stole forward, until the light glared full upon his eyes. At one extremity of an open space, hemmed in by the dark wall of the forest, arose a rock, bearing some rude, natural resemblance either to an altar or a pulpit, and surrounded by four blazing pines, their tops aflame, their stems untouched, like candles at an evening meeting. The mass of foliage, that had overgrown the summit of the rock, was all on fire, blazing high into the night, and fitfully illuminating the whole field. Each pendent twig and leafy festoon was in a blaze. As the red light arose and fell, a numerous congregation alternately shone forth, then disappeared in shadow, and again grew, as it were, out of the darkness, peopling the heart of the solitary woods at once.

"A grave and dark-clad company!" quoth Goodman Brown.

In truth, they were such. Among them, quivering to-and-fro, between gloom and splendor, appeared faces that would be seen, next day, at the council board of the province, and others which, Sabbath after Sabbath, looked devoutly heavenward, and benignantly over the crowded pews, from the holiest pulpits in the land. Some affirm that the lady of the governor was there. At least, there were high dames well known to her, and wives of honored husbands, and widows a great multitude, and ancient maidens, all of excellent repute, and fair young girls, who trembled lest their mothers should espy them. Either the sudden gleams of light, flashing over the obscure field, bedazzled Goodman Brown, or he recognized a score of the church members of Salem village, famous for their especial sanctity. Good old Deacon Gookin had arrived, and waited at the skirts of that venerable saint, his reverend pastor. But, irreverently consorting with these grave, reputable, and pious people, these elders of the church, these chaste dames and dewy virgins, there were men of dissolute lives and women of spotted fame, wretches given over to all mean and filthy vice, and suspected even of horrid crimes. It was strange to see, that the good shrank not from the wicked, nor were the sinners abashed by the saints. Scattered, also, among their pale-faced enemies, were the Indian priests, or powwows, who had often scared their native forest with more hideous incantations than any known to English witchcraft.

"But, where is Faith?" thought Goodman Brown; and, as hope came into his heart, he trembled.

Another verse of the hymn arose, a slow and mournful strain, such as the pious love, but joined to words which expressed all that our nature can conceive of sin, and darkly hinted at far more. Unfathomable to mere mortals is the lore of fiends. Verse after verse was sung, and still the chorus of the desert swelled between, like the deepest tone of a mighty organ. And, with the final peal of that dreadful anthem, there came a sound, as if the roaring wind, the rushing streams, the howling beasts, and every other voice of the unconverted wilderness, were mingling and according with the voice of guilty man, in homage to the prince of all. The four blazing pines threw up a loftier flame, and obscurely discovered shapes and visages of horror on the smoke-wreaths, above the impious assembly. At the same moment, the fire on the rock shot redly forth, and formed a glowing arch above its base, where now appeared a figure. With reverence be it spoken, the apparition bore no slight similitude, both in garb and manner, to some grave divine of the New England churches.

"Bring forth the converts!" cried a voice, that echoed through the field and rolled into the forest.

At the word, Goodman Brown stepped forth from the shadow of the trees, and approached the congregation, with whom he felt a loathful brotherhood, by the sympathy of all that was wicked in his heart. He could have well-nigh sworn, that the shape of his own dead father beckoned him to advance, looking downward from a smoke-wreath, while a woman, with dim features of despair, threw out her hand to warn him back. Was it his mother? But he had no power to retreat one step, nor to resist, even in thought, when the minister and good old Deacon Gookin seized his arms, and led him to the blazing rock. Thither came also the slender form of a veiled female, led between Goody Cloyse, that pious teacher of the catechism, and Martha Carrier, who had received the devil's promise to be queen of hell. A rampant hag was she! And there stood the proselytes, beneath the canopy of fire.

"Welcome, my children," said the dark figure, "to the communion of your race! Ye have found, thus young, your nature and your destiny. My children, look behind you!"

They turned; and flashing forth, as it were, in a sheet of flame, the fiend-worshippers were seen; the smile of welcome gleamed darkly on every visage.

"There," resumed the sable form, "are all whom ye have reverenced from youth. Ye deemed them holier than yourselves, and shrank from your own sin, contrasting it with their lives of righteousness and prayerful aspirations heavenward. Yet, here are they all, in my worshipping assembly! This night it shall be granted you to know their secret deeds; how hoary-bearded elders of the church have whispered wanton words to the young maids of their households; how many a woman, eager for widow's weeds, has given her husband a drink at bedtime, and let him sleep his last sleep in her bosom; how beardless youths have made haste to inherit their father's wealth; and how fair damsels—blush not, sweet ones!—have dug little graves in the garden, and bidden me, the sole guest, to an infant's funeral. By the sympathy of your human hearts for sin, ye shall scent out all the places—whether in church, bed-chamber, street, field, or forest—where crime has been committed, and shall exult to behold the whole earth one stain of guilt, one mighty blood-spot. Far more than this! It shall be yours to penetrate, in every bosom, the deep mystery of sin, the fountain of all wicked arts, and which inexhaustibly supplies more evil impulses than human power—than my power, at its utmost!—can make manifest in deeds. And now, my children, look upon each other."

They did so; and, by the blaze of the hell-kindled torches, the wretched man beheld his Faith, and the wife her husband, trembling before that unhallowed altar.

"Lo! there ye stand, my children," said the figure, in a deep and solemn tone, almost sad, with its despairing awfulness, as if his once angelic nature could yet mourn for our miserable race. "Depending upon one another's hearts, ye had still hoped that virtue were not all a dream! Now are ye undeceived!—Evil is the nature of mankind. Evil must be your only happiness. Welcome, again, my children, to the communion of your race!"

"Welcome!" repeated the fiend-worshippers, in one cry of despair and triumph.

And there they stood, the only pair, as it seemed, who were yet hesitating on the verge of wickedness, in this dark world. A basin was hollowed, naturally, in the rock. Did it contain water, reddened by the lurid light? or was it blood? or, perchance, a liquid flame? Herein did the Shape of Evil dip his hand, and prepare to lay the mark of baptism upon their foreheads, that they might be partakers of the mystery of sin, more conscious of the secret guilt of others, both in deed and thought, than they could now be of their own. The husband cast one look at his pale wife, and Faith at him. What polluted wretches would the next glance show them to each other, shuddering alike at what they disclosed and what they saw!

"Faith! Faith!" cried the husband. "Look up to Heaven, and resist the Wicked One!"

Whether Faith obeyed, he knew not. Hardly had he spoken, when he found himself amid calm night and solitude, listening to a roar of the wind, which died heavily away through the forest. He staggered against the rock, and felt it chill and damp, while a hanging twig, that had been all on fire, besprinkled his cheek with the coldest dew.

The next morning, young Goodman Brown came slowly into the street of Salem village, staring around him like a bewildered man. The good old minister was taking a walk along the graveyard, to get an appetite for breakfast and meditate his sermon, and bestowed a blessing, as he passed, on Goodman Brown. He shrank from the venerable saint, as if to avoid an anathema. Old Deacon Gookin was at domestic worship, and the holy words of his prayer were heard through the open window. "What God doth the wizard pray to?" quoth Goodman Brown. Goody Cloyse, that excellent old Christian, stood in the early sunshine, at her own lattice, catechizing a little girl, who had brought her a pint of morning's milk. Goodman Brown snatched away the child, as from the grasp of the fiend himself. Turning the corner by the meeting-house, he spied the head of Faith, with the pink ribbons, gazing anxiously forth, and bursting into such joy at sight of him, that she skipt along the street, and almost kissed her husband before the whole village. But Goodman Brown looked sternly and sadly into her face, and passed on without a greeting.

Had Goodman Brown fallen asleep in the forest, and only dreamed a wild dream of a witch-meeting?

Be it so, if you will. But, alas! it was a dream of evil omen for young Goodman Brown. A stern, a sad, a darkly meditative, a distrustful, if not a desperate man did he become, from the night of that fearful dream. On the Sabbath day, when the congregation were singing a holy psalm, he could not listen, because an anthem of sin rushed loudly upon his ear, and drowned all the blessed strain. When the minister spoke from the pulpit, with power and fervid eloquence, and with his hand on the open Bible, of the sacred truths of our religion, and of saint-like lives and triumphant deaths, and of future bliss or misery unutterable, then did Goodman Brown turn pale, dreading lest the roof should thunder down upon the gray blasphemer and his hearers. Often, awaking suddenly at midnight, he shrank from the bosom of Faith, and at morning or eventide, when the family knelt down at prayer, he scowled, and muttered to himself, and gazed sternly at his wife, and turned away. And when he had lived long, and was borne to his grave, a hoary corpse, followed by Faith, an aged woman, and children and grand-children, a goodly procession, besides neighbors not a few, they carved no hopeful verse upon his tombstone; for his dying hour was gloom.

II

WILKIE COLLINS

Brother Morgan's Story OF THE *Dead Hand*

1857

When this present nineteenth century was younger by a good many years than it is now, a certain friend of mine, named Arthur Holliday, happened to arrive in the town of Doncaster exactly in the middle of the race-week, or, in other words, in the middle of the month of September.

He was one of those reckless, rattlepated, open-hearted, and open-mouthed young gentlemen who possess the gift of familiarity in its highest perfection, and who scramble carelessly along the journey of life, making friends, as the phrase is, wherever they go. His father was a rich manufacturer, and had bought landed property enough in one of the midland counties to make all the born squires in his neighborhood thoroughly envious of him. Arthur was his only son, possessor in prospect of the great estate and the great business after his father's death; well supplied with money, and not too rigidly looked after, during his father's lifetime. Report, or scandal, whichever you please, said that the old gentleman had been rather wild in his youthful days, and that, unlike most parents, he was not disposed to be violently indignant when he found that his son took after him. This may be true or not. I myself only knew the elder Mr. Holliday when he was getting on in years, and then he was as quiet and as respectable a gentleman as ever I met with.

Well, one September, as I told you, young Arthur comes to Doncaster, having suddenly decided, in his hare-brained way, that he would go to the races. He did not reach the town till towards the close of evening, and he went at once to see about his dinner and bed at the principal hotel. Dinner they were ready enough to give him; but as for a bed, they laughed when he mentioned it. In the race-week at Doncaster, it is no uncommon thing for visitors who have not bespoken apartments to pass the night in their carriages at the inn doors. As for the lower sort of strangers, I myself have often seen them, at that full time, sleeping out on the door-steps for want of a covered place to creep under. Rich as he was, Arthur's chance of getting a night's lodging (seeing that he had not written beforehand to secure one) was more than doubtful. He tried the second hotel, and the third hotel, and two of the inferior inns after that; and was met everywhere with the same form of answer. No accommodation for the night of any sort was left. All the bright golden sovereigns in his pocket would not buy him a bed at Doncaster in the race-week.

To a young fellow of Arthur's temperament, the novelty of being turned away into the street like a penniless vagabond, at every house where he asked for a lodging, presented itself in the light of a new and highly amusing piece of experience. He went on with his carpet-bag in his hand, applying for a bed at every place of entertainment for travelers that he could find in Doncaster, until he wandered into the outskirts of the town.

By this time the last glimmer of twilight had faded out, the moon was rising dimly in a mist, the wind was getting cold, the clouds were gathering heavily, and there was every prospect that it was soon going to rain.

The look of the night had rather a lowering effect on young Holliday's good spirits. He began to contemplate the houseless situation in which he was placed, from the serious rather than the humorous point of view; and he looked about him for another public-house to inquire at, with something very like downright anxiety in his mind on the subject of a lodging for the night.

The suburban part of the town towards which he had now strayed was hardly lighted at all, and he could see nothing of the houses as he passed them, except that they got progressively smaller and dirtier the farther he went. Down the winding road before him shone the dull gleam of an oil lamp, the one faint lonely light that struggled ineffectually with the foggy darkness all round him. He resolved to go on as far as this lamp; and then, if it showed him nothing in the shape of an inn, to return to the central part of the town, and to try if he could not at least secure a chair to sit down on, through the night, at one of the principal hotels.

As he got near the lamp, he heard voices; and, walking close under it, found that it lighted the entrance to a narrow court, on the wall of which was painted a long hand in faded flesh color, pointing, with a lean forefinger, to this inscription:—

THE TWO ROBINS.

Arthur turned into the court without hesitation, to see what The Two Robins could do for him. Four or five men were standing together round the door of the house, which was at the bottom of the court, facing the entrance from the street. The men were all listening to one other man, better dressed than the rest, who was telling his audience something, in a low voice, in which they were apparently very much interested.

On entering the passage, Arthur was passed by a stranger with a knapsack in his hand, who was evidently leaving the house.

"No," said the traveler with the knapsack, turning round and addressing himself cheerfully to a fat, sly-looking, bald-headed man, with a dirty white apron on, who had followed him down the passage. "No, Mr. Landlord, I am not easily scared by trifles; but I don't mind confessing that I can't quite stand *that*."

It occurred to young Holliday, the moment he heard these words, that the stranger had been asked an exorbitant price for a bed at The Two Robins; and that he was unable, or unwilling to pay it. The moment his back was turned, Arthur, comfortably conscious of his own well-filled pockets, addressed himself in a great hurry, for fear any other benighted traveler should slip in and forestall him, to the sly-looking landlord with the dirty apron and the bald head.

"If you have got a bed to let," he said, "and if that gentleman who has just gone out won't pay your price for it, I will."

The sly landlord looked hard at Arthur.

"Will you, sir?" he asked, in a meditative, doubtful way.

"Name your price," said young Holliday; thinking that the landlord's hesitation sprang from some boorish distrust of him. "Name your price, and I'll give you the money at once, if you like."

"Are you game for five shillings?" inquired the landlord, rubbing his stubbly double chin, and looking up thoughtfully at the ceiling above him.

Arthur nearly laughed in the man's face; but thinking it prudent to control himself, offered the five shillings as seriously as he could. The sly landlord held out his hand, then suddenly drew it back again.

"You're acting all fair and above-board by me," he said; "and, before I take your money, I'll do the same by you. Look here, this is how it stands. You can have a bed all to yourself for five shillings; but you can't have more than a half share of the room it stands in. Do you see what I mean, young gentleman?"

"Of course I do," returned Arthur, a little irritably. "You mean that it is a double-bedded room, and that one of the beds is occupied?"

The landlord nodded his head, and rubbed his double chin harder than ever. Arthur hesitated, and mechanically moved back a step or two towards the door. The idea of sleeping in the same room with a total stranger did not present an attractive prospect to him. He felt more than half inclined to drop his five shillings into his pocket, and to go out into the street once more.

"Is it yes, or no?" asked the landlord. "Settle it as quick as you can, because there's lots of people wanting a bed at Doncaster, to-night, besides you."

Arthur looked towards the court, and heard the rain falling heavily in the street outside. He thought he would ask a question or two before he rashly decided on leaving the shelter of The Two Robins.

"What sort of man is it who has got the other bed?" he inquired. "Is he a gentleman? I mean is he a quiet, well-behaved person?"

"The quietest man I ever came across," said the landlord, rubbing his fat hands stealthily one over the other. "As sober as a judge, and as regular as clock-work in his habits. It hasn't struck nine, not ten minutes ago, and he's in his bed already. I don't know whether that comes up to your notion of a quiet man: it goes a long way a-head of mine, I can tell you."

"Is he asleep, do you think?" asked Arthur.

"I know he's asleep," returned the landlord. "And what's more, he's gone off so fast, that I'll warrant you don't wake him. This way, sir," said the landlord, speaking over young Holliday's shoulder, as if he was addressing some new guest who was approaching the house.

"Here you are," said Arthur, determined to be before-hand with the stranger, whoever he might be. "I'll take the bed." And he handed the five shillings to the landlord, who nodded, dropped the money carelessly into his waistcoat-pocket, and lighted a candle.

"Come up and see the room," said the host of The Two Robins, leading the way to the staircase quite briskly, considering how fat he was.

They mounted to the second floor of the house. The landlord half opened a door, fronting the landing, then stopped, and turned round to Arthur.

"It's a fair bargain, mind, on my side as well as on yours," he said. "You give me five shillings; I will give you in return a clean, comfortable bed; and I warrant, before-hand, that you won't be interfered with, or annoyed in any way, by the man who sleeps in the same room with you." Saying those words, he looked hard, for a moment, in young Holliday's face, and then led the way into the room.

It was larger and cleaner than Arthur expected it would be. The two beds stood parallel with each other—a space of about six feet intervening between them. They were both of the same medium size, and both had the same plain white curtains, made to draw, if necessary, all round them.

The occupied bed was the bed nearest the window. The curtains were all drawn round it, except the half curtain at the bottom, on the side of the bed farthest from the window. Arthur saw the feet of the sleeping man raising the scanty clothes into a sharp little eminence, as if he were lying flat on his back. He took the candle, and advanced softly to draw the curtain—stopped half way, and listened for a moment—then turned to the landlord.

"He is a very quiet sleeper," said Arthur.

"Yes," said the landlord, "very quiet."

Young Holliday advanced with the candle, and looked in at the man cautiously.

"How pale he is," said Arthur.

"Yes," returned the landlord, "pale enough, isn't he?"

Arthur looked closer at the man. The bedclothes were drawn up to his chin, and they lay perfectly still over the region of his chest. Surprised and vaguely startled, as he noticed this, Arthur stooped down closer over the stranger; looked at his ashy, parted lips; listened breathlessly for an instant; looked again at the still face, and the motionless lips and chest; and turned round suddenly on the landlord, with his own cheeks as pale, for the moment, as the hollow cheeks of the man on the bed.

"Come here," he whispered, under his breath. "Come here, for God's sake! The man's not asleep—he is dead."

"You have found that out sooner than I thought you would," said the landlord composedly. "Yes, he's dead, sure enough. He died at five o'clock to-day."

"How did he die? Who is he?" asked Arthur, staggered for the moment by the audacious coolness of the answer.

"As to who he is," rejoined the landlord, "I know no more about him than you do. There are his books and letters and things, all sealed up in that brown paper parcel, for the Coroner's inquest to open to-morrow or next day. He's been here a week, paying his way fairly enough, and stopping indoors, for the most part, as if he was ailing. My girl brought up his tea at five to-day, and as he was pouring of it out, he fell down in a faint, or a fit, or a compound of both, for anything I know. We couldn't bring him to—and I said he was dead. And the doctor couldn't bring him to—and the doctor said he was dead. And there he is. And the Coroner's inquest's coming as soon as it can. And that's as much as I know about it."

Arthur held the candle close to the man's lips. The flame still burnt straight up, as steadily as ever. There was a moment of silence; and the rain pattered drearily through it against the panes of the window.

"If you haven't got nothing more to say to me," continued the landlord, "I suppose I may go. You don't expect your five shillings back, do you? There's the bed I promised you, clean and comfortable. There's the man I warranted not to disturb you, quiet in this world forever. If you're frightened to stop alone with him, that's not my look-out. I've kept my part of the bargain, and I mean to keep the money. I'm not Yorkshire myself, young gentleman; but I've lived long enough in these parts to have my wits sharpened; and I shouldn't wonder if you found out the way to brighten up yours, next time you come among us."

With those words, the landlord turned towards the door, and laughed to himself softly, in high satisfaction at his own sharpness.

Startled and shocked as he was, Arthur had by this time sufficiently recovered himself to feel indignant at the trick that had been played on him, and at the insolent manner in which the landlord exulted in it.

"Don't laugh, till you are quite sure you have got the laugh against me," he said sharply. "You shan't have the five shillings for nothing, my man. I'll keep the bed."

"Will you?" said the landlord. "Then I wish you a good night's rest." With that brief farewell, he went out, and shut the door after him.

A good night's rest! The words had hardly been spoken, the door had hardly been closed, before Arthur half repented the hasty words that had just escaped him. Though not naturally over-sensitive, and not wanting in courage of the moral as well as the physical sort, the presence of the dead man had an instantaneously chilling effect on his mind when he found himself alone in the room—alone, and bound by his own rash words to stay there till the next morning. An older man would have thought nothing of those words, and would have acted without reference to them, as his calmer sense suggested. But Arthur was too young to treat the ridicule, even of his inferiors, with contempt—too young not to fear the momentary humiliation of falsifying his own foolish boast, more than he feared the trial of watching out the long night in the same chamber with the dead.

"It is but a few hours," he thought to himself, "and I can get away the first thing in the morning."

He was looking towards the occupied bed, as that idea passed through his mind, and the sharp angular eminence made in the clothes by the dead man's upturned feet, again caught his eye. He advanced and drew the curtains, purposely abstaining, as he did so, from looking at the face of the corpse, lest he might unnerve himself at the outset by fastening some ghastly impression of it on his mind. He drew the curtain very gently, and sighed involuntarily as he closed it.

"Poor fellow!" he said, almost as sadly as if he had known the man. "Ah, poor fellow!"

He went next to the window. The night was black, and he could see nothing from it. The rain still pattered heavily against the glass. He inferred, from hearing it, that the window was at the back of the house; remembering that the front was sheltered from the weather by the court and the buildings over it.

While he was still standing at the window—for even the dreary rain was a relief, because of the sound it made; a relief, also, because it moved, and had some faint suggestion, in consequence, of life and companionship in it—while he was standing at the window, and looking vacantly into the black darkness outside, he heard a distant church-clock strike ten. Only ten! How was he to pass the time till the house was astir the next morning?

Under any other circumstances, he would have gone down to the public-house parlor, would have called for his grog, and would have laughed and talked with the company assembled as familiarly as if he had known them all his life. But the very thought of whiling away the time in this manner was now distasteful to him. The new situation in which he was placed seemed to have altered him to himself already. Thus far, his life had been the common, trifling, prosaic surface-life of a prosperous young man, with no troubles to conquer, and no trials to face. He had lost no relation whom he loved, no friend whom he treasured. Till this night, what share he had of the immortal inheritance that is divided amongst us all, had lain dormant with him. Till this night, Death and he had not once met, even in thought.

He took a few turns up and down the room—then stopped. The noise made by his boots on the poorly carpeted floor jarred on his ear. He hesitated a little, and ended by taking the boots off, and walking backwards and forwards noiselessly.

All desire to sleep or to rest had left him. The bare thought of lying down on the unoccupied bed, instantly drew the picture on his mind of a dreadful mimicry of the position of the dead man. Who was he? What was the story of his past life? Poor he must have been, or he would not have stopped at such a place as The Two Robins Inn—and weakened, probably, by long illness, or he could hardly have died in the manner which the landlord had described. Poor, ill, lonely—dead in a strange place; dead, with nobody but a stranger to pity him. A sad story: truly, on the mere face of it, a very sad story.

While these thoughts were passing through his mind, he had stopped insensibly at the window, close to which stood the foot of the bed with the closed curtains. At first he looked at it absently; then he became conscious that his eyes were fixed on it; and then, a perverse desire took possession of him to do the very thing which he had resolved not to do, up to this time—to look at the dead man.

He stretched out his hand towards the curtains; but checked himself in the very act of undrawing them, turned his back sharply on the bed, and walked towards the chimney-piece, to see what things were placed on it, and to try if he could keep the dead man out of his mind that way.

There was a pewter inkstand on the chimney-piece, with some mildewed remains of ink in the bottle. There were two coarse china ornaments of the commonest kind; and there was a square of embossed card, dirty and fly-blown, with a collection of wretched riddles printed on it, in all sorts of zigzag directions, and in variously colored inks. He took the card and went away to read it at the table on which the candle was placed; sitting down, with his back resolutely turned to the curtained bed.

He read the first riddle, the second, the third, all in one corner of the card—then turned it round impatiently to look at another. Before he could begin reading the riddles printed here, the sound of the church clock stopped him.

Eleven.

He had got through an hour of the time, in the room with the dead man.

Once more he looked at the card. It was not easy to make out the letters printed on it, in consequence of the dimness of the light which the landlord had left him—a common tallow candle, furnished with a pair of heavy old-fashioned steel snuffers. Up to this time, his mind had been too much occupied to think of the light. He had left the wick of the candle unsnuffed, till it had risen higher than the flame, and had burnt into an odd penthouse shape at the top, from which morsels of the charred cotton fell off, from time to time, in little flakes. He took up the snuffers now, and trimmed the wick. The light brightened directly, and the room became less dismal.

Again he turned to the riddles; reading them doggedly and resolutely, now in one corner of the card, now in another. All his efforts, however, could not fix his attention on them. He pursued his occupation mechanically, deriving no sort of impression from what he was reading. It was as if a shadow from the curtained bed had got between his mind and the gaily printed letters—a shadow that nothing could dispel. At last, he gave up the struggle, threw the card from him impatiently, and took to walking softly up and down the room again.

The dead man, the dead man, the *hidden* dead man on the bed!

There was the one persistent idea still haunting him. Hidden! Was it only the body being there—or was it the body being there, *concealed*, that was preying on his mind? He stopped at the window, with that doubt in him; once more listening to the pattering rain, once more looking out into the black darkness.

Still the dead man!

The darkness forced his mind back upon itself, and set his memory at work, reviving, with a painfully vivid distinctness, the momentary impression it had received from his first sight of the corpse. Before long, the face seemed to be hovering out in the middle of the rain and darkness, confronting him through the window, with the paleness whiter, with the dreadful dull line of light between the imperfectly closed eye-lids broader than he had seen it—with the parted lips slowly dropping farther and farther away from each other—with the features growing larger and moving closer, till they seemed to fill the window, and silence the rain, and shut out the night.

The sound of a voice shouting below stairs, woke him suddenly from the dream of his own distempered fancy. He recognized it as the voice of the landlord.

"Shut up at twelve, Ben," he heard it say. "I'm off to bed."

He wiped away the damp that had gathered on his forehead, reasoned with himself for a little while, and resolved to shake his mind free of the ghastly counterfeit which still clung to it, by forcing himself to confront, if it was only for a moment, the solemn reality. Without allowing himself an instant to hesitate, he parted the curtains at the foot of the bed, and looked through.

There was the sad, peaceful, white face, with the awful mystery of stillness on it, laid back upon the pillow. No stir, no change there! He only looked at it for a moment before he closed the curtains again; but that moment steadied him, calmed him, restored him—mind and body—to himself.

He returned to his old occupation of walking up and down the room; persevering in it, this time, till the clock struck again.

Twelve.

As the sound of the clock bell died away, it was succeeded by the confused noise, downstairs, of the drinkers in the taproom leaving the house. The next sound, after an interval of silence, was caused by the barring of the door, and the closing of the shutters at the back of the Inn. Then the silence followed again, and was disturbed no more.

He was alone now—absolutely, hopelessly alone with the dead man, till the next morning.

The wick of the candle wanted trimming again. He took up the snuffers—but paused suddenly on the very point of using them, and looked attentively at the candle—then back, over his shoulder, at the curtained bed—then again at the candle. It had been lighted, for the first time, to show him the way upstairs, and three parts of it, at least, were already consumed. In another hour it would be burnt out. In another hour—unless he called at once to the man who had shut up the Inn, for a fresh candle—he would be left in the dark.

Strongly as his mind had been affected since he had entered the room, his unreasonable dread of encountering ridicule, and of exposing his courage to suspicion, had not altogether lost its influence over him yet.

He lingered irresolutely by the table, waiting till he could prevail on himself to open the door, and call from the landing to the man who had shut up the Inn. In his present hesitating frame of mind, it was a kind of relief to gain a few moments only by engaging in the trifling occupation of snuffing the candle. His hand trembled a little, and the snuffers were heavy and awkward to use. When he closed them on the wick, he closed them a hair's breadth too low. In an instant the candle was out, and the room was plunged in pitch darkness.

The one impression which the absence of light immediately produced on his mind, was distrust of the curtained bed—distrust which shaped itself into no distinct idea, but which was powerful enough, in its very vagueness, to bind him down to his chair, to make his heart beat fast, and to set him listening intently. No sound stirred in the room but the familiar sound of the rain against the window, louder and sharper now than he had heard it yet.

Still the vague distrust, the inexpressible dread, possessed him, and kept him in his chair. He had put his carpet-bag on the table when he first entered the room; and he now took the key from his pocket, reached out his hand softly, opened the bag, and groped in it for his traveling writing-case, in which he knew that there was a small store of matches. When he had got one of the matches, he waited before he struck it on the coarse wooden table, and listened intently again, without knowing why. Still there was no sound in the room but the steady, ceaseless, rattling sound of the rain.

He lighted the candle again, without another moment of delay; and, on the instant of its burning up, the first object in the room that his eyes sought for was the curtained bed.

Just before the light had been put out, he had looked in that direction, and had seen no change, no disarrangement of any sort, in the folds of the closely drawn curtains.

When he looked at the bed now, he saw, hanging over the side of it—a long white hand.

It lay perfectly motionless, midway on the side of the bed, where the curtain at the head and the curtain at the foot met. Nothing more was visible. The clinging curtains hid everything but the long white hand.

He stood looking at it, unable to stir, unable to call out; feeling nothing, knowing nothing; every faculty he possessed gathered up and lost in the one seeing faculty. How long that first panic held him, he never could tell afterwards. It might have been only for a moment; it might have been for many minutes together. How he got to the bed—whether he ran to it headlong, or whether he approached it slowly—how he wrought himself up to unclose the curtains and look in, he never has remembered, and never will remember, to his dying day. It is enough that he did go to the bed, and that he did look inside the curtains.

The man had moved. One of his arms was outside the clothes; his face was turned a little on the pillow; his eyelids were wide open. Changed as to position, and as to one of the features, the face was otherwise fearfully and wonderfully unaltered. The dead paleness and the dead quiet were on it still.

One glance showed Arthur this—one glance before he flew breathlessly to the door, and alarmed the house.

The man whom the landlord called "Ben" was the first to appear on the stairs. In three words, Arthur told him what had happened, and sent him for the nearest doctor.

I, who tell you this story, was then staying with a medical friend of mine, in practice at Doncaster, taking care of his patients for him during his absence in London; and I, for the time being, was the nearest doctor. They had sent for me from the Inn, when the stranger was taken ill in the afternoon; but I was not at home, and medical assistance was sought for elsewhere. When the man from The Two Robins rang the night-bell, I was just thinking of going to bed. Naturally enough, I did not believe a word of his story about "a dead man who had come to life again." However, I put on my hat, armed myself with one or two bottles of restorative medicine, and ran to the Inn, expecting to find nothing more remarkable, when I got there, than a patient in a fit.

My surprise at finding that the man had spoken the literal truth was almost, if not quite, equaled by my astonishment at finding myself face to face with Arthur Holliday as soon as I entered the bedroom. It was no time then for giving or seeking explanations. We just shook hands amazedly; and then I ordered everybody but Arthur out of the room, and hurried to the man on the bed.

The kitchen fire had not been long out. There was plenty of hot water in the boiler, and plenty of flannel to be had. With these, with my medicines, and with such help as Arthur could render under my direction, I dragged the man, literally, out of the jaws of death. In less than an hour from the time when I had been called in, he was alive and talking, in the bed on which he had been laid out to wait for the Coroner's inquest.

You will naturally ask me what had been the matter with him; and I might treat you, in reply, to a long theory, plentifully sprinkled with what the children call hard words. I prefer telling you that, in this case, cause and effect could not be satisfactorily joined together by any theory whatever. There are mysteries in life, and in the conditions of it, which human science has not fathomed yet; and I candidly confess to you that, in bringing that man back to existence, I was, morally speaking, groping hap-hazard in the dark. I know (from the testimony of the doctor who attended him in the afternoon) that the vital machinery, so far as its action is appreciable by our senses, had, in this case, unquestionably stopped; and I am equally certain (seeing that I recovered him) that the vital principle was not extinct. When I add that he had suffered from a long and complicated illness, and that his whole nervous system was utterly deranged, I have told you all I really know of the physical condition of my dead-alive patient at The Two Robins Inn.

When he "came to," as the phrase goes, he was a startling object to look at, with his colorless face, his sunken cheeks, his wild black eyes, and his long black hair. The first question he asked me about himself, when he could speak, made me suspect that I had been called in to a man in my own profession. I mentioned to him my surmise, and he told me that I was right.

He said he had come last from Paris, where he had been attached to a hospital. That he had lately returned to England, on his way to Edinburgh, to continue his studies; that he had been taken ill on the journey; and that he had stopped to rest and recover himself at Doncaster. He did not add a word about his name, or who he was, and of course I did not question him on the subject. All I inquired, when he ceased speaking, was what branch of the profession he intended to follow.

"Any branch," he said, bitterly, "which will put bread into the mouth of a poor man."

At this, Arthur, who had been hitherto watching him in silent curiosity, burst out impetuously in his usual good-humored way:—

"My dear fellow!" (everybody was "my dear fellow" with Arthur) "now you have come to life again, don't begin by being down-hearted about your prospects. I'll answer for it, I can help you to some capital thing in the medical line—or, if I can't, I know my father can."

The medical student looked at him steadily.

"Thank you," he said coldly; then added, "May I ask who your father is?"

"He's well enough known all about this part of the country," replied Arthur. "He is a great manufacturer, and his name is Holliday."

My hand was on the man's wrist during this brief conversation. The instant the name of Holliday was pronounced, I felt the pulse under my fingers flutter, stop, go on suddenly with a bound, and beat afterwards for a minute or two at the fever rate.

"How did you come here?" asked the stranger, quickly, excitably, passionately almost.

Arthur related briefly what had happened from the time of his first taking the bed at the Inn.

"I am indebted to Mr. Holliday's son then, for the help that has saved my life," said the medical student, speaking to himself, with a singular sarcasm in his voice. "Come here!"

He held out, as he spoke, his long, white, bony right hand.

"With all my heart," said Arthur, taking his hand cordially. "I may confess it now," he continued, laughing; "upon my honor you almost frightened me out of my wits."

The stranger did not seem to listen. His wild black eyes were fixed with a look of eager interest on Arthur's face, and his long bony fingers kept tight hold of Arthur's hand. Young Holliday, on his side, returned the gaze, amazed and puzzled by the medical student's odd language and manners. The two faces were close together; I looked at them; and, to my amazement, I was suddenly impressed by the sense of a likeness between them—not in features or complexion, but solely in expression. It must have been a strong likeness, or I should certainly not have found it out, for I am naturally slow at detecting resemblances between faces.

"You have saved my life," said the strange man, still looking hard in Arthur's face, still holding tightly by his hand. "If you had been my own brother, you could not have done more for me than that."

He laid a singularly strong emphasis on those three words, "my own brother," and a change passed over his face as he pronounced them—a change that no language of mine is competent to describe.

"I hope I have not done being of service to you yet," said Arthur. "I'll speak to my father as soon as I get home."

"You seem to be fond and proud of your father," said the medical student. "I suppose, in return, he is fond and proud of you?"

"Of course he is," answered Arthur, laughing. "Is there anything wonderful in that? Isn't *your* father fond——"

The stranger suddenly dropped young Holliday's hand, and turned his face away.

"I beg your pardon," said Arthur. "I hope I have not unintentionally pained you. I hope you have not lost your father?"

"I can't well lose what I have never had," retorted the medical student, with a harsh mocking laugh.

"What you have never had!"

The strange man suddenly caught Arthur's hand again, suddenly looked once more hard in his face.

"Yes," he said, with a repetition of the bitter laugh. "You have brought a poor devil back into the world, who has no business there. Do I astonish you? Well! I have a fancy of my own for telling you what men in my situation generally keep a secret. I have no name and no father. The merciful law of Society tells me I am Nobody's son! Ask your father if he will be my father too, and help me on in life with the family name."

Arthur looked at me more puzzled than ever.

I signed to him to say nothing, and then laid my fingers again on the man's wrist. No! In spite of the extraordinary speech that he had just made, he was not, as I had been disposed to suspect, beginning to get light-headed. His pulse, by this time, had fallen back to a quiet, slow beat, and his skin was moist and cool. Not a symptom of fever or agitation about him.

Finding that neither of us answered him, he turned to me, and began talking of the extraordinary nature of his case, and asking my advice about the future course of medical treatment to which he ought to subject himself. I said the matter required careful thinking over, and suggested that I should send him a prescription a little later. He told me to write it at once, as he would, most likely, be leaving Doncaster in the morning, before I was up. It was quite useless to represent to him the folly and danger of such a proceeding as this. He heard me politely and patiently, but held to his resolution, without offering any reasons or explanations, and repeated to me, that if I wished to give him a chance of seeing my prescription, I must write it at once.

Hearing this, Arthur volunteered the loan of a traveling writing-case, which, he said, he had with him; and, bringing it to the bed, shook the note paper out of the pocket of the case forthwith in his usual careless way. With the paper, there fell out, on the counterpane of the bed, a small packet of sticking-plaster and a little water-color drawing of a landscape.

The medical student took up the drawing and looked at it. His eye fell on some initials, neatly written in cipher, in one corner. He started, and trembled; his pale face grew whiter than ever; his wild black eyes turned on Arthur, and looked through and through him.

"A pretty drawing," he said, in a remarkably quiet tone of voice.

"Ah! and done by such a pretty girl," said Arthur. "Oh, such a pretty girl! I wish it was not a landscape—I wish it was a portrait of her!"

"You admire her very much?"

Arthur, half in jest, half in earnest, kissed his hand for answer.

"Love at first sight," said young Holliday, putting the drawing away again. "But the course of it doesn't run smooth. It's the old story. She's monopolized, as usual. Trammeled by a rash engagement to some poor man who is never likely to get money enough to marry her. It was lucky I heard of it in time, or I should certainly have risked a declaration when she gave me that drawing. Here, doctor! Here is pen, ink, and paper, all ready for you."

"When she gave you that drawing! Gave it. Gave it."

He repeated the words slowly to himself, and suddenly closed his eyes. A momentary distortion passed across his face, and I saw one of his hands clutch up the bedclothes and squeeze them hard. I thought he was going to be ill again, and begged that there might be no more talking. He opened his eyes when I spoke, fixed them once more, searchingly, on Arthur, and said, slowly and distinctly:—

"You like her, and she likes you. The poor man may die out of your way. Who can tell that she may not give you herself as well as her drawing, after all?"

Before young Holliday could answer, he turned to me, and said in a whisper, "Now for the prescription." From that time, though he spoke to Arthur again, he never looked at him more.

When I had written the prescription, he examined it, approved of it, and then astonished us both by abruptly wishing us good night. I offered to sit up with him, and he shook his head. Arthur offered to sit up with him, and he said, shortly, with his face turned away, "No." I insisted on having somebody left to watch him. He gave way when he found I was determined, and said he would accept the services of the waiter at the Inn.

"Thank you both," he said, as we rose to go. "I have one last favor to ask—not of you, doctor, for I leave you to exercise your professional discretion—but of Mr. Holliday." His eyes, while he spoke, still rested steadily on me, and never once turned towards Arthur. "I beg that Mr. Holliday will not mention to any one—least of all to his father—the events that have occurred, and the words that have passed, in this room. I entreat him to bury me in his memory, as, but for him, I might have been buried in my grave. I cannot give my reasons for making this strange request. I can only implore him to grant it."

His voice faltered for the first time, and he hid his face on the pillow. Arthur, completely bewildered, gave the required pledge. I took young Holliday away with me, immediately afterwards, to the house of my friend; determining to go back to the Inn, and to see the medical student again before he had left in the morning.

I returned to the Inn at eight o'clock, purposely abstaining from waking Arthur, who was sleeping off the past night's excitement on one of my friend's sofas. A suspicion had occurred to me, as soon as I was alone in my bedroom, which made me resolve that Holliday and the stranger whose life he had saved should not meet again, if I could prevent it.

I have already alluded to certain reports, or scandals, which I knew of, relating to the early life of Arthur's father. While I was thinking, in my bed, of what had passed at the Inn—of the change in the student's pulse when he heard the name of Holliday; of the resemblance of expression that I had discovered between his face and Arthur's; of the emphasis he had laid on those three words, "my own brother"; and of his incomprehensible acknowledgment of his own illegitimacy—while I was thinking of these things, the reports I have mentioned suddenly flew into my mind, and linked themselves fast to the chain of my previous reflections. Something within me whispered, "It is best that those two young men should not meet again." I felt it before I slept; I felt it when I woke; and I went, as I told you, alone to the Inn the next morning.

I had missed my only opportunity of seeing my nameless patient again. He had been gone nearly an hour when I inquired for him.

I have now told you everything that I know for certain, in relation to the man whom I brought back to life in the double-bedded room of the Inn at Doncaster. What I have next to add is matter for inference and surmise, and is not, strictly speaking, matter of fact.

I have to tell you, first, that the medical student turned out to be strangely and unaccountably right in assuming it as more than probable that Arthur Holliday would marry the young lady who had given him the water-color drawing of the landscape. That marriage took place a little more than a year after the events occurred which I have just been relating.

The young couple came to live in the neighborhood in which I was then established in practice. I was present at the wedding, and was rather surprised to find that Arthur was singularly reserved with me, both before and after his marriage, on the subject of the young lady's prior engagement. He only referred to it once, when we were alone, merely telling me, on that occasion, that his wife had done all that honor and duty required of her in the matter, and that the engagement had been broken off with the full approval of her parents. I never heard more from him than this. For three years he and his wife lived together happily. At the expiration of that time, the symptoms of a serious illness first declared themselves in Mrs. Arthur Holliday. It turned out to be a long, lingering, hopeless malady. I attended her throughout. We had been great friends when she was well, and we became more attached to each other than ever when she was ill. I had many long and interesting conversations with her in the intervals when she suffered least. The result of one of those conversations I may briefly relate, leaving you to draw any inferences from it that you please.

The interview to which I refer, occurred shortly before her death.

I called one evening, as usual, and found her alone, with a look in her eyes which told me she had been crying. She only informed me, at first, that she had been depressed in spirits; but, by little and little, she became more communicative, and confessed to me that she had been looking over some old letters, which had been addressed to her, before she had seen Arthur, by a man to whom she had been engaged to be married. I asked her how the engagement came to be broken off. She replied that it had not been broken off, but that it had died out in a very mysterious manner. The person to whom she was engaged—her first love, she called him—was poor, and there was no immediate prospect of their being married. He followed my profession, and went abroad to study. They had corresponded regularly, until the time when, as she believed, he had returned to England. From that period she heard no more of him. He was of a fretful, sensitive temperament; and she feared that she might have inadvertently done or said something to offend him.

However that might be, he had never written to her again; and, after waiting a year, she had married Arthur. I asked when the first estrangement had begun, and found that the time at which she ceased to hear anything of her first lover, exactly corresponded with the time at which I had been called in to my mysterious patient at The Two Robins Inn.

A fortnight after that conversation, she died. In course of time Arthur married again. Of late years, he has lived principally in London, and I have seen little or nothing of him.

I have some years to pass over before I can approach to anything like a conclusion of this fragmentary narrative. And even when that later period is reached, the little that I have to say will not occupy your attention for more than a few minutes.

One rainy autumn evening, while I was still practicing as a country doctor, I was sitting alone, thinking over a case then under my charge which sorely perplexed me, when I heard a low knock at the door of my room.

"Come in," I cried, looking up curiously to see who wanted me.

After a momentary delay, the lock moved, and a long, white, bony hand stole round the door as it opened, gently pushing it over a fold in the carpet which hindered it from working freely on the hinges. The hand was followed by a man whose face instantly struck me with a very strange sensation. There was something familiar to me in the look of him; and yet it was also something that suggested the idea of change.

He quietly introduced himself as "Mr. Lorn"; presented to me some excellent professional recommendations; and proposed to fill the place, then vacant, of my assistant. While he was speaking, I noticed it as singular that we did not appear to be meeting each other like strangers; and that, while I was certainly startled at seeing him, he did not appear to be at all startled at seeing me.

It was on the tip of my tongue to say that I thought I had met with him before. But there was something in his face, and something in my recollections—I can hardly say what—which unaccountably restrained me from speaking, and which, as unaccountably, attracted me to him at once, and made me feel ready and glad to accept his proposal.

He took his assistant's place on that very day. We got on together as if we had been old friends from the first; but, throughout the whole time of his residence in my house, he never volunteered any confidences on the subject of his past life; and

I never approached the forbidden topic except by hints, which he resolutely refused to understand.

I had long had a notion that my patient at the Inn might have been a natural son of the elder Mr. Holliday's, and that he might also have been the man who was engaged to Arthur's first wife. And, now, another idea occurred to me, that Mr. Lorn was the only person in existence who could, if he chose, enlighten me on both those doubtful points. But he never did choose—and I was never enlightened. He remained with me till I removed to London to try my fortune there, as a physician, for the second time; and then he went his way, and I went mine, and we have never seen one another since.

I can add no more. I may have been right in my suspicion, or I may have been wrong. All I know is, that, in those days of my country practice, when I came home late, and found my assistant asleep, and woke him, he used to look, in coming to, wonderfully like the stranger at Doncaster, as he raised himself in the bed on that memorable night.

III

SIR ARTHUR CONAN DOYLE

The Captain OF THE *"Pole-Star"*

1883

Being an extract from the singular journal of John M'Alister Ray, student of medicine.

September 11th.—Lat. 81° 40´ N; long. 2° E. Still lying-to amid enormous ice fields. The one which stretches away to the north of us, and to which our ice-anchor is attached, cannot be smaller than an English county. To the right and left unbroken sheets extend to the horizon. This morning the mate reported that there were signs of pack ice to the southward. Should this form of sufficient thickness to bar our return, we shall be in a position of danger, as the food, I hear, is already running somewhat short. It is late in the season, and the nights are beginning to reappear. This morning I saw a star twinkling just over the fore-yard, the first since the beginning of May. There is considerable discontent among the crew, many of whom are anxious to get back home to be in time for the herring season, when labor always commands a high price upon the Scotch coast. As yet their displeasure is only signified by sullen countenances and black looks, but I heard from the second mate this afternoon that they contemplated sending a deputation to the Captain to explain their grievance. I much doubt how he will receive it, as he is a man of fierce temper, and very sensitive about anything approaching to an infringement of his rights. I shall venture after dinner to say a few words to him upon the subject. I have always found that he will tolerate from me what he would resent from any other member of the crew. Amsterdam Island, at the north-west corner of Spitzbergen, is visible upon our starboard quarter—a rugged line of volcanic rocks, intersected by white seams, which represent glaciers. It is curious to think that at the present moment there is probably no human being nearer to us than the Danish settlements in the south of Greenland—a good nine hundred miles as the crow flies. A captain takes a great responsibility upon himself when he risks his vessel under such circumstances. No whaler has ever remained in these latitudes till so advanced a period of the year.

9 p.m.—I have spoken to Captain Craigie, and though the result has been hardly satisfactory, I am bound to say that he listened to what I had to say very quietly and even deferentially. When I had finished he put on that air of iron determination which I have frequently observed upon his face, and paced rapidly backwards and forwards across the narrow cabin for some minutes. At first I feared that I had seriously offended him, but he dispelled the idea by sitting down again, and putting his hand upon my arm with a gesture which almost amounted to a caress. There was a depth of tenderness too in his wild dark eyes which surprised me considerably. "Look here, Doctor," he said, "I'm sorry I ever took you—I am indeed—and I would give fifty pounds this minute to see you standing safe upon the Dundee quay. It's hit or miss with me this time. There are fish to the north of us. How dare you shake your head, sir, when I tell you I saw them blowing from the masthead?"—this in a sudden burst of fury, though I was not conscious of having shown any signs of doubt. "Two-and-twenty fish in as many minutes as I am a living man, and not one under ten foot.[1] Now, Doctor, do you think I can leave the country when there is only one infernal strip of ice between me and my fortune? If it came on to blow from the north to-morrow we could fill the ship and be away before the frost could catch us. If it came on to blow from the south—well, I suppose the men are paid for risking their lives, and as for myself it matters but little to me, for I have more to bind me to the other world than to this one. I confess that I am sorry for *you*, though. I wish I had old Angus Tait who was with me last voyage, for he was a man that would never be missed, and you—you said once that you were engaged, did you not?"

---

1 A whale is measured among whalers not by the length of its body, but by the length of its whalebone.

"Yes," I answered, snapping the spring of the locket which hung from my watch-chain, and holding up the little vignette of Flora.

"Curse you!" he yelled, springing out of his seat, with his very beard bristling with passion. "What is your happiness to me? What have I to do with her that you must dangle her photograph before my eyes?" I almost thought that he was about to strike me in the frenzy of his rage, but with another imprecation he dashed open the door of the cabin and rushed out upon deck, leaving me considerably astonished at his extraordinary violence. It is the first time that he has ever shown me anything but courtesy and kindness. I can hear him pacing excitedly up and down overhead as I write these lines.

I should like to give a sketch of the character of this man, but it seems presumptuous to attempt such a thing upon paper, when the idea in my own mind is at best a vague and uncertain one. Several times I have thought that I grasped the clue which might explain it, but only to be disappointed by his presenting himself in some new light which would upset all my conclusions. It may be that no human eye but my own shall ever rest upon these lines, yet as a psychological study I shall attempt to leave some record of Captain Nicholas Craigie.

A man's outer case generally gives some indication of the soul within. The Captain is tall and well-formed, with dark, handsome face, and a curious way of twitching his limbs, which may arise from nervousness, or be simply an outcome of his excessive energy. His jaw and whole cast of countenance is manly and resolute, but the eyes are the distinctive feature of his face. They are of the very darkest hazel, bright and eager, with a singular mixture of recklessness in their expression, and of something else which I have sometimes thought was more allied with horror than any other emotion. Generally the former predominated, but on occasions, and more particularly when he was thoughtfully inclined, the look of fear would spread and deepen until it imparted a new character to his whole countenance. It is at these times that he is most subject to tempestuous fits of anger, and he seems to be aware of it, for I have known him lock himself up so that no one might approach him until his dark hour was passed. He sleeps badly, and I have heard him shouting during the night, but his cabin is some little distance from mine, and I could never distinguish the words which he said.

This is one phase of his character, and the most disagreeable one. It is only through my close association with him, thrown together as we are day after day, that I have observed it. Otherwise he is an agreeable companion, well-read and entertaining, and as gallant a seaman as ever trod a deck. I shall not easily forget the way in which he handled the ship when we were caught by a gale among the loose ice at the beginning of April. I have never seen him so cheerful, and even hilarious, as he was that night, as he paced backwards and forwards upon the bridge amid the flashing of the lightning and the howling of the wind. He has told me several times that the thought of death was a pleasant one to him, which is a sad thing for a young man to say; he cannot be much more than thirty, though his hair and moustache are already slightly grizzled. Some great sorrow must have overtaken him and blighted his whole life. Perhaps I should be the same if I lost my Flora—God knows! I think if it were not for her that I should care very little whether the wind blew from the north or the south to-morrow. There, I hear him come down the companion, and he has locked himself up in his room, which shows that he is still in an unamiable mood. And so to bed, as old Pepys would say, for the candle is burning down (we have to use them now since the nights are closing in), and the steward has turned in, so there are no hopes of another one.

September 12th.—Calm, clear day, and still lying in the same position. What wind there is comes from the south-east, but it is very slight. Captain is in a better humor, and apologized to me at breakfast for his rudeness. He still looks somewhat distrait, however, and retains that wild look in his eyes which in a Highlander would mean that he was "fey"—at least so our chief engineer remarked to me, and he has some reputation among the Celtic portion of our crew as a seer and expounder of omens.

It is strange that superstition should have obtained such mastery over this hard-headed and practical race. I could not have believed to what an extent it is carried had I not observed it for myself. We have had a perfect epidemic of it this voyage, until I have felt inclined to serve out rations of sedatives and nerve-tonics with the Saturday allowance of grog. The first symptom of it was that shortly after leaving Shetland the men at the wheel used to complain that they heard plaintive cries and screams in the wake of the ship, as if something were following it and were unable to overtake it. This fiction has been kept up during the whole voyage, and on dark nights at the beginning of the seal-fishing it was only with great difficulty that men could be induced to do their spell. No doubt what they heard was either the creaking of the rudder-chains, or the cry of some passing sea-bird. I have been fetched out of bed several times to listen to it, but I need hardly say that I was never able to distinguish anything unnatural. The men, however, are so absurdly positive upon the subject that it is hopeless to argue with them. I mentioned the matter to the Captain once, but to my surprise he took it very gravely, and indeed appeared to be considerably disturbed by what I told him. I should have thought that he at least would have been above such vulgar delusions.

All this disquisition upon superstition leads me up to the fact that Mr. Manson, our second mate, saw a ghost last night—or, at least, says that he did, which of course is the same thing. It is quite refreshing to have some new topic of conversation after the eternal routine of bears and whales which has served us for so many months. Manson swears the ship is haunted, and that he would not stay in her a day if he had any other place to go to. Indeed the fellow is honestly frightened, and I had to give him some chloral and bromide of potassium this morning to steady him down. He seemed quite indignant when I suggested that he had been having an extra glass the night before, and I was obliged to pacify him by keeping as grave a countenance as possible during his story, which he certainly narrated in a very straight-forward and matter-of-fact way.

"I was on the bridge," he said, "about four bells in the middle watch, just when the night was at its darkest. There was a bit of a moon, but the clouds were blowing across it so that you couldn't see far from the ship. John M'Leod, the harpooner, came aft from the foc'sle-head and reported a strange noise on the starboard bow. I went forrard and we both heard it, sometimes like a bairn crying and sometimes like a wench in pain. I've been seventeen years to the country and I never heard seal, old or young, make a sound like that. As we were standing there on the foc'sle-head the moon came out from behind a cloud, and we both saw a sort of white figure moving across the ice field in the same direction that we had heard the cries. We lost sight of it for a while, but it came back on the port bow, and we could just make it out like a shadow on the ice. I sent a hand aft for the rifles, and M'Leod and I went down on to the pack, thinking that maybe it might be a bear. When we got on the ice I lost sight of M'Leod, but I pushed on in the direction where I could still hear the cries. I followed them for a mile or maybe more, and then running round a hummock I came right on to the top of it standing and waiting for me seemingly. I don't know what it was. It wasn't a bear any way. It was tall and white and straight, and if it wasn't a man nor a woman, I'll stake my davy it was something worse. I made for the ship as hard as I could run, and precious glad I was to find myself aboard. I signed articles to do my duty by the ship, and on the ship I'll stay, but you don't catch me on the ice again after sundown."

That is his story, given as far as I can in his own words. I fancy what he saw must, in spite of his denial, have been a young bear erect upon its hind legs, an attitude which they often assume when alarmed. In the uncertain light this would bear a resemblance to a human figure, especially to a man whose nerves were already somewhat shaken. Whatever it may have been, the occurrence is unfortunate, for it has produced a most unpleasant effect upon the crew. Their looks are more sullen than before, and their discontent more open. The double grievance of being debarred from the herring fishing and of being detained in what they choose to call a haunted vessel, may lead them to do something rash. Even the harpooners, who are the oldest and steadiest among them, are joining in the general agitation.

Apart from this absurd outbreak of superstition, things are looking rather more cheerful. The pack which was forming to the south of us has partly cleared away, and the water is so warm as to lead me to believe that we are lying in one of those branches of the gulf-stream which run up between Greenland and Spitzbergen. There are numerous small Medusae and sea lemons about the ship, with abundance of shrimps, so that there is every possibility of "fish" being sighted. Indeed one was seen blowing about dinner-time, but in such a position that it was impossible for the boats to follow it.

September 13th.—Had an interesting conversation with the chief mate, Mr. Milne, upon the bridge. It seems that our Captain is as great an enigma to the seamen, and even to the owners of the vessel, as he has been to me. Mr. Milne tells me that when the ship is paid off, upon returning from a voyage, Captain Craigie disappears, and is not seen again until the approach of another season, when he walks quietly into the office of the company, and asks whether his services will be required. He has no friend in Dundee, nor does any one pretend to be acquainted with his early history. His position depends entirely upon his skill as a seaman, and the name for courage and coolness which he had earned in the capacity of mate, before being entrusted with a separate command. The unanimous opinion seems to be that he is not a Scotchman, and that his name is an assumed one. Mr. Milne thinks that he has devoted himself to whaling simply for the reason that it is the most dangerous occupation which he could select, and that he courts death in every possible manner. He mentioned several instances of this, one of which is rather curious, if true. It seems that on one occasion he did not put in an appearance at the office, and a substitute had to be selected in his place. That was at the time of the last Russian and Turkish war. When he turned up again next spring he had a puckered wound in the side of his neck which he used to endeavor to conceal with his cravat. Whether the mate's inference that he had been engaged in the war is true or not I cannot say. It was certainly a strange coincidence.

The wind is veering round in an easterly direction, but is still very slight. I think the ice is lying closer than it did yesterday. As far as the eye can reach on every side there is one wide expanse of spotless white, only broken by an occasional rift or the dark shadow of a hummock. To the south there is the narrow lane of blue water which is our sole means of escape, and which is closing up every day. The Captain is taking a heavy responsibility upon himself. I hear that the tank of potatoes has been finished, and even the biscuits are running short, but he preserves the same impassible countenance, and spends the greater part of the day at the crow's nest, sweeping the horizon with his glass. His manner is very variable, and he seems to avoid my society, but there has been no repetition of the violence which he showed the other night.

7.30 p.m.—My deliberate opinion is that we are commanded by a madman. Nothing else can account for the extraordinary vagaries of Captain Craigie. It is fortunate that I have kept this journal of our voyage, as it will serve to justify us in case we have to put him under any sort of restraint, a step which I should only consent to as a last resource. Curiously enough it was he himself who suggested lunacy and not mere eccentricity as the secret of his strange conduct. He was standing upon the bridge about an hour ago, peering as usual through his glass, while I was walking up and down the quarterdeck. The majority of the men were below at their tea, for the watches have not been regularly kept of late. Tired of walking, I leaned against the bulwarks, and admired the mellow glow cast by the sinking sun upon the great ice fields which surround us. I was suddenly aroused from the reverie into which I had fallen by a hoarse voice at my elbow, and starting round I found that the Captain had descended and was standing by my side. He was staring out over the ice with an expression in which horror, surprise, and something approaching to joy were contending for the mastery. In spite of the cold, great drops of perspiration were coursing down his forehead, and he was evidently fearfully excited. His limbs twitched like those of a man upon the verge of an epileptic fit, and the lines about his mouth were drawn and hard.

"Look!" he gasped, seizing me by the wrist, but still keeping his eyes upon the distant ice, and moving his head slowly in a horizontal direction, as if following some object which was moving across the field of vision. "Look! There, man, there! Between the hummocks! Now coming out from behind the far one! You see her—you *must* see her! There still! Flying from me, by God, flying from me—and gone!"

He uttered the last two words in a whisper of concentrated agony which shall never fade from my remembrance. Clinging to the ratlines he endeavored to climb up upon the top of the bulwarks as if in the hope of obtaining a last glance at the departing object. His strength was not equal to the attempt, however, and he staggered back against the saloon skylights, where he leaned panting and exhausted. His face was so livid that I expected him to become unconscious, so lost no time in leading him down the companion, and stretching him upon one of the sofas in the cabin. I then poured him out some brandy, which I held to his lips, and which had a wonderful effect upon him, bringing the blood back into his white face and steadying his poor shaking limbs. He raised himself up upon his elbow, and looking round to see that we were alone, he beckoned to me to come and sit beside him.

"You saw it, didn't you?" he asked, still in the same subdued awesome tone so foreign to the nature of the man.

"No, I saw nothing."

His head sank back again upon the cushions. "No, he wouldn't without the glass," he murmured. "He couldn't. It was the glass that showed her to me, and then the eyes of love—the eyes of love. I say, Doc, don't let the steward in! He'll think I'm mad. Just bolt the door, will you!"

I rose and did what he had commanded.

He lay quiet for a while, lost in thought apparently, and then raised himself up upon his elbow again, and asked for some more brandy.

"You don't think I am, do you, Doc?" he asked, as I was putting the bottle back into the after-locker. "Tell me now, as man to man, do you think that I am mad?"

"I think you have something on your mind," I answered, "which is exciting you and doing you a good deal of harm."

"Right there, lad!" he cried, his eyes sparkling from the effects of the brandy.

"Plenty on my mind—plenty! But I can work out the latitude and the longitude, and I can handle my sextant and manage my logarithms. You couldn't prove me mad in a court of law, could you, now?" It was curious to hear the man lying back and coolly arguing out the question of his own sanity.

"Perhaps not," I said; "but still I think you would be wise to get home as soon as you can, and settle down to a quiet life for a while."

"Get home, eh?" he muttered, with a sneer upon his face. "One word for me and two for yourself, lad. Settle down with Flora—pretty little Flora. Are bad dreams signs of madness?"

"Sometimes," I answered.

"What else? What would be the first symptoms?"

"Pains in the head, noises in the ears, flashes before the eyes, delusions"——

"Ah! what about them?" he interrupted. "What would you call a delusion?"

"Seeing a thing which is not there is a delusion."

"But she *was* there!" he groaned to himself. "She *was* there!" and rising, he unbolted the door and walked with slow and uncertain steps to his own cabin, where I have no doubt that he will remain until to-morrow morning. His system seems to have received a terrible shock, whatever it may have been that he imagined himself to have seen. The man becomes a greater mystery every day, though I fear that the solution which he has himself suggested is the correct one, and that his reason is affected. I do not think that a guilty conscience has anything to do with his behavior. The idea is a popular one among the officers, and, I believe, the crew; but I have seen nothing to support it. He has not the air of a guilty man, but of one who has had terrible usage at the hands of fortune, and who should be regarded as a martyr rather than a criminal.

The wind is veering round to the south to-night. God help us if it blocks that narrow pass which is our only road to safety! Situated as we are on the edge of the main Arctic pack, or the "barrier" as it is called by the whalers, any wind from the north has the effect of shredding out the ice around us and allowing our escape, while a wind from the south blows up all the loose ice behind us and hems us in between two packs. God help us, I say again!

September 14th.—Sunday, and a day of rest. My fears have been confirmed, and the thin strip of blue water has disappeared from the southward. Nothing but the great motionless ice fields around us, with their weird hummocks and fantastic pinnacles. There is a deathly silence over their wide expanse which is horrible. No lapping of the waves now, no cries of seagulls or straining of sails, but one deep universal silence in which the murmurs of the seamen, and the creak of their boots upon the white shining deck, seem discordant and out of place. Our only visitor was an Arctic fox, a rare animal upon the pack, though common enough upon the land. He did not come near the ship, however, but after surveying us from a distance fled rapidly across the ice. This was curious conduct, as they generally know nothing of man, and being of an inquisitive nature, become so familiar that they are easily captured. Incredible as it may seem, even this little incident produced a bad effect upon the crew. "Yon puir beastie kens mair, ay, an' sees mair nor you nor me!" was the comment of one of the leading harpooners, and the others nodded their acquiescence. It is vain to attempt to argue against such puerile superstition. They have made up their minds that there is a curse upon the ship, and nothing will ever persuade them to the contrary.

The Captain remained in seclusion all day except for about half an hour in the afternoon, when he came out upon the quarterdeck. I observed that he kept his eye fixed upon the spot where the vision of yesterday had appeared, and was quite prepared for another outburst, but none such came. He did not seem to see me although I was standing close beside him. Divine service was read as usual by the chief engineer. It is a curious thing that in whaling vessels the Church of England Prayer-book is always employed, although there is never a member of that Church among either officers or crew. Our men are all Roman Catholics or Presbyterians, the former predominating. Since a ritual is used which is foreign to both, neither can complain that the other is preferred to them, and they listen with all attention and devotion, so that the system has something to recommend it.

A glorious sunset, which made the great fields of ice look like a lake of blood. I have never seen a finer and at the same time more weird effect. Wind is veering round. If it will blow twenty-four hours from the north all will yet be well.

September 15th.—To-day is Flora's birthday. Dear lass! it is well that she cannot see her boy, as she used to call me, shut up among the ice fields with a crazy captain and a few weeks' provisions. No doubt she scans the shipping list in the *Scotsman* every morning to see if we are reported from Shetland. I have to set an example to the men and look cheery and unconcerned; but God knows, my heart is very heavy at times.

The thermometer is at nineteen Fahrenheit to-day. There is but little wind, and what there is comes from an unfavorable quarter. Captain is in an excellent humor; I think he imagines he has seen some other omen or vision, poor fellow, during the night, for he came into my room early in the morning, and stooping down over my bunk, whispered, "It wasn't a delusion, Doc; it's all right!" After breakfast he asked me to find out how much food was left, which the second mate and I proceeded to do. It is even less than we had expected. Forward they have half a tank full of biscuits, three barrels of salt meat, and a very limited supply of coffee beans and sugar. In the after-hold and lockers there are a good many luxuries, such as tinned salmon, soups, haricot mutton, &c., but they will go a very short way among a crew of fifty men. There are two barrels of flour in the store-room, and an unlimited supply of tobacco. Altogether there is about enough to keep the men on half rations for eighteen or twenty days—certainly not more. When we reported the state of things to the Captain, he ordered all hands to be piped, and addressed them from the quarterdeck. I never saw him to better advantage. With his tall, well-knit figure, and dark animated face, he seemed a man born to command, and he discussed the situation in a cool sailor-like way which showed that while appreciating the danger he had an eye for every loophole of escape.

"My lads," he said, "no doubt you think I brought you into this fix, if it is a fix, and maybe some of you feel bitter against me on account of it. But you must remember that for many a season no ship that comes to the country has brought in as much oil-money as the old *Pole-Star*, and every one of you has had his share of it. You can leave your wives behind you in comfort while other poor fellows come back to find their lasses on the parish. If you have to thank me for the one you have to thank me for the other, and we may call it quits. We've tried a bold venture before this and succeeded, so now that we've tried one and failed we've no cause to cry out about it. If the worst comes to the worst, we can make the land across the ice, and lay in a stock of seals which will keep us alive until the spring. It won't come to that, though, for you'll see the Scotch coast again before three weeks are out. At present every man must go on half rations, share and share alike, and no favor to any. Keep up your hearts and you'll pull through this as you've pulled through many a danger before." These few simple words of his had a wonderful effect upon the crew. His former unpopularity was forgotten, and the old harpooner whom I have already mentioned for his superstition, led off three cheers, which were heartily joined in by all hands.

September 16th.—The wind has veered round to the north during the night, and the ice shows some symptoms of opening out. The men are in a good humor in spite of the short allowance upon which they have been placed. Steam is kept up in the engine-room, that there may be no delay should an opportunity for escape present itself. The Captain is in exuberant spirits, though he still retains that wild "fey" expression which I have already remarked upon. This burst of cheerfulness puzzles me more than his former gloom. I cannot understand it. I think I mentioned in an early part of this journal that one of his oddities is that he never permits any person to enter his cabin, but insists upon making his own bed, such as it is, and performing every other office for himself. To my surprise he handed me the key to-day and requested me to go down there and take the time by his chronometer while he measured the altitude of the sun at noon. It is a bare little room, containing a washing-stand and a few books, but little else in the way of luxury, except some pictures upon the walls. The majority of these are small cheap oleographs, but there was one water-color sketch of the head of a young lady which arrested my attention. It was evidently a portrait, and not one of those fancy types of female beauty which sailors particularly affect. No artist could have evolved from his own mind such a curious mixture of character and weakness. The languid, dreamy eyes, with their drooping lashes, and the broad, low brow, unruffled by thought or care, were in strong contrast with the clean-cut, prominent jaw, and the resolute set of the lower lip. Underneath it in one of the corners was written, "M. B., aet. 19." That any one in the short space of nineteen years of existence could develop such strength of will as was stamped upon her face seemed to me at the time to be well-nigh incredible. She must have been an extraordinary woman. Her features have thrown such a glamor over me that, though I had but a fleeting glance at them, I could, were I a draftsman, reproduce them line for line upon this page of the journal. I wonder what part she has played in our Captain's life. He has hung her picture at the end of his berth, so that his eyes continually rest upon it. Were he a less reserved man I should make some remark upon the subject. Of the other things in his cabin there was nothing worthy of mention—uniform coats, a camp-stool, small looking-glass, tobacco-box, and numerous pipes, including an oriental hookah—which, by-the-bye, gives some color to Mr. Milne's story about his participation in the war, though the connection may seem rather a distant one.

11.20 p.m.—Captain just gone to bed after a long and interesting conversation on general topics. When he chooses he can be a most fascinating companion, being remarkably well-read, and having the power of expressing his opinion forcibly without appearing to be dogmatic. I hate to have my intellectual toes trod upon. He spoke about the nature of the soul, and sketched out the views of Aristotle and Plato upon the subject in a masterly manner. He seems to have a leaning for metempsychosis and the doctrines of Pythagoras. In discussing them we touched upon modern spiritualism, and I made some joking allusion to the impostures of Slade, upon which, to my surprise, he warned me most impressively against confusing the innocent with the guilty, and argued that it would be as logical to brand Christianity as an error because Judas, who professed that religion, was a villain. He shortly afterwards bade me good-night and retired to his room.

The wind is freshening up, and blows steadily from the north. The nights are as dark now as they are in England. I hope to-morrow may set us free from our frozen fetters.

September 17th.—The Bogie again. Thank Heaven that I have strong nerves! The superstition of these poor fellows, and the circumstantial accounts which they give, with the utmost earnestness and self-conviction, would horrify any man not accustomed to their ways. There are many versions of the matter, but the sum-total of them all is that something uncanny has been flitting round the ship all night, and that Sandie M'Donald of Peterhead and "lang" Peter Williamson of Shetland saw it, as also did Mr. Milne on the bridge—so, having three witnesses, they can make a better case of it than the second mate did. I spoke to Milne after breakfast, and told him that he should be above such nonsense, and that as an officer he ought to set the men a better example. He shook his weather-beaten head ominously, but answered with characteristic caution, "Mebbe aye, mebbe na, Doctor," he said; "I didna ca' it a ghaist. I canna' say I preen my faith in sea-bogles an' the like, though there's a mony as claims to ha' seen a' that and waur. I'm no easy feared, but maybe your ain bluid would run a bit cauld, mun, if instead o' speerin' aboot it in daylicht ye were wi' me last night, an' seed an awfu' like shape, white an' gruesome, whiles here, whiles there, an' it greetin' and ca'ing in the darkness like a bit lambie that hae lost its mither. Ye would na' be sae ready to put it a' doon to auld wives' clavers then, I'm thinkin'." I saw it was hopeless to reason with him, so contented myself with begging him as a personal favor to call me up the next time the specter appeared—a request to which he acceded with many ejaculations expressive of his hopes that such an opportunity might never arise.

As I had hoped, the white desert behind us has become broken by many thin streaks of water which intersect it in all directions. Our latitude to-day was 80° 52´ N, which shows that there is a strong southerly drift upon the pack. Should the wind continue favorable it will break up as rapidly as it formed. At present we can do nothing but smoke and wait and hope for the best. I am rapidly becoming a fatalist. When dealing with such uncertain factors as wind and ice a man can be nothing else. Perhaps it was the wind and sand of the Arabian deserts which gave the minds of the original followers of Mahomet their tendency to bow to kismet.

These spectral alarms have a very bad effect upon the Captain. I feared that it might excite his sensitive mind, and endeavored to conceal the absurd story from him, but unfortunately he overheard one of the men making an allusion to it, and insisted upon being informed about it. As I had expected, it brought out all his latent lunacy in an exaggerated form. I can hardly believe that this is the same man who discoursed philosophy last night with the most critical acumen and coolest judgment. He is pacing backwards and forwards upon the quarterdeck like a caged tiger, stopping now and again to throw out his hands with a yearning gesture, and stare impatiently out over the ice. He keeps up a continual mutter to himself, and once he called out, "But a little time, love—but a little time!" Poor fellow, it is sad to see a gallant seaman and accomplished gentleman reduced to such a pass, and to think that imagination and delusion can cow a mind to which real danger was but the salt of life. Was ever a man in such a position as I, between a demented captain and a ghost-seeing mate? I sometimes think I am the only really sane man aboard the vessel—except perhaps the second engineer, who is a kind of ruminant, and would care nothing for all the fiends in the Red Sea so long as they would leave him alone and not disarrange his tools.

The ice is still opening rapidly, and there is every probability of our being able to make a start to-morrow morning. They will think I am inventing when I tell them at home all the strange things that have be-fallen me.

12 p.m.—I have been a good deal startled, though I feel steadier now, thanks to a stiff glass of brandy. I am hardly myself yet, however, as this handwriting will testify. The fact is, that I have gone through a very strange experience, and am beginning to doubt whether I was justified in branding every one on board as madmen because they professed to have seen things which did not seem reasonable to my understanding. Pshaw! I am a fool to let such a trifle unnerve me; and yet, coming as it does after all these alarms, it has an additional significance, for I cannot doubt either Mr. Manson's story or that of the mate, now that I have experienced that which I used formerly to scoff at.

After all it was nothing very alarming—a mere sound, and that was all. I cannot expect that any one reading this, if any one ever should read it, will sympathize with my feelings, or realize the effect which it produced upon me at the time. Supper was over, and I had gone on deck to have a quiet pipe before turning in. The night was very dark—so dark that, standing under the quarter-boat, I was unable to see the officer upon the bridge. I think I have already mentioned the extraordinary silence which prevails in these frozen seas. In other parts of the world, be they ever so barren, there is some slight vibration of the air—some faint hum, be it from the distant haunts of men, or from the leaves of the trees, or the wings of the birds, or even the faint rustle of the grass that covers the ground. One may not actively perceive the sound, and yet if it were withdrawn it would be missed. It is only here in these Arctic seas that stark, unfathomable stillness obtrudes itself upon you in all its gruesome reality. You find your tympanum straining to catch some little murmur, and dwelling eagerly upon every accidental sound within the vessel. In this state I was leaning against the bulwarks when there arose from the ice almost directly underneath me a cry, sharp and shrill, upon the silent air of the night, beginning, as it seemed to me, at a note such as prima donna never reached, and mounting from that ever higher and higher until it culminated in a long wail of agony, which might have been the last cry of a lost soul. The ghastly scream is still ringing in my ears. Grief, unutterable grief, seemed to be expressed in it, and a great longing, and yet through it all there was an occasional wild note of exultation. It shrilled out from close beside me, and yet as I glared into the darkness I could discern nothing. I waited some little time, but without hearing any repetition of the sound, so I came below, more shaken than I have ever been in my life before. As I came down the companion I met Mr. Milne coming up to relieve the watch. "Weel, Doctor," he said, "maybe that's auld wives' clavers tae? Did ye no hear it skirling? Maybe that's a supersteetion? What d'ye think o't noo?" I was obliged to apologize to the honest fellow, and acknowledge that I was as puzzled by it as he was. Perhaps to-morrow things may look different. At present I dare hardly write all that I think. Reading it again in days to come, when I have shaken off all these associations, I should despise myself for having been so weak.

September 18th.—Passed a restless and uneasy night, still haunted by that strange sound. The Captain does not look as if he had had much repose either, for his face is haggard and his eyes bloodshot. I have not told him of my adventure of last night, nor shall I. He is already restless and excited, standing up, sitting down, and apparently utterly unable to keep still.

A fine lead appeared in the pack this morning, as I had expected, and we were able to cast off our ice-anchor, and steam about twelve miles in a west-sou'-westerly direction. We were then brought to a halt by a great floe as massive as any which we have left behind us. It bars our progress completely, so we can do nothing but anchor again and wait until it breaks up, which it will probably do within twenty-four hours, if the wind holds. Several bladder-nosed seals were seen swimming in the water, and one was shot, an immense creature more than eleven feet long. They are fierce, pugnacious animals, and are said to be more than a match for a bear. Fortunately they are slow and clumsy in their movements, so that there is little danger in attacking them upon the ice.

The Captain evidently does not think we have seen the last of our troubles, though why he should take a gloomy view of the situation is more than I can fathom, since every one else on board considers that we have had a miraculous escape, and are sure now to reach the open sea.

"I suppose you think it's all right now, Doctor?" he said, as we sat together after dinner.

"I hope so," I answered.

"We mustn't be too sure—and yet no doubt you are right. We'll all be in the arms of our own true loves before long, lad, won't we? But we mustn't be too sure—we mustn't be too sure."

He sat silent a little, swinging his leg thoughtfully backwards and forwards. "Look here," he continued; "it's a dangerous place this, even at its best—a treacherous, dangerous place. I have known men cut off very suddenly in a land like this. A slip would do it sometimes—a single slip, and down you go through a crack, and only a bubble on the green water to show where it was that you sank. It's a queer thing," he continued with a nervous laugh, "but all the years I've been in this country I never once thought of making a will—not that I have anything to leave in particular, but still when a man is exposed to danger he should have everything arranged and ready—don't you think so?"

"Certainly," I answered, wondering what on earth he was driving at.

"He feels better for knowing it's all settled," he went on. "Now if anything should ever befall me, I hope that you will look after things for me. There is very little in the cabin, but such as it is I should like it to be sold, and the money divided in the same proportion as the oil-money among the crew. The chronometer I wish you to keep yourself as some slight remembrance of our voyage. Of course all this is a mere precaution, but I thought I would take the opportunity of speaking to you about it. I suppose I might rely upon you if there were any necessity?"

"Most assuredly," I answered; "and since you are taking this step, I may as well"——

"You! you!" he interrupted. "*You're* all right. What the devil is the matter with *you?* There, I didn't mean to be peppery, but I don't like to hear a young fellow, that has hardly began life, speculating about death. Go up on deck and get some fresh air into your lungs instead of talking nonsense in the cabin, and encouraging me to do the same."

The more I think of this conversation of ours the less do I like it. Why should the man be settling his affairs at the very time when we seem to be emerging from all danger? There must be some method in his madness. Can it be that he contemplates suicide? I remember that upon one occasion he spoke in a deeply reverent manner of the heinousness of the crime of self-destruction. I shall keep my eye upon him, however, and though I cannot obtrude upon the privacy of his cabin, I shall at least make a point of remaining on deck as long as he stays up.

Mr. Milne pooh-poohs my fears, and says it is only the "skipper's little way."

He himself takes a very rosy view of the situation. According to him we shall be out of the ice by the day after to-morrow, pass Jan Meyen two days after that, and sight Shetland in little more than a week. I hope he may not be too sanguine. His opinion may be fairly balanced against the gloomy precautions of the Captain, for he is an old and experienced seaman, and weighs his words well before uttering them.

The long-impending catastrophe has come at last. I hardly know what to write about it. The Captain is gone. He may come back to us again alive, but I fear me—I fear me. It is now seven o'clock of the morning of the 19th of September. I have spent the whole night traversing the great ice-floe in front of us with a party of seamen in the hope of coming upon some trace of him, but in vain. I shall try to give some account of the circumstances which attended upon his disappearance. Should any one ever chance to read the words which I put down, I trust they will remember that I do not write from conjecture or from hearsay, but that I, a sane and educated man, am describing accurately what actually occurred before my very eyes. My inferences are my own, but I shall be answerable for the facts.

The Captain remained in excellent spirits after the conversation which I have recorded. He appeared to be nervous and impatient, however, frequently changing his position, and moving his limbs in an aimless choreic way which is characteristic of him at times. In a quarter of an hour he went upon deck seven times, only to descend after a few hurried paces. I followed him each time, for there was something about his face which confirmed my resolution of not letting him out of my sight. He seemed to observe the effect which his movements had produced, for he endeavored by an over-done hilarity, laughing boisterously at the very smallest of jokes, to quiet my apprehensions.

After supper he went on to the poop once more, and I with him. The night was dark and very still, save for the melancholy soughing of the wind among the spars. A thick cloud was coming up from the north-west, and the ragged tentacles which it threw out in front of it were drifting across the face of the moon, which only shone now and again through a rift in the wrack. The Captain paced rapidly backwards and forwards, and then seeing me still dogging him, he came across and hinted that he thought I should be better below—which, I need hardly say, had the effect of strengthening my resolution to remain on deck.

I think he forgot about my presence after this, for he stood silently leaning over the taffrail, and peering out across the great desert of snow, part of which lay in shadow, while part glittered mistily in the moonlight. Several times I could see by his movements that he was referring to his watch, and once he muttered a short sentence, of which I could only catch the one word "ready." I confess to having felt an eerie feeling creeping over me as I watched the loom of his tall figure through the darkness, and noted how completely he fulfilled the idea of a man who is keeping a tryst. A tryst with whom? Some vague perception began to dawn upon me as I pieced one fact with another, but I was utterly unprepared for the sequel.

By the sudden intensity of his attitude I felt that he saw something. I crept up behind him. He was staring with an eager questioning gaze at what seemed to be a wreath of mist, blown swiftly in a line with the ship. It was a dim, nebulous body, devoid of shape, sometimes more, sometimes less apparent, as the light fell on it. The moon was dimmed in its brilliancy at the moment by a canopy of thinnest cloud, like the coating of an anemone.

"Coming, lass, coming," cried the skipper, in a voice of unfathomable tenderness and compassion, like one who soothes a beloved one by some favor long looked for, and as pleasant to bestow as to receive.

What followed happened in an instant. I had no power to interfere. He gave one spring to the top of the bulwarks, and another which took him on to the ice, almost to the feet of the pale misty figure. He held out his hands as if to clasp it, and so ran into the darkness with outstretched arms and loving words. I still stood rigid and motionless, straining my eyes after his retreating form, until his voice died away in the distance. I never thought to see him again, but at that moment the moon shone out brilliantly through a chink in the cloudy heaven, and illuminated the great field of ice. Then I saw his dark figure already a very long way off, running with prodigious speed across the frozen plain. That was the last glimpse which we caught of him—perhaps the last we ever shall. A party was organized to follow him, and I accompanied them, but the men's hearts were not in the work, and nothing was found. Another will be formed within a few hours. I can hardly believe I have not been dreaming, or suffering from some hideous nightmare, as I write these things down.

7.30 p.m.—Just returned dead beat and utterly tired out from a second unsuccessful search for the Captain. The floe is of enormous extent, for though we have traversed at least twenty miles of its surface, there has been no sign of its coming to an end. The frost has been so severe of late that the overlying snow is frozen as hard as granite, otherwise we might have had the footsteps to guide us. The crew are anxious that we should cast off and steam round the floe and so to the southward, for the ice has opened up during the night, and the sea is visible upon the horizon. They argue that Captain Craigie is certainly dead, and that we are all risking our lives to no purpose by remaining when we have an opportunity of escape. Mr. Milne and I have had the greatest difficulty in persuading them to wait until to-morrow night, and have been compelled to promise that we will not under any circumstances delay our departure longer than that. We propose therefore to take a few hours' sleep, and then to start upon a final search.

September 20th, evening.—I crossed the ice this morning with a party of men exploring the southern part of the floe, while Mr. Milne went off in a northerly direction. We pushed on for ten or twelve miles without seeing a trace of any living thing except a single bird, which fluttered a great way over our heads, and which by its flight I should judge to have been a falcon. The southern extremity of the ice field tapered away into a long narrow spit which projected out into the sea. When we came to the base of this promontory, the men halted, but I begged them to continue to the extreme end of it, that we might have the satisfaction of knowing that no possible chance had been neglected.

We had hardly gone a hundred yards before M'Donald of Peterhead cried out that he saw something in front of us, and began to run. We all got a glimpse of it and ran too. At first it was only a vague darkness against the white ice, but as we raced along together it took the shape of a man, and eventually of the man of whom we were in search. He was lying face downwards upon a frozen bank. Many little crystals of ice and feathers of snow had drifted on to him as he lay, and sparkled upon his dark seaman's jacket. As we came up some wandering puff of wind caught these tiny flakes in its vortex, and they whirled up into the air, partially descended again, and then, caught once more in the current, sped rapidly away in the direction of the sea. To my eyes it seemed but a snow-drift, but many of my companions averred that it started up in the shape of a woman, stooped over the corpse and kissed it, and then hurried away across the floe. I have learned never to ridicule any man's opinion, however strange it may seem. Sure it is that Captain Nicholas Craigie had met with no painful end, for there was a bright smile upon his blue pinched features, and his hands were still outstretched as though grasping at the strange visitor which had summoned him away into the dim world that lies beyond the grave.

We buried him the same afternoon with the ship's ensign around him, and a thirty-two pound shot at his feet. I read the burial service, while the rough sailors wept like children, for there were many who owed much to his kind heart, and who showed now the affection which his strange ways had repelled during his lifetime. He went off the grating with a dull, sullen splash, and as I looked into the green water I saw him go down, down, down until he was but a little flickering patch of white hanging upon the outskirts of eternal darkness. Then even that faded away, and he was gone. There he shall lie, with his secret and his sorrows and his mystery all still buried in his breast, until that great day when the sea shall give up its dead, and Nicholas Craigie come out from among the ice with the smile upon his face, and his stiffened arms outstretched in greeting. I pray that his lot may be a happier one in that life than it has been in this.

I shall not continue my journal. Our road to home lies plain and clear before us, and the great ice field will soon be but a remembrance of the past. It will be some time before I get over the shock produced by recent events. When I began this record of our voyage I little thought of how I should be compelled to finish it. I am writing these final words in the lonely cabin, still starting at times and fancying I hear the quick nervous step of the dead man upon the deck above me. I entered his cabin to-night, as was my duty, to make a list of his effects in order that they might be entered in the official log. All was as it had been upon my previous visit, save that the picture which I have described as having hung at the end of his bed had been cut out of its frame, as with a knife, and was gone. With this last link in a strange chain of evidence I close my diary of the voyage of the *Pole-Star*.

NOTE BY DR. JOHN M'ALISTER RAY, SENIOR.—I have read over the strange events connected with the death of the Captain of the *Pole-Star,* as narrated in the journal of my son. That everything occurred exactly as he describes it I have the fullest confidence, and, indeed, the most positive certainty, for I know him to be a strong-nerved and unimaginative man, with the strictest regard for veracity. Still, the story is, on the face of it, so vague and so improbable, that I was long opposed to its publication. Within the last few days, however, I have had independent testimony upon the subject which throws a new light upon it. I had run down to Edinburgh to attend a meeting of the British Medical Association, when I chanced to come across Dr. P——, an old college chum of mine, now practicing at Saltash, in Devonshire. Upon my telling him of this experience of my son's, he declared to me that he was familiar with the man, and proceeded, to my no small surprise, to give me a description of him, which tallied remarkably well with that given in the journal, except that he depicted him as a younger man. According to his account, he had been engaged to a young lady of singular beauty residing upon the Cornish coast. During his absence at sea his betrothed had died under circumstances of peculiar horror.

IV

LOUISA BALDWIN

The Empty Picture Frame

1895

It was a wild day in September. An equinoctial gale had raged since dawn, shaking doors and windows, and battering the walls of Eastwick Court. The orchards were strewed with bruised fruit plucked by the rude hand of the wind. The gardens that yesterday, neat and trim, basked in autumn sunshine, today were littered with branches stript from the trees, and melancholy with uprooted flowers. The paths were cut into channels by torrents of rain, that washed the loose sand on the grass, where, as the water subsided, it lay in red patches. At sunset there came a sudden lull. The gale fell to a whisper, and the rain ceased. But no flush of light overspread the gray sky. No western glow shone on the somber walls, or reflected its red light on the rain-washed windows of the old house.

Within doors it was too dark to read or work, and in the enforced idleness of twilight, Miss Swinford laid down her book, and seated herself on a low chair by the fire.

Katherine Swinford was alone in the great drawing-room. As she leaned forward with hands clasped in her lap, watching the bickering flames that played about the logs on the hearth, there was something pathetic as well as dignified in her appearance. The mistress of Eastwick Court was no longer young. Her thick hair was streaked with white, and sundry lines on her brow, and about her clear gray eyes, showed where time's finger had touched her and left its mark. Her features were large but finely formed, her expression firm and self-reliant. Miss Swinford had lived so long alone, mistress of a large property, and a law unto herself in her own domain, that she had acquired the somewhat imperious manner of one who exercises a benevolent tyranny, and has an unquestioned right to be obeyed. She was the only child and heiress of Sir John Swinford who had been dead some twelve years, and she had lost her mother in her infancy.

No one could have supposed that Miss Swinford, like Queen Elizabeth, was destined to reign alone. She had had as many suitors as the Virgin Queen herself, and they might be classed in three orders. The first, and most numerous, was attracted by the estate to which the lady seemed but the necessary appendage. The second felt the charm of the heiress, and the still greater charm of her wealth, while the third order of suitor was represented by one man only, who loved Katherine for her own sake, and would have sought her for his wife if she had been penniless. No need to tell the story—"es ist ein altes Liedchen"—the true love died long ago, and his fever-worn body lay buried in the hot sand of a tropic shore, and Katherine Swinford was still and would always remain Katherine Swinford.

Perhaps as she sat by her lonely hearth in the gathering dusk, she was thinking of what might have been, of the strong arm she might have leaned on, of the children that might have called her mother. She sighed, and rising abruptly, rang for lights. "This will never do! I shall grow melancholy if I sit by myself in the twilight. It is peopled with ghosts, and with might-have-beens, the worst of all ghosts. I have been too much alone lately. I ought to keep up a succession of visitors. By the way, I wonder why I have not heard from Sir Piers Hammersley. It is ten days since I wrote to him inviting his daughter to come and stay with me." And an air of bright energy succeeded to her momentary depression, and when the lamps were brought into the room Miss Swinford was looking ten years younger than she had done a short time before.

Sir Piers Hammersley was a cousin of the late Sir John Swinford, and both descended from a common ancestor, Sir Miles Swinford, who lived at Eastwick Court in the time of Charles the First. The Hammersleys were originally Swinfords. But Sir Miles's second son Adam had married an heiress in Cumberland, Anne Hammersley, on the condition that he should bear her name as well as share her fortune. When Adam went to live in the north he took with him his sister Joceline, whose lover Colonel Dacres had been wounded fighting for his king, and died in her father's house, since when she had pined and drooped at Eastwick Court. Joceline was only three-and-twenty years old, and her family thought that absence from home and its tragic associations would restore her to health and cheerfulness.

And in this hope she made what was then the long wild journey out of Herefordshire into Cumberland. But no change of air or scene could arrest the decline into which she had fallen. Before the spring came she was laid in the vault of the Hammersleys.

Her sad story and the tradition of her beauty, confirmed by a portrait still preserved at Eastwick Court, had caused her to be remembered both by the Swinfords and Hammersleys, and the name of Joceline had not been allowed to die out in the family. The very reason why Miss Swinford had bestirred herself to write to her father's cousin whom she had not seen since she was a girl, was that his only daughter was named Joceline. Her heart had warmed towards her unknown kinswoman in her loneliness, and she had written asking Sir Piers to allow his daughter to visit her at the house that was the birthplace of the original Joceline. The Hammersleys still lived in Cumberland, and Miss Swinford's letter must have reached its destination the day after it was posted. But she had received no answer to her friendly invitation. She was astonished and almost affronted by chilling silence where she had hoped to meet with a cordial response.

"My cousin Joceline is so much younger than I that perhaps she does not feel very eager about spending a few weeks alone with me," she argued with herself. "But at least she should be wishful to see the home of her ancestors, and the portrait of Joceline Swinford, whom she is fortunate if she resembles in personal appearance."

Here Miss Swinford's soliloquy was cut short by an unexpected interruption. A sound of heavy wheels driving slowly up the avenue by which the house was approached from the high road, and the carriage, wagon, or whatever it was that could be so ponderous, came to a standstill at the front door. "The storm must have cut the gravel up terribly," thought Miss Swinford; "I never heard wheels sound so heavy in the avenue before. Who can be paying an afternoon call so late, just when I am about to dress for dinner!" and the heavy carriage drove slowly away. Immediately afterwards the drawing-room door was thrown open, and Bennet the old butler announced "Miss Hammersley." Miss Swinford started with surprise, and advanced to welcome a young and tall lady dressed in black, some fifteen years her junior. She was of a mortal pallor of complexion, with dreamy brown eyes and fair hair, and bearing the most extraordinary resemblance to the portrait of Joceline Swinford.

"My dear cousin! You have dropped upon me from the clouds! I have received no intimation that I should have the pleasure of seeing you to-day, or I would have driven to the station to meet you myself," and she kissed her young kinswoman's pale cheek.

"How cold you are, my dear! Come and sit near the fire before you take off your cloak." And she led Joceline to a low chair, and she sat down by the flickering fire, with her back to the lamp.

"What sort of a journey have you had this stormy day? I'm afraid you had to change trains rather often between Cumberland and our little village station."

Joceline Hammersley raised her eyes with a strange uncomprehending gaze, as though she were listening to a language she did not understand, and instead of replying to her question merely said, "I have come a long way, I am very tired."

"You are not strong, my dear, I am afraid, you look so pale and weary. It is a pity I cannot give you a little of my superfluous strength," and Miss Swinford smiled kindly on her young cousin. She could not take her eyes from the white oval face with its high marble brow, large dark eyes and heavy eyelids, delicate nose and small mouth with lips too pale for health. "It is astounding, perfectly astounding!" at length she said. "Do you know that you are the living image of our common ancestress Joceline Swinford! You are exactly like the Van Dyke portrait in the library! I must show it to you!"

"Oh, not to-night! not to-night!" pleaded her cousin.

"Very well then, not to-night, but first thing in the morning. By candle-light it might startle you, it would be like looking at the reflection of your face in a mirror. But let me unfasten your cloak for you, my dear." For her guest was enveloped in a long black silk cloak, with a hood drawn over her fair curls, a quaint garment becoming her so well as to suggest the idea, that the pale silent lady was an artist in dress, and studied effects very successfully.

"Do not let me trouble you," she replied, throwing her hood back upon her shoulders, "my waiting woman will give me the help I require."

"Your waiting woman! Dear child, what an antiquated phrase! But I suppose odd words and expressions still linger in the wilds of Cumberland. Your maid, yes, I will ring for her, and I will show you to your room, where I am afraid the fire can hardly be lighted yet. It should have been burning all day if you had only done me the honor to announce your arrival beforehand." And Miss Swinford opened the drawing-room door, when to her amazement her guest with unhesitating step as though she knew her way perfectly, turned towards the old part of the house, that was full of empty rooms.

"Not that way, my dear! You are going to the disused part of the building, that has not been inhabited since my grandfather's time, and belongs now-a-days entirely to ghosts and rats. Let me lead you to our comfortable modern rooms, less historically interesting, but better suited to the requirements of a tired traveler like yourself." And her guest turned to follow her with an expression of disappointment on her pale face.

"May I not see the old rooms?"

"Certainly. I will show you everything, beginning with your own portrait, to-morrow morning. But here is your maid and this is your room, as we dine in half an hour I will leave you now to dress." And mistress and maid were left together.

Miss Hammersley's maid was no less remarkable looking than her mistress, with the same extreme pallor, though here the resemblance ended, for the mistress was beautiful and the maid distinctly ugly. Her gray hair was drawn away from her dark bony forehead under a close-fitting white cap. Her eyes were small and black, and her mouth large, with thin compressed lips. Like her mistress, she was dressed in entire disregard of existing fashion, in a dark woollen material, with a deep linen collar and long white apron. At first the sight of a maid wearing a cap that a modern cook would scorn, and an apron suitable in size for a scullion, occasioned rude mirth among Miss Swinford's servants. But their laughter was brief, and succeeded by uneasy fear, for Mistress Galt (as Miss Hammersley called her maid) had queer unaccountable ways, in harmony with her strange and repellent appearance.

The morning after Miss Hammersley's arrival at Eastwick Court, the sun shone brightly on the destruction caused by the storm of the previous day, and the gardeners were busy repairing the damage done by the wind and rain.

When Miss Swinford entered the breakfast room, her guest was walking on the terrace, dressed in a white close-fitting gown low and open at the front, and her bare neck exposed to the chilly morning air. Miss Swinford hastened to her from the open window, exclaiming, "My dear child, you will catch your death of cold! Come back and put a shawl over your neck. Is it still the fashion to come down to breakfast in a low dress as my grandmother used to do!" and she led her into the house, and wrapped a soft shawl about her shoulders.

"How cold you are! And the morning air has brought no color to your face! My dear child, are you always as cold as this?"

"Yes, always," she replied quietly. Then adding as though speaking to herself, "yet I am clothed in woollen and sheltered from wind and rain."

"Drink your coffee, you make me cold to look at you! And after breakfast I will take you upstairs to the library to show you the portrait of your namesake, and you shall tell me if you see the resemblance to yourself which I think so striking. It is an odd coincidence, the dress you are wearing might have been copied from that in the picture. But you shall see for yourself," and Miss Swinford, pleased to have someone to talk to, continued chatting, and did not notice how silent her cousin remained.

After breakfast she took Joceline's cold hand in hers, and led her upstairs.

"The library was my father's favorite room, and I have made no alteration in it since his time. It was there that I last saw your father, and I remember how greatly he admired Joceline Swinford's portrait. He said he should like to have a copy of it, but he does not need that as long as he has you to look at, my dear." And Miss Swinford flung the door of the library wide open with a triumphant "there!"

But she started with astonishment, for over the fireplace, where the portrait of Joceline Swinford had been, hung only the empty frame, its tarnished gilding in somber harmony with the square of blackened wall that had been covered by the canvas.

Miss Swinford rang the bell impetuously, and ran into the corridor to second its summons with her voice.

"Bennet, Bennet! there is the most extraordinary thing! The old portrait of Miss Joceline Swinford has been taken out of the frame, and carried away bodily! The house has been broken into during the night! Search everywhere, and find out by what door or window it has been entered."

The servants gathered in a cluster round the library door, looking up at the empty frame with awe-stricken faces, and Miss Swinford sat down and fairly burst into tears. Joceline gently laid her hand on her shoulder, and said in a low voice, "Do not weep, the picture will be restored to you!" and raising her eyes her cousin beheld the very embodiment of Joceline Swinford's portrait standing beside her. The shawl had slipped from her shoulders, leaving her neck uncovered, and in face, attitude, and costume, she was so amazingly like the figure in the missing picture that Miss Swinford started. And the servants, still peering in at the door, looked from the empty frame to the pale lady, and then at each other with indefinable fear.

No trace of the thieves could be discovered. No lock, bolt or bar on door or window had been tampered with, and the picture was hung so high that whoever had stolen it, must have accomplished the theft by the help of a ladder. The local superintendent of police came to examine the house, and to take down a description of the missing picture from Miss Swinford's lips, and she advertised a large reward for its discovery or for such information as should lead to the detection of the thief.

"The picture will be restored to you," repeated Joceline.

"I am afraid not, my dear. The stolen portrait of the beautiful Duchess of Devonshire has never been recovered, and how can I hope to get my picture back again, and to unravel the mystery of its disappearance?" Miss Swinford telegraphed tidings of her loss to her lawyer in London, and followed it up by a long letter of instructions. He was to send a description of the missing portrait to all the picture dealers, and an advertisement was put in the papers warning pawnbrokers to detain the bearer, as well as the picture, if it was offered to them. And having done everything in her power to recover her treasure, Miss Swinford remained inconsolable under her loss.

The excitement in the servants' hall was intense, and the physical difficulty of abstracting from its frame, a picture hung at such a height was dilated upon at great length. Finally they all agreed with old Bennet when he gave it as his opinion, "that it was like as if it had been spirited away!"

Only one person in the house appeared indifferent to the prevailing distress and anxiety, and this was Mistress Galt, who went about chuckling to herself with eldritch laughter.

Several days passed in which Miss Swinford did little but lament her loss, and exhaust conjecture as to how the picture could have been so mysteriously removed. But neither search nor enquiry threw any light on the matter. The portrait had vanished, leaving no more trace than if it had melted into thin air.

Her distraction of mind at first prevented Miss Swinford from noticing her guest, as she otherwise would have done. But as she became less preoccupied, she observed in Joceline Hammersley numberless little peculiarities, that, taken all together, convinced her she was unlike anyone she had ever met before. She had none of the ardor and impetuosity of youth, she was silent and reticent. She was ignorant of everyday matters that a child would know, and yet surprised her by considerable out of the way knowledge, and acquaintance with by-gone times, though she knew nothing of contemporary history. Her phraseology was often amusingly antiquated. Sometimes too she would misunderstand the plainest language, and require it to be translated into another form before she appeared to grasp its meaning.

"Does your father never take you to London, my dear?" asked Miss Swinford, thinking it a pity that so lovely a young creature should not see more society than her country home afforded.

"He took me thither once on a time when I was but a child, and I call to mind that while we were at our lodging in Whitehall the Queen was brought to bed of a son, and the rejoicing thereat."

"My dear Joceline, you positively must not make use of such an old-fashioned, countrified expression as 'brought to bed!'" said Miss Swinford, "it is only fit for an old nurse! Ladies may have spoken in that way a century ago, but it is purely rustic now. If you must date your visit to London by royal domestic events, you should say you were there when the Queen was confined."

"But that would not be the truth," replied Joceline, raising her dark eyes and folding her hands in her lap, "for it was not the Queen's but the King's majesty that was confined in Carisbrook Castle," and she sighed heavily.

Miss Swinford was confounded. Could it be that her beautiful young kinswoman was mildly deranged? She looked into the dreamy brown eyes fixed upon her, and merely saying, "I think you have lived too much alone in the country," lapsed into thoughtful silence.

That night when Miss Swinford was retiring to rest and her maid was about to leave the room, she lingered at the door and said, "There's something I want to speak to you about, miss, but I hardly know how to, for it's about Miss Hammersley."

"What is it, Dapper? What can you have to say that concerns my cousin?"

"There's something strange about the young lady, miss, and about Mistress Galt too, as she calls her. They walk in their sleep or something as bad. Last night when I was lying awake I heard footsteps, and I got up and opened my door, and crossed the gallery and looked over the banisters, and there below if there wasn't

Miss Hammersley and her maid going into the empty rooms in the old part of the house. I saw them quite plain in the moonlight through the big window. They were in their day dresses, they hadn't undressed for bed though it was past two o'clock, and Miss Hammersley was crying and sobbing. They seemed to know their way about the house in the dark as well as we do by daylight! I felt frightened and went back to bed, and it would be a good half hour before I heard them creep back to their rooms again. I thought I'd better tell you about it, miss."

"You amaze me, Dapper! It's impossible that they both walk in their sleep. But perhaps my cousin does, and her maid follows her lest she should meet with some accident, or wake suddenly and be alarmed."

"I hope, miss, that if you hear anything tonight you'll please to get up and see for yourself. I'll put your dressing-gown by the candle and matches, and if you want me I'm a light sleeper, I should wake if you only scratched on the door." And Dapper retired, leaving her mistress profoundly uneasy.

Many uncomfortable thoughts were suggested to Miss Swinford's mind by what she had heard. She rose and locked the door, that if Joceline walked in her sleep, at all events she would not be startled by her entering the room in the night with wide unseeing eyes. She thought over all her cousin's peculiarities, her strange inanimate expression, her deadly pallor and coldness, her silence and dreamy look, and decided that she was a very likely subject to be a somnambulist. Having settled this painful matter to her satisfaction, Miss Swinford's mind reverted to its favorite theme—the inexplicable loss of the portrait. And she fell asleep to dream that her cousin stood in the tarnished frame over the library mantel-shelf, saying, "I told you that Joceline Swinford's portrait would come back to you!" when she woke suddenly, the clock struck two, and she heard gentle steps in the carpeted gallery.

In a moment she had put on her dressing-gown and opened the door. Dapper had left a lamp burning, and by its light she saw Joceline Hammersley in the gallery on the opposite side of the hall, followed by her maid, walking towards the door leading to the old part of the house.

Miss Swinford hastened along the gallery that ran round the four sides of the hall, till she was close behind the dim figures that had now passed beyond the light of the lamp. Mistress Galt was silent and rigid, but Joceline, pale as death, walked with clasped hands, moaning to herself. They left the door open as they entered the deserted rooms, and Miss Swinford followed unperceived. They passed quickly across stretches of pallid moonlight falling through the dusty windows, alternating with breadths of blackest shadow, opening door after door till they came to a corner room, looking out to the front and end of the house. Then they paused, and Joceline lifted up her face that no moonlight could bleach whiter, and cried, "It was here that he died! On this spot my love died! Here he lay till they bore him to his last resting place, but far from me! He alone in my narrow bed!" and Miss Swinford, terrified, and convinced that her cousin was either a mad woman or a somnambulist, turned and fled.

She did not pause or look behind her till she had locked herself in her room, when she fell half fainting upon the bed. "My poor cousin is insane! She has heard the story of the death of Joceline Swinford's lover in this house, and has brooded over it, till with her peculiar temperament it has turned her brain. And that strange woman Galt is her keeper, I see it all now! How shall I get rid of her? I shall become mad myself if we stay together much longer in this old house. How could she know the room in which Colonel Dacres died? I have not told her, and she has not been at Eastwick Court before. It is hateful, it is uncanny!" and Miss Swinford shuddered.

Presently she heard light footsteps once more, and opening the door saw the dim figures of her cousin and her maid returning to their room. They had made a complete circuit of the house, and regained the gallery by means of a disused staircase, the door leading to which was kept locked. When all was once more silent, Miss Swinford crossed the gallery, candle in hand, to examine for herself if the lock had been tampered with. But the door was fastened as it had been for many years, and the paper pasted round it to prevent drafts was undisturbed. Yet there was no other means of reaching the side of the gallery by which Joceline Hammersley and Mistress Galt had returned to their rooms, except by this staircase.

Miss Swinford slept no more that night, and when she closed her eyes, it was only to open them and assure herself that the pale-faced Joceline was not standing by her side.

At length when morning light filled the room, she drew aside the curtain and looked into the garden. She was startled to see Joceline and Mistress Galt standing together under the window. Neither of them wore hood or kerchief in the keen morning air, and Joceline's bare neck looked white and cold as marble. "She is as like the old portrait as though she were the original Joceline come back from the dead!" exclaimed Miss Swinford.

Mistress and maid were looking fixedly at a spot in the garden, towards which first one pointed and then another, and in the silence of the early morning Miss Swinford could hear every word.

"And I say, Mistress Joceline, that the bowling green lay yonder!"

"Nay, be not so confident. You were here but for a few months when all was sorrow and confusion, while I dwelt here for three-and-twenty years, and till the cruel wars came had great joy and pleasure in my home. The bowling green was by the sundial, and lay to the north of the maze. But that is gone too. All is changed, the very flowers wear strange faces."

"Shall you not rest, Mistress, since you have seen that which you prayed to see once more?"

"Yes, I shall rest. I shall sleep till we all wake together."

"Mad! Stark mad!" ejaculated her cousin as she dropped the curtain and turned from the window.

The day proved wet and stormy, and Miss Swinford had to pass the heavy hours indoors with her uncanny guest. She was now so fully convinced of her cousin's insanity that she felt nervous in her presence, and unable to question her about her mysterious conduct. Joceline was, if possible, quieter and more reserved than ever. She looked fearfully ill, at times scarcely conscious, and as though her dark eyes moved with difficulty from one object to another.

"I am afraid you did not rest well last night, you seem so tired," Miss Swinford ventured to say.

"I have not slept of late, but soon I shall rest again." And she seemed almost to fall asleep as she spoke. Only once did she show spontaneous interest in anything, when turning over the leaves of a book, she came upon an engraving of the celebrated portrait of Strafford. Then her pale face seemed to radiate light. "My Lord Strafford!" she exclaimed, "and yet how unlike, for no picture can give the dark fire of his eye! O noble soul, that gave thy life for thy king, and yet wast powerless to avert his doom!"

At length the tedious day drew to an end. The two ladies were sitting in silence in the drawing-room, Miss Swinford wondering when her strange cousin would depart. She was resolved that she would write to Sir Piers to say that the change back to the bracing air of the north would be beneficial to his daughter's health, when Joceline rose noiselessly and left the room. "How shall I get through another night with that unaccountable being wandering about the house, asleep or insane!" she thought looking after her with a troubled expression. "I cannot bear the strain of her company! It will be long indeed before I invite a stranger again to pay me a visit!" when the door opened and her cousin stood before her pale as a lily, dressed in her black traveling cloak and hood. Miss Swinford rose in amazement. "My dear, what is the meaning of this! You came unannounced, you cannot surely be leaving me as abruptly as you arrived!"

"I must go, I am wanted," she said. And as she spoke the sound of heavy wheels was heard approaching the house. An inexplicable fear fell upon Miss Swinford.

"But how shall you travel? You are too late for any train to-night."

"I go as I came. I shall soon be at my journey's end. Farewell, cousin Katherine, and be of good cheer, the portrait of Joceline Swinford will be restored to you!" Miss Swinford mechanically followed her downstairs, where Mistress Galt was already waiting, and the servants peering over the banisters to watch the departure. Miss Swinford stept into the porch with her guest, and there stood waiting a huge coach, drawn by four black horses. By the light of the moon, issuing from beneath a cloud, she saw that the coachman was dressed in as antique a style as his mistress, and that his face like hers was deadly pale.

"Farewell, cousin, farewell!" said Joceline, touching Miss Swinford's cheek with her cold lips, "the missing picture will be restored to its place." And followed by Mistress Galt she stepped into the coach, in which six persons could have seated themselves with ease. She leaned out of the window, and bowed to her hostess with solemn formality. Then the horses moving at a heavy trot drew the lumbering vehicle down the avenue towards the high road. Miss Swinford, Bennet, Dapper and a couple of grooms attracted by the extraordinary sound of the heavy carriage approaching the house, stood awestruck watching it depart. Not one of them could have expressed his fear in words, and the terror each felt was the greater for being unspoken. The huge coach rumbled along the avenue, when it turned into the high road, and still they could hear the heavy wagon-like sound of its wheels.

"They have taken the turning to the left!" cried Miss Swinford, the first to break silence. "That great carriage and four horses can never cross the Brook Bridge. They should have turned to the right. See if you can overtake them before the road is too narrow for them to turn!" and the grooms ran down a side path that was used as a shortcut to the road. The heavy sound of wheels grew duller and more distant, and suddenly ceased. "Thank goodness they are stopped in time, they will turn now!" said Miss Swinford. But still no sound was heard. Presently the grooms came back breathless with running, the younger of them looking ready to faint.

"You stopped them in time, Landon, I hope?" asked Miss Swinford of the elder of the two men.

"O Lord, O Lord, ma'am, there's no coach nor nothing to stop! As I'm a living sinner there's nothing but a three-mile stretch o' road clear as day in the moonlight, and not so much as a wheelbarrow on it, and neither man nor beast to be seen! That big coach and four's clean gone, same as if it had sunk into the ground!"

"Come into the house, madam," said Dapper, supporting her mistress, for she staggered as though she would fall, "and thank God, however they're gone, those white-faced witches are out of the place at last!" And sick with amazement Miss Swinford suffered herself to be led indoors.

When she had recovered herself, she said with her usual determination, "Dapper and Bennet, come with me into the library, I want you both!" And they followed their mistress in silence. Miss Swinford paused for an instant on the threshold, then opening wide the door all three entered the room. The lamp stood on the table, a cheerful fire burned on the hearth. Everything was in its accustomed order, and Dapper and Bennet looked vaguely about them wondering why they were wanted. But their mistress pointed to the wall above the mantel-shelf. From its tarnished frame the portrait of Joceline Swinford looked down on them once more, as though it had never been missing from its place. Dapper screamed shrilly, Bennet gazed open-mouthed, Miss Swinford buried her face in her hands and said in a tremulous voice, "This is dreadful! What does it mean, what can it mean!"

The next morning's post brought Miss Swinford a letter fron Sir Piers Hammersly, at Carlsbad, where he and his daughter were staying, apologizing for her letter remaining so long unanswered, but it had been carelessly overlooked and only forwarded to him that day. He was exceedingly annoyed to think how uncourteous he must have appeared. Joceline, too, was as sorry as himself. She hoped that her cousin would renew her kind invitation some future time, to give her the pleasure of making her acquaintance, and of visiting the old home of the family.

Then the strange beautiful girl who had come and gone so mysteriously, whose visit had corresponded with the absence of the portrait of Joceline Swinford, was not her cousin after all! Who then was she, or *what* was she? Miss Swinford believed that she knew who her strange guest had been. But she dared not express her conviction in words. Her friends would have thought her mad. She kept her secret locked in her breast. But she was a changed woman from that time forward, and within twelve months the last of the Swinfords was laid to rest in the family burial place. The old servants still tell the story of the pale lady's visit, and her weird ways, and how their mistress fell into pining health from the very night of her mysterious departure.

V

W. W. JACOBS

The Monkey's Paw

1902

I.

Without, the night was cold and wet, but in the small parlor of Laburnam Villa the blinds were drawn and the fire burned brightly. Father and son were at chess, the former, who possessed ideas about the game involving radical changes, putting his king into such sharp and unnecessary perils that it even provoked comment from the white-haired old lady knitting placidly by the fire.

"Hark at the wind," said Mr. White, who, having seen a fatal mistake after it was too late, was amiably desirous of preventing his son from seeing it.

"I'm listening," said the latter, grimly surveying the board as he stretched out his hand. "Check."

"I should hardly think that he'd come tonight," said his father, with his hand poised over the board.

"Mate," replied the son.

"That's the worst of living so far out," bawled Mr. White, with sudden and unlooked-for violence; "of all the beastly, slushy, out-of-the-way places to live in, this is the worst. Pathway's a bog, and the road's a torrent. I don't know what people are thinking about. I suppose because only two houses in the road are let, they think it doesn't matter."

"Never mind, dear," said his wife, soothingly; "perhaps you'll win the next one."

Mr. White looked up sharply, just in time to intercept a knowing glance between mother and son. The words died away on his lips, and he hid a guilty grin in his thin gray beard.

"There he is," said Herbert White, as the gate banged to loudly and heavy footsteps came toward the door.

The old man rose with hospitable haste, and opening the door, was heard condoling with the new arrival. The new arrival also condoled with himself, so that Mrs. White said, "Tut, tut!" and coughed gently as her husband entered the room, followed by a tall, burly man, beady of eye and rubicund of visage.

"Sergeant-Major Morris," he said, introducing him.

The sergeant-major shook hands, and taking the proffered seat by the fire, watched contentedly while his host got out whiskey and tumblers and stood a small copper kettle on the fire.

At the third glass his eyes got brighter, and he began to talk, the little family circle regarding with eager interest this visitor from distant parts, as he squared his broad shoulders in the chair and spoke of wild scenes and doughty deeds; of wars and plagues and strange peoples.

"Twenty-one years of it," said Mr. White, nodding at his wife and son. "When he went away he was a slip of a youth in the warehouse. Now look at him."

"He don't look to have taken much harm," said Mrs. White, politely.

"I'd like to go to India myself," said the old man, "just to look round a bit, you know."

"Better where you are," said the sergeant-major, shaking his head. He put down the empty glass, and sighing softly, shook it again.

"I should like to see those old temples and fakirs and jugglers," said the old man. "What was that you started telling me the other day about a monkey's paw or something, Morris?"

"Nothing," said the soldier, hastily. "Leastways nothing worth hearing."

"Monkey's paw?" said Mrs. White, curiously.

"Well, it's just a bit of what you might call magic, perhaps," said the sergeant-major, off-handedly.

His three listeners leaned forward eagerly. The visitor absentmindedly put his empty glass to his lips and then set it down again. His host filled it for him.

"To look at," said the sergeant-major, fumbling in his pocket, "it's just an ordinary little paw, dried to a mummy."

He took something out of his pocket and proffered it. Mrs. White drew back with a grimace, but her son, taking it, examined it curiously.

"And what is there special about it?" inquired Mr. White as he took it from his son, and having examined it, placed it upon the table.

"It had a spell put on it by an old fakir," said the sergeant-major, "a very holy man. He wanted to show that fate ruled people's lives, and that those who interfered with it did so to their sorrow. He put a spell on it so that three separate men could each have three wishes from it."

His manner was so impressive that his hearers were conscious that their light laughter jarred somewhat.

"Well, why don't you have three, sir?" said Herbert White, cleverly.

The soldier regarded him in the way that middle age is wont to regard presumptuous youth. "I have," he said, quietly, and his blotchy face whitened.

"And did you really have the three wishes granted?" asked Mrs. White.

"I did," said the sergeant-major, and his glass tapped against his strong teeth.

"And has anybody else wished?" persisted the old lady.

"The first man had his three wishes. Yes," was the reply; "I don't know what the first two were, but the third was for death. That's how I got the paw."

His tones were so grave that a hush fell upon the group.

"If you've had your three wishes, it's no good to you now, then, Morris," said the old man at last. "What do you keep it for?"

The soldier shook his head. "Fancy, I suppose," he said, slowly. "I did have some idea of selling it, but I don't think I will. It has caused enough mischief already. Besides, people won't buy. They think it's a fairy tale; some of them, and those who do think anything of it want to try it first and pay me afterward."

"If you could have another three wishes," said the old man, eyeing him keenly, "would you have them?"

"I don't know," said the other. "I don't know."

He took the paw, and dangling it between his forefinger and thumb, suddenly threw it upon the fire. White, with a slight cry, stooped down and snatched it off.

"Better let it burn," said the soldier, solemnly.

"If you don't want it, Morris," said the other, "give it to me."

"I won't," said his friend, doggedly. "I threw it on the fire. If you keep it, don't blame me for what happens. Pitch it on the fire again like a sensible man."

The other shook his head and examined his new possession closely. "How do you do it?" he inquired.

"Hold it up in your right hand and wish aloud," said the sergeant-major, "but I warn you of the consequences."

"Sounds like the *Arabian Nights,*" said Mrs. White, as she rose and began to set the supper. "Don't you think you might wish for four pairs of hands for me?"

Her husband drew the talisman from his pocket, and then all three burst into laughter as the sergeant-major, with a look of alarm on his face, caught him by the arm.

"If you must wish," he said, gruffly, "wish for something sensible."

Mr. White dropped it back in his pocket, and placing chairs, motioned his friend to the table. In the business of supper the talisman was partly forgotten, and afterward the three sat listening in an enthralled fashion to a second installment of the soldier's adventures in India.

"If the tale about the monkey's paw is not more truthful than those he has been telling us," said Herbert, as the door closed behind their guest, just in time for him to catch the last train, "we sha'nt make much out of it."

"Did you give him anything for it, father?" inquired Mrs. White, regarding her husband closely.

"A trifle," said he, coloring slightly. "He didn't want it, but I made him take it. And he pressed me again to throw it away."

"Likely," said Herbert, with pretended horror. "Why, we're going to be rich, and famous and happy. Wish to be an emperor, father, to begin with; then you can't be henpecked."

He darted round the table, pursued by the maligned Mrs. White armed with an antimacassar.

Mr. White took the paw from his pocket and eyed it dubiously. "I don't know what to wish for, and that's a fact," he said, slowly. "It seems to me I've got all I want."

"If you only cleared the house, you'd be quite happy, wouldn't you?" said Herbert, with his hand on his shoulder. "Well, wish for two hundred pounds, then; that'll just do it."

His father, smiling shamefacedly at his own credulity, held up the talisman, as his son, with a solemn face, somewhat marred by a wink at his mother, sat down at the piano and struck a few impressive chords.

"I wish for two hundred pounds," said the old man distinctly.

A fine crash from the piano greeted the words, interrupted by a shuddering cry from the old man. His wife and son ran toward him.

"It moved," he cried, with a glance of disgust at the object as it lay on the floor. "As I wished, it twisted in my hand like a snake."

"Well, I don't see the money," said his son as he picked it up and placed it on the table, "and I bet I never shall."

"It must have been your fancy, father," said his wife, regarding him anxiously.

He shook his head. "Never mind, though; there's no harm done, but it gave me a shock all the same."

They sat down by the fire again while the two men finished their pipes. Outside, the wind was higher than ever, and the old man started nervously at the sound of a door banging upstairs. A silence unusual and depressing settled upon all three, which lasted until the old couple rose to retire for the night.

"I expect you'll find the cash tied up in a big bag in the middle of your bed," said Herbert, as he bade them good-night, "and something horrible squatting up on top of the wardrobe watching you as you pocket your ill-gotten gains."

He sat alone in the darkness, gazing at the dying fire, and seeing faces in it. The last face was so horrible and so simian that he gazed at it in amazement. It got so vivid that, with a little uneasy laugh, he felt on the table for a glass containing a little water to throw over it. His hand grasped the monkey's paw, and with a little shiver he wiped his hand on his coat and went up to bed.

II.

In the brightness of the wintry sun next morning as it streamed over the breakfast table he laughed at his fears. There was an air of prosaic wholesomeness about the room which it had lacked on the previous night, and the dirty, shriveled little paw was pitched on the sideboard with a carelessness which betokened no great belief in its virtues.

"I suppose all old soldiers are the same," said Mrs. White. "The idea of our listening to such nonsense! How could wishes be granted in these days? And if they could, how could two hundred pounds hurt you, father?"

"Might drop on his head from the sky," said the frivolous Herbert.

"Morris said the things happened so naturally," said his father, "that you might if you so wished attribute it to coincidence."

"Well, don't break into the money before I come back," said Herbert as he rose from the table. "I'm afraid it'll turn you into a mean, avaricious man, and we shall have to disown you."

His mother laughed, and following him to the door, watched him down the road; and returning to the breakfast table, was very happy at the expense of her husband's credulity. All of which did not prevent her from scurrying to the door at the postman's knock, nor prevent her from referring somewhat shortly to retired sergeant-majors of bibulous habits when she found that the post brought a tailor's bill.

"Herbert will have some more of his funny remarks, I expect, when he comes home," she said, as they sat at dinner.

"I dare say," said Mr. White, pouring himself out some beer; "but for all that, the thing moved in my hand; that I'll swear to."

"You thought it did," said the old lady soothingly.

"I say it did," replied the other. "There was no thought about it; I had just—— What's the matter?"

His wife made no reply. She was watching the mysterious movements of a man outside, who, peering in an undecided fashion at the house, appeared to be trying to make up his mind to enter. In mental connection with the two hundred pounds, she noticed that the stranger was well dressed, and wore a silk hat of glossy newness. Three times he paused at the gate, and then walked on again. The fourth time he stood with his hand upon it, and then with sudden resolution flung it open and walked up the path. Mrs. White at the same moment placed her hands behind her, and hurriedly unfastening the strings of her apron, put that useful article of apparel beneath the cushion of her chair.

She brought the stranger, who seemed ill at ease, into the room. He gazed at her furtively, and listened in a preoccupied fashion as the old lady apologized for the appearance of the room, and her husband's coat, a garment which he usually reserved for the garden. She then waited as patiently as her sex would permit, for him to broach his business, but he was at first strangely silent.

"I—was asked to call," he said at last, and stooped and picked a piece of cotton from his trousers. "I come from 'Maw and Meggins.'"

The old lady started. "Is anything the matter?" she asked, breathlessly. "Has anything happened to Herbert? What is it? What is it?"

Her husband interposed. "There, there, mother," he said, hastily. "Sit down, and don't jump to conclusions. You've not brought bad news, I'm sure, sir"; and he eyed the other wistfully.

"I'm sorry——" began the visitor.

"Is he hurt?" demanded the mother, wildly.

The visitor bowed in assent. "Badly hurt," he said, quietly, "but he is not in any pain."

"Oh, thank God!" said the old woman, clasping her hands. "Thank God for that! Thank——"

She broke off suddenly as the sinister meaning of the assurance dawned upon her and she saw the awful confirmation of her fears in the other's perverted face. She caught her breath, and turning to her slower-witted husband, laid her trembling old hand upon his. There was a long silence.

"He was caught in the machinery," said the visitor at length in a low voice.

"Caught in the machinery," repeated Mr. White, in a dazed fashion, "yes."

He sat staring blankly out at the window, and taking his wife's hand between his own, pressed it as he had been wont to do in their old courting-days nearly forty years before.

"He was the only one left to us," he said, turning gently to the visitor. "It is hard."

The other coughed, and rising, walked slowly to the window. "The firm wished me to convey their sincere sympathy with you in your great loss," he said, without looking round. "I beg that you will understand I am only their servant and merely obeying orders."

There was no reply; the old woman's face was white, her eyes staring, and her breath inaudible; on the husband's face was a look such as his friend the sergeant might have carried into his first action.

"I was to say that Maw and Meggins disclaim all responsibility," continued the other. "They admit no liability at all, but in consideration of your son's services, they wish to present you with a certain sum as compensation."

Mr. White dropped his wife's hand, and rising to his feet, gazed with a look of horror at his visitor. His dry lips shaped the words, "How much?"

"Two hundred pounds," was the answer.

Unconscious of his wife's shriek, the old man smiled faintly, put out his hands like a sightless man, and dropped, a senseless heap, to the floor.

III.

In the huge new cemetery, some two miles distant, the old people buried their dead, and came back to a house steeped in shadow and silence. It was all over so quickly that at first they could hardly realize it, and remained in a state of expectation as though of something else to happen—something else which was to lighten this load, too heavy for old hearts to bear.

But the days passed, and expectation gave place to resignation—the hopeless resignation of the old, sometimes miscalled, apathy. Sometimes they hardly exchanged a word, for now they had nothing to talk about, and their days were long to weariness.

It was about a week after that the old man, waking suddenly in the night, stretched out his hand and found himself alone. The room was in darkness, and the sound of subdued weeping came from the window. He raised himself in bed and listened.

"Come back," he said, tenderly. "You will be cold."

"It is colder for my son," said the old woman, and wept afresh.

The sound of her sobs died away on his ears. The bed was warm, and his eyes heavy with sleep. He dozed fitfully, and then slept until a sudden wild cry from his wife awoke him with a start.

"The paw!" she cried wildly. "The monkey's paw!"

He started up in alarm. "Where? Where is it? What's the matter?"

She came stumbling across the room toward him. "I want it," she said, quietly. "You've not destroyed it?"

"It's in the parlor, on the bracket," he replied, marveling. "Why?"

She cried and laughed together, and bending over, kissed his cheek.

"I only just thought of it," she said, hysterically. "Why didn't I think of it before? Why didn't *you* think of it?"

"Think of what?" he questioned.

"The other two wishes," she replied, rapidly. "We've only had one."

"Was not that enough?" he demanded, fiercely.

"No," she cried, triumphantly; "we'll have one more. Go down and get it quickly, and wish our boy alive again."

The man sat up in bed and flung the bedclothes from his quaking limbs. "Good God, you are mad" he cried, aghast.

"Get it," she panted; "get it quickly, and wish——Oh, my boy, my boy!"

Her husband struck a match and lit the candle. "Get back to bed," he said, unsteadily. "You don't know what you are saying."

"We had the first wish granted," said the old woman, feverishly; "why not the second?"

"A coincidence," stammered the old man.

"Go and get it and wish," cried his wife, quivering with excitement.

The old man turned and regarded her, and his voice shook. "He has been dead ten days, and besides he—I would not tell you else, but—I could only recognize him by his clothing. If he was too terrible for you to see then, how now?"

"Bring him back," cried the old woman, and dragged him toward the door. "Do you think I fear the child I have nursed?"

He went down in the darkness, and felt his way to the parlor, and then to the mantelpiece. The talisman was in its place, and a horrible fear that the unspoken wish might bring his mutilated son before him ere he could escape from the room seized upon him, and he caught his breath as he found that he had lost the direction of the door. His brow cold with sweat, he felt his way round the table, and groped along the wall until he found himself in the small passage with the unwholesome thing in his hand.

Even his wife's face seemed changed as he entered the room. It was white and expectant, and to his fears seemed to have an unnatural look upon it. He was afraid of her.

"*Wish!*" she cried, in a strong voice.

"It is foolish and wicked," he faltered.

"*Wish!*" repeated his wife.

He raised his hand. "I wish my son alive again."

The talisman fell to the floor, and he regarded it fearfully. Then he sank trembling into a chair as the old woman, with burning eyes, walked to the window and raised the blind.

He sat until he was chilled with the cold, glancing occasionally at the figure of the old woman peering through the window. The candle-end, which had burned below the rim of the china candlestick, was throwing pulsating shadows on the ceiling and walls, until, with a flicker larger than the rest, it expired. The old man, with an unspeakable sense of relief at the failure of the talisman, crept back to his bed, and a minute or two afterward the old woman came silently and apathetically beside him.

Neither spoke, but lay silently listening to the ticking of the clock. A stair creaked, and a squeaky mouse scurried noisily through the wall. The darkness was oppressive, and after lying for some time screwing up his courage, he took the box of matches, and striking one, went downstairs for a candle.

At the foot of the stairs the match went out, and he paused to strike another; and at the same moment a knock, so quiet and stealthy as to be scarcely audible, sounded on the front door.

The matches fell from his hand and spilled in the passage. He stood motionless, his breath suspended until the knock was repeated. Then he turned and fled swiftly back to his room, and closed the door behind him. A third knock sounded through the house.

"What's that?" cried the old woman, starting up.

"A rat," said the old man in shaking tones—"a rat. It passed me on the stairs."

His wife sat up in bed listening. A loud knock resounded through the house.

"It's Herbert!" she screamed. "It's Herbert!"

She ran to the door, but her husband was before her, and catching her by the arm, held her tightly.

"What are you going to do?" he whispered hoarsely.

"It's my boy; it's Herbert!" she cried, struggling mechanically. "I forgot it was two miles away. What are you holding me for? Let go. I must open the door."

"For God's sake don't let it in," cried the old man, trembling.

"You're afraid of your own son," she cried, struggling. "Let me go. I'm coming, Herbert; I'm coming."

There was another knock, and another. The old woman with a sudden wrench broke free and ran from the room. Her husband followed to the landing, and called after her appealingly as she hurried downstairs. He heard the chain rattle back and the bottom bolt drawn slowly and stiffly from the socket. Then the old woman's voice, strained and panting.

"The bolt," she cried, loudly. "Come down. I can't reach it."

But her husband was on his hands and knees groping wildly on the floor in search of the paw. If he could only find it before the thing outside got in. A perfect fusillade of knocks reverberated through the house, and he heard the scraping of a chair as his wife put it down in the passage against the door. He heard the creaking of the bolt as it came slowly back, and at the same moment he found the monkey's paw, and frantically breathed his third and last wish.

The knocking ceased suddenly, although the echoes of it were still in the house. He heard the chair drawn back, and the door opened. A cold wind rushed up the staircase, and a long loud wail of disappointment and misery from his wife gave him courage to run down to her side, and then to the gate beyond. The street lamp flickering opposite shone on a quiet and deserted road.

VI

AMBROSE BIERCE

An Inhabitant OF *Carcosa*

1886

For there be divers sorts of death—some wherein the body remaineth; and in some it vanisheth quite away with the spirit. This commonly occurreth only in solitude (such is God's will) and, none seeing the end, we say the man is lost, or gone on a long journey—which indeed he hath; but sometimes it hath happened in sight of many, as abundant testimony showeth. In one kind of death the spirit also dieth, and this it hath been known to do while yet the body was in vigor for many years. Sometimes, as is veritably attested, it dieth with the body, but after a season it is raised up again in that place that the body did decay.

Pondering these words of Hali (whom God rest) and questioning their full meaning, as one who, having an intimation yet doubts if there be not something behind other than that which he has discerned, I noted not whither I had strayed until a sudden chill wind striking my face revived in me a sense of my surroundings. I observed with astonishment that everything seemed unfamiliar. On every side of me stretched a bleak and desolate expanse of plain, covered with a tall overgrowth of sere grass, which rustled and whistled in the autumn wind with heaven knows what mysterious and disquieting suggestion. Protruded at long intervals above it, stood strangely shaped and somber-colored rocks, which seemed to have an understanding with one another and to exchange looks of uncomfortable significance, as if they had reared their heads to watch the issue of some foreseen event. A few blasted trees here and there appeared as leaders in this malevolent conspiracy of silent expectation. The day, I thought, must be far advanced, though the sun was invisible; and although sensible that the air was raw and chill, my consciousness of that fact was rather mental than physical—I had no feeling of discomfort. Over all the dismal landscape a canopy of low, lead-colored clouds hung like a visible curse. In everything there were a menace and a portent—a hint of crime, an intimation of doom. Bird, beast, or insect there was none. The wind sighed in the bare branches of the dead trees and the gray grass bent to whisper its dread secret to the earth; but no other sound or motion broke the awful repose of that dismal place.

I observed in the herbage a number of weatherworn stones, evidently shaped with tools. They were broken, covered with moss and half sunken in the earth. Some lay prostrate, some leaned at various angles, none were vertical. They were obviously headstones of graves, though the graves themselves no longer existed as either mounds or depressions; the years had leveled all. Scattered here and there, more massive blocks showed where some pompous tomb or ambitious monument had once flung its feeble defiance at oblivion. So old seemed these relics, these vestiges of vanity and memorials of affection and piety—so battered and worn and stained, so neglected, deserted, forgotten the place, that I could not help thinking myself the discoverer of the burial-ground of a prehistoric race of men—a nation whose very name was long extinct.

Filled with these reflections, I was for some time heedless of the sequence of my own experiences, but soon I thought, "How came I hither?" A moment's reflection seemed to make this all clear, and explain at the same time, though in a disquieting way, the singularly weird character with which my fancy had invested all that I saw and heard. I was ill. I remembered now how I had been prostrated by a sudden fever, and how my family had told me that in my periods of delirium I had constantly cried out for liberty and air, and had been held in bed to prevent my escape out-of-doors. Now I had eluded the vigilance of my attendants, and had wandered hither to—to where? I could not conjecture. Clearly I was at a considerable distance from the city where I dwelt—the ancient and famous city of Carcosa. No signs of human life were anywhere visible or audible; no rising smoke, no watchdog's bark, no lowing of cattle, no shouts of children at play—nothing but this dismal burial-place, with its air of mystery and dread, due to my own disordered brain. Was I not becoming again delirious, there, beyond human aid? Was it not indeed *all* an illusion of my madness? I called aloud the names of my wife and sons, reached out my hands in search of theirs, even as I walked among the crumbling stones and in the withered grass.

A noise behind me caused me to turn about. A wild animal—a lynx—was approaching. The thought came to me: If I break down here in the desert—if the fever returns and I fail, this beast will be at my throat. I sprang toward it, shouting. It trotted tranquilly by, within a hand's breadth of me, and disappeared behind a rock. A moment later a man's head appeared to rise out of the ground a short distance away. He was ascending the far slope of a low hill whose crest was hardly to be distinguished from the general level. His whole figure soon came into view against the background of gray cloud. He was half naked, half clad in skins. His hair was unkempt, his beard long and ragged. In one hand he carried a bow and arrow; the other held a blazing torch with a long trail of black smoke. He walked slowly and with caution, as if he feared falling into some open grave concealed by the tall grass. This strange apparition surprised but did not alarm, and, taking such a course as to intercept him, I met him almost face to face, accosting him with the salutation, "God keep you!"

He gave no heed, nor did he arrest his pace.

"Good stranger," I continued, "I am ill and lost. Direct me, I beseech you, to Carcosa?"

The man broke into a barbarous chant in an unknown tongue, passing on and away. An owl on the branch of a decayed tree hooted dismally, and was answered by another in the distance. Looking upward I saw, through a sudden rift in the clouds, Aldebaran and the Hyades! In all this there was a hint of night—the lynx, the man with a torch, the owl. Yet I saw—I saw even the stars in absence of the darkness. I saw, but was apparently not seen nor heard. Under what awful spell did I exist?

I seated myself at the root of a great tree, seriously to consider what it was best to do. That I was mad I could no longer doubt, yet recognized a ground of doubt in the conviction. Of fever I had no trace. I had, withal, a sense of exhilaration and vigor altogether unknown to me—a feeling of mental and physical exaltation. My senses seemed all alert; I could feel the air as a ponderous substance, I could hear the silence.

A great root of the giant tree against whose trunk I leaned as I sat, held enclosed in its grasp a slab of granite, a portion of which protruded into a recess formed by another root. The stone was thus partly protected from the weather, though greatly decomposed. Its edges were worn round, its corners eaten away, its face deeply furrowed and scaled. Glittering particles of mica were visible in the earth beneath it—vestiges of its decomposition. This stone had apparently marked the grave out of which the tree had sprung ages ago. The tree's exacting roots had robbed the grave and made the stone a prisoner.

A sudden wind pushed some dry leaves and twigs from the uppermost face of the stone; I saw the low-relief letters of an inscription and bent to read it. God in heaven! *my* name in full!—the date of *my* birth!—the date of *my* death!

A level shaft of rosy light illuminated the whole side of the tree as I sprang to my feet in terror. The sun was rising in the east. I stood between the tree and his broad red disk—no shadow darkened the trunk! A chorus of howling wolves saluted the dawn. I saw them sitting on their haunches, singly and in groups, on the summits of irregular mounds and tumuli, filling a half of my desert prospect and extending to the horizon; and then I knew that these were the ruins of the ancient and famous city of Carcosa.

Such are the facts imparted to the medium Bayrolles by the spirit Hoseib Alar Robardin.

VII

EDGAR ALLAN POE

The Fall OF THE *House of Usher*

1839

Son cœur est un luth suspendu;
Sitôt qu'on le touche il résonne.
—DE BÉRANGER

During the whole of a dull, dark, and soundless day in the autumn of the year, when the clouds hung oppressively low in the heavens, I had been passing alone, on horseback, through a singularly dreary tract of country; and at length found myself, as the shades of the evening drew on, within view of the melancholy House of Usher. I know not how it was—but, with the first glimpse of the building, a sense of insufferable gloom pervaded my spirit. I say insufferable; for the feeling was unrelieved by any of that half-pleasurable, because poetic, sentiment, with which the mind usually receives even the sternest natural images of the desolate or terrible. I looked upon the scene before me—upon the mere house, and the simple landscape features of the domain—upon the bleak walls—upon the vacant eyelike windows—upon a few rank sedges—and upon a few white trunks of decayed trees—with an utter depression of soul which I can compare to no earthly sensation more properly than to the after-dream of the reveler upon opium—the bitter lapse into common life—the hideous dropping off of the veil. There was an iciness, a sinking, a sickening of the heart—an unredeemed dreariness of thought which no goading of the imagination could torture into aught of the sublime. What was it—I paused to think—what was it that so unnerved me in the contemplation of the House of Usher? It was a mystery all insoluble; nor could I grapple with the shadowy fancies that crowded upon me as I pondered. I was forced to fall back upon the unsatisfactory conclusion, that while, beyond doubt, there *are* combinations of very simple natural objects which have the power of thus affecting us, still the reason, and the analysis, of this power, lie among considerations beyond our depth. It was possible, I reflected, that a mere different arrangement of the particulars of the scene, of the details of the picture, would be sufficient to modify, or perhaps to annihilate its capacity for sorrowful impression; and, acting upon this idea, I reined my horse to the precipitous brink of a black and lurid tarn that lay in unruffled luster by the dwelling, and gazed down—but with a shudder even more thrilling than before—upon the remodeled and inverted images of the gray sedge, and the ghastly tree-stems, and the vacant and eyelike windows.

Nevertheless, in this mansion of gloom I now proposed to myself a sojourn of some weeks. Its proprietor, Roderick Usher, had been one of my boon companions in boyhood; but many years had elapsed since our last meeting. A letter, however, had lately reached me in a distant part of the country—a letter from him—which, in its wildly importunate nature, had admitted of no other than a personal reply. The MS. gave evidence of nervous agitation. The writer spoke of acute bodily illness—of a pitiable mental idiosyncrasy which oppressed him—and of an earnest desire to see me, as his best, and indeed, his only personal friend, with a view of attempting, by the cheerfulness of my society, some alleviation of his malady. It was the manner in which all this, and much more, was said—it was the apparent *heart* that went with his request—which allowed me no room for hesitation—and I accordingly obeyed, what I still considered a very singular summons, forthwith.

Although, as boys, we had been even intimate associates, yet I really knew little of my friend. His reserve had been always excessive and habitual. I was aware, however, that his very ancient family had been noted, time out of mind, for a peculiar sensibility of temperament, displaying itself, through long ages, in many works of exalted art, and manifested, of late, in repeated deeds of munificent yet unobtrusive charity, as well as in a passionate devotion to the intricacies, perhaps even more than to the orthodox and easily recognizable beauties, of musical science. I had learned, too, the very remarkable fact, that the stem of the Usher race, all time-honored as it was, had put forth, at no period, any enduring branch; in other words, that the entire family lay in the direct line of descent, and had always, with very trifling and very temporary variation, so lain. It was this deficiency, I considered, while running over in thought the perfect keeping of the character of the premises with the accredited character of the people, and while speculating upon the possible influence which the one, in the long lapse of centuries, might have exercised upon the other—it was this deficiency, perhaps, of collateral issue, and the consequent undeviating transmission, from sire to son, of the patrimony with the name, which had, at length, so identified the two as to merge the original title of the estate in the quaint and equivocal appellation of the "House of Usher"—an appellation which seemed to include, in the minds of the peasantry who used it, both the family and the family mansion.

I have said that the sole effect of my somewhat childish experiment, of looking down within the tarn, had been to deepen the first singular impression. There can be no doubt that the consciousness of the rapid increase of my superstition—for why should I not so term it?—served mainly to accelerate the increase itself. Such, I have long known, is the paradoxical law of all sentiments having terror as a basis. And it might have been for this reason only, that, when I again uplifted my eyes to the house itself, from its image in the pool, there grew in my mind a strange fancy—a fancy so ridiculous, indeed, that I but mention it to show the vivid force of the sensations which oppressed me. I had so worked upon my imagination as really to believe that around about the whole mansion and domain there hung an atmosphere peculiar to themselves and their immediate vicinity—an atmosphere which had no affinity with the air of heaven, but which had reeked up from the decayed trees, and the gray wall, and the silent tarn, in the form of an inelastic vapor or gas—dull, sluggish, faintly discernible, and leaden-hued. Shaking off from my spirit what *must* have been a dream, I scanned more narrowly the real aspect of the building. Its principal feature seemed to be that of an excessive antiquity. The discoloration of ages had been great. Minute fungi overspread the whole exterior, hanging in a fine tangled web-work from the eaves. Yet all this was apart from any extraordinary dilapidation. No portion of the masonry had fallen; and there appeared to be a wild inconsistency between its still perfect adaptation of parts, and the utterly porous, and evidently decayed condition of the individual stones. In this there was much that reminded me of the specious totality of old wood-work which has rotted for long years in some neglected vault, with no disturbance from the breath of the external air. Beyond this indication of extensive decay, however, the fabric gave little token of instability. Perhaps the eye of a scrutinizing observer might have discovered a barely perceptible fissure, which, extending from the roof of the building in front, made its way down the wall in a zigzag direction, until it became lost in the sullen waters of the tarn.

Noticing these things, I rode over a short causeway to the house. A servant in waiting took my horse, and I entered the Gothic archway of the hall. A valet, of stealthy step, thence conducted me, in silence, through many dark and intricate passages in my progress to the studio of his master. Much that I encountered on the way contributed, I know not how, to heighten the vague sentiments of which I have already spoken. While the objects around me—while the carvings of the ceilings, the somber tapestries of the walls, the ebon blackness of the floors, and the phantasmagoric armorial trophies which rattled as I strode, were but matters to which, or to such as which, I had been accustomed from my infancy—while I hesitated not to acknowledge how familiar was all this—I still wondered to find how unfamiliar were the fancies which ordinary images were stirring up. On one of the staircases, I met the physician of the family. His countenance, I thought, wore a mingled expression of low cunning and perplexity. He accosted me with trepidation and passed on. The valet now threw open a door and ushered me into the presence of his master.

The room in which I found myself was very large and excessively lofty. The windows were long, narrow, and pointed, and at so vast a distance from the black oaken floor as to be altogether inaccessible from within. Feeble gleams of encrimsoned light made their way through the trellised panes, and served to render sufficiently distinct the more prominent objects around; the eye, however, struggled in vain to reach the remoter angles of the chamber, or the recesses of the vaulted and fretted ceiling. Dark draperies hung upon the walls. The general furniture was profuse, comfortless, antique, and tattered. Many books and musical instruments lay scattered about, but failed to give any vitality to the scene. I felt that I breathed an atmosphere of sorrow. An air of stern, deep, and irredeemable gloom hung over and pervaded all.

Upon my entrance, Usher arose from a sofa upon which he had been lying at full length, and greeted me with a vivacious warmth which had much in it, I at first thought, of an overdone cordiality—of the constrained effort of the *ennuyé* man of the world. A glance, however, at his countenance convinced me of his perfect sincerity. We sat down; and for some moments, while he spoke not, I gazed upon him with a feeling half of pity, half of awe. Surely, man had never before so terribly altered, in so brief a period, as had Roderick Usher! It was with difficulty that I could bring myself to admit the identity of the wan being before me with the companion of my early boyhood. Yet the character of his face had been at all times remarkable. A cadaverousness of complexion; an eye large, liquid, and luminous beyond comparison; lips somewhat thin and very pallid, but of a surpassingly beautiful curve; a nose of a delicate Hebrew model, but with a breadth of nostril unusual in similar formations; a finely molded chin, speaking, in its want of prominence, of a want of moral energy; hair of a more than weblike softness and tenuity; these features, with an inordinate expansion above the regions of the temple, made up altogether a countenance not easily to be forgotten. And now in the mere exaggeration of the prevailing character of these features, and of the expression they were wont to convey, lay so much of change that I doubted to whom I spoke. The now ghastly pallor of the skin, and the now miraculous luster of the eye, above all things startled and even awed me. The silken hair, too, had been suffered to grow all unheeded, and as, in its wild gossamer texture, it floated rather than fell about the face, I could not, even with effort, connect its arabesque expression with any idea of simple humanity.

In the manner of my friend I was at once struck with an incoherence—an inconsistency; and I soon found this to arise from a series of feeble and futile struggles to overcome an habitual trepidancy, an excessive nervous agitation. For something of this nature I had indeed been prepared, no less by his letter, than by reminiscences of certain boyish traits, and by conclusions deduced from his peculiar physical conformation and temperament. His action was alternately vivacious and sullen. His voice varied rapidly from a tremulous indecision (when the animal spirits seemed utterly in abeyance) to that species of energetic concision—that abrupt, weighty, unhurried, and hollow-sounding enunciation—that leaden, self-balanced and perfectly modulated guttural utterance, which may be observed in the moments of the intensest excitement of the lost drunkard, or the irreclaimable eater of opium.

It was thus that he spoke of the object of my visit, of his earnest desire to see me, and of the solace he expected me to afford him. He entered, at some length, into what he conceived to be the nature of his malady. It was, he said, a constitutional and a family evil, and one for which he despaired to find a remedy—a mere nervous affection, he immediately added, which would undoubtedly soon pass off. It displayed itself in a host of unnatural sensations. Some of these, as he detailed them, interested and bewildered me—although, perhaps, the terms, and the general manner of the narration had their weight. He suffered much from a morbid acuteness of the senses; the most insipid food was alone endurable; he could wear only garments of certain texture; the odors of all flowers were oppressive; his eyes were tortured by even a faint light; and there were but peculiar sounds, and these from stringed instruments, which did not inspire him with horror.

To an anomalous species of terror I found him a bounden slave. "I shall perish," said he, "I *must* perish in this deplorable folly. Thus, thus, and not otherwise, shall I be lost. I dread the events of the future, not in themselves, but in their results. I shudder at the thought of any, even the most trivial, incident, which may operate upon this intolerable agitation of soul. I have, indeed, no abhorrence of danger, except in its absolute effect—in terror. In this unnerved—in this pitiable condition—I feel that I must inevitably abandon life and reason together in my struggles with some fatal demon of fear."

I learned, moreover, at intervals, and through broken and equivocal hints, another singular feature of his mental condition. He was enchained by certain superstitious impressions in regard to the dwelling which he tenanted, and from which, for many years, he had never ventured forth—in regard to an influence whose supposititious force was conveyed in terms too shadowy here to be restated—an influence which some peculiarities in the mere form and substance of his family mansion, had, by dint of long sufferance, he said, obtained over his spirit—an effect which the *physique* of the gray walls and turrets, and of the dim tarn into which they all looked down, had, at length, brought about upon the *morale* of his existence.

He admitted, however, although with hesitation, that much of the peculiar gloom which thus afflicted him could be traced to a more natural and far more palpable origin—to the severe and long-continued illness—indeed to the evidently approaching dissolution—of a tenderly beloved sister; his sole companion for long years—his last and only relative on earth. "Her decease," he said, with a bitterness which I can never forget, "would leave him (him the hopeless and the frail) the last of the ancient race of the Ushers." As he spoke the lady Madeline (for so was she called) passed slowly through a remote portion of the apartment, and, without having noticed my presence, disappeared. I regarded her with an utter astonishment not unmingled with dread. Her figure, her air, her features—all, in their very minutest development were those—were identically, (I can use no other sufficient term,) were identically those of the Roderick Usher who sat beside me. A feeling of stupor oppressed me, as my eyes followed her retreating steps. As a door, at length, closed upon her exit, my glance sought instinctively and eagerly the countenance of the brother—but he had buried his face in his hands, and I could only perceive that a far more than ordinary wanness had overspread the emaciated fingers through which trickled many passionate tears.

The disease of the lady Madeline had long baffled the skill of her physicians. A settled apathy, a gradual wasting away of the person, and frequent although transient affections of a partially cataleptical character, were the unusual diagnosis. Hitherto she had steadily borne up against the pressure of her malady, and had not betaken herself finally to bed; but, on the closing in of the evening of my arrival at the house, she succumbed, as her brother told me at night with inexpressible agitation, to the prostrating power of the destroyer—and I learned that the glimpse I had obtained of her person would thus probably be the last I should obtain—that the lady, at least while living, would be seen by me no more.

For several days ensuing, her name was unmentioned by either Usher or myself; and during this period, I was busied in earnest endeavors to alleviate the melancholy of my friend. We painted and read together—or I listened, as if in a dream, to the wild improvisations of his speaking guitar. And thus, as a closer and still closer intimacy admitted me more unreservedly into the recesses of his spirit, the more bitterly did I perceive the futility of all attempt at cheering a mind from which darkness, as if an inherent positive quality, poured forth upon all objects of the moral and physical universe, in one unceasing radiation of gloom.

I shall ever bear about me a memory of the many solemn hours I thus spent alone with the master of the House of Usher. Yet I should fail in any attempt to convey an idea of the exact character of the studies, or of the occupations, in which he involved me, or led me the way. An excited and highly distempered ideality threw a sulphurous luster over all. His long improvised dirges will ring forever in my ears. Among other things, I bear painfully in mind a certain singular perversion and amplification of the wild air of the last waltz of Von Weber. From the paintings over which his elaborate fancy brooded, and which grew, touch by touch, into vaguenesses at which I shuddered the more thrillingly, because I shuddered knowing not why, from these paintings (vivid as their images now are before me) I would in vain endeavor to educe more than a small portion which should lie within the compass of merely written words. By the utter simplicity, by the nakedness of his designs, he arrested and overawed attention. If ever mortal painted an idea, that mortal was Roderick Usher. For me at least—in the circumstances then surrounding me—there arose out of the pure abstractions which the hypochondriac contrived to throw upon his canvas, an intensity of intolerable awe, no shadow of which felt I ever yet in the contemplation of the certainly glowing yet too concrete reveries of Fuseli.

One of the phantasmagoric conceptions of my friend, partaking not so rigidly of the spirit of abstraction, may be shadowed forth, although feebly, in words. A small picture presented the interior of an immensely long and rectangular vault or tunnel, with low walls, smooth, white, and without interruption or device. Certain accessory points of the design served well to convey the idea that this excavation lay at an exceeding depth below the surface of the earth. No outlet was observed in any portion of its vast extent, and no torch, or other artificial source of light was discernible—yet a flood of intense rays rolled throughout, and bathed the whole in a ghastly and inappropriate splendor.

I have just spoken of that morbid condition of the auditory nerve which rendered all music intolerable to the sufferer, with the exception of certain effects of stringed instruments. It was, perhaps, the narrow limits to which he thus confined himself upon the guitar, which gave birth, in great measure, to the fantastic character of his performances. But the fervid *facility* of his impromptus could not be so accounted for. They must have been, and were, in the notes, as well as in the words of his wild fantasias, (for he not unfrequently accompanied himself with rhymed verbal improvisations), the result of that intense mental collectedness and concentration to which I have previously alluded as observable only in particular moments of the highest artificial excitement. The words of one of these rhapsodies I have easily borne away in memory. I was, perhaps, the more forcibly impressed with it, as he gave it, because, in the under or mystic current of its meaning, I fancied that I perceived, and for the first time, a full consciousness on the part of Usher, of the tottering of his lofty reason upon her throne. The verses, which were entitled "The Haunted Palace," ran very nearly, if not accurately, thus:

I.

In the greenest of our valleys,
By good angels tenanted,
Once a fair and stately palace—
Snow-white palace—reared its head.
In the monarch Thought's dominion—
It stood there!
Never seraph spread a pinion
Over fabric half so fair.

II.

Banners yellow, glorious, golden,
On its roof did float and flow;
(This—all this—was in the olden
Time long ago);
And every gentle air that dallied,
In that sweet day,
Along the ramparts plumed and pallid,
A winged odor went away.

III.

Wanderers in that happy valley
Through two luminous windows saw
Spirits moving musically
To a lute's well-tunèd law,
Round about a throne, where sitting
(Porphyrogene!)
In state his glory well befitting,
The sovereign of the realm was seen.

IV.

And all with pearl and ruby glowing
Was the fair palace door,
Through which came flowing, flowing, flowing,

And sparkling evermore,
A troop of Echoes whose sweet duty
Was but to sing,
In voices of surpassing beauty,
The wit and wisdom of their king.

V.

But evil things, in robes of sorrow,
Assailed the monarch's high estate;
(Ah, let us mourn, for never morrow
Shall dawn upon him, desolate!)
And, round about his home, the glory
That blushed and bloomed
Is but a dim-remembered story
Of the old time entombed.

VI.

And travelers now within that valley,
Through the red-litten windows, see
Vast forms that move fantastically
To a discordant melody;
While, like a rapid ghastly river,
Through the pale door,
A hideous throng rush out forever,
And laugh—but smile no more.

I well remember that suggestions arising from this ballad led us into a train of thought wherein there became manifest an opinion of Usher's which I mention not so much on account of its novelty, (for other men have thought thus,) as on account of the pertinacity with which he maintained it. This opinion, in its general form, was that of the sentience of all vegetable things. But, in his disordered fancy, the idea had assumed a more daring character, and trespassed, under certain conditions, upon the kingdom of inorganization. I lack words to express the full extent, or the earnest *abandon* of his persuasion. The belief, however, was connected (as I have previously hinted) with the gray stones of the home of his forefathers. The conditions of the sentience had been here, he imagined, fulfilled in the method of collocation of these stones—in the order of their arrangement, as well as in that of the many fungi which overspread them, and of the decayed trees which stood around—above all, in the long undisturbed endurance of this arrangement, and in its reduplication in the still waters of the tarn. Its evidence—the evidence of the sentience—was to be seen, he said, (and I here started as he spoke,) in *the gradual yet certain condensation of an atmosphere of their own about the waters and the walls.* The result was discoverable, he added, in that silent, yet importunate and terrible influence which for centuries had molded the destinies of his family, and which made *him* what I now saw him—what he was. Such opinions need no comment, and I will make none.

Our books—the books which, for years, had formed no small portion of the mental existence of the invalid—were, as might be supposed, in strict keeping with this character of phantasm. We pored together over such works as the Ververt et Chartreuse of Gresset; the Belphegor of Machiavelli; the Selenography of Brewster; the Heaven and Hell of Swedenborg; the Subterranean Voyage of Nicholas Klimm de Holberg; the Chiromancy of Robert Flud, of Jean d'Indaginé, and of De la Chambre; the Journey into the Blue Distance of Tieck; and the City of the Sun of Campanella. One favorite volume was a small octavo edition of the Directorium Inquisitorium, by the Dominican Eymeric de Gironne; and there were passages in Pomponius Mela, about the old African Satyrs and Œgipans, over which Usher would sit dreaming for hours. His chief delight, however, was found in the earnest and repeated perusal of an exceedingly rare and curious book in quarto Gothic—the manual of a forgotten church—the *Vigilae Mortuorum secundum Chorum Ecclesiae Maguntinae.*

I could not help thinking of the wild ritual of this work, and of its probable influence upon the hypochondriac, when, one evening, having informed me abruptly that the lady Madeline was no more, he stated his intention of preserving her corpse for a fortnight, (previously to its final interment,) in one of the numerous vaults within the main walls of the building. The worldly reason, however, assigned for this singular proceeding, was one which I did not feel at liberty to dispute. The brother had been led to his resolution (so he told me) by considerations of the unusual character of the malady of the deceased, of certain obtrusive and eager inquiries on the part of her medical men, and of the remote and exposed situation of the burial-ground of the family. I will not deny that when I called to mind the sinister countenance of the person whom I met upon the staircase, on the day of my arrival at the house, I had no desire to oppose what I regarded as at best but a harmless, and not by any means an unnatural, precaution.

At the request of Usher, I personally aided him in the arrangements for the temporary entombment. The body having been encoffined, we two alone bore it to its rest. The vault in which we placed it (and which had been so long unopened that our torches, half smothered in its oppressive atmosphere, gave us little opportunity for investigation) was small, damp, and entirely without means of admission for light; lying, at great depth, immediately beneath that portion of the building in which was my own sleeping apartment. It had been used, apparently, in remote feudal times, for the worst purposes of a donjon-keep, and, in later days, as a place of deposit for powder, or other highly combustible substance, as a portion of its floor, and the whole interior of a long archway through which we reached it, were carefully sheathed with copper. The door, of massive iron, had been, also, similarly protected. Its immense weight caused an unusually sharp grating sound, as it moved upon its hinges.

Having deposited our mournful burden upon tressels within this region of horror, we partially turned aside the yet unscrewed lid of the coffin, and looked upon the face of the tenant. The exact similitude between the brother and sister even here again startled and confounded me. Usher, divining, perhaps, my thoughts, murmured out some few words from which I learned that the deceased and himself had been twins, and that sympathies of a scarcely intelligible nature had always existed between them. Our glances, however, rested not long upon the dead—for we could not regard her unawed. The disease which had thus entombed the lady in the maturity of youth, had left, as usual in all maladies of a strictly cataleptical character, the mockery of a faint blush upon the bosom and the face, and that suspiciously lingering smile upon the lip which is so terrible in death. We replaced and screwed down the lid, and, having secured the door of iron, made our way, with toil, into the scarcely less gloomy apartments of the upper portion of the house.

And now, some days of bitter grief having elapsed, an observable change came over the features of the mental disorder of my friend. His ordinary manner had vanished. His ordinary occupations were neglected or forgotten. He roamed from chamber to chamber with hurried, unequal, and objectless step. The pallor of his countenance had assumed, if possible, a more ghastly hue—but the luminousness of his eye had utterly gone out. The once occasional huskiness of his tone was heard no more; and a tremulous quaver, as if of extreme terror, habitually characterized his utterance.—There were times, indeed, when I thought his unceasingly agitated mind was laboring with an oppressive secret, to divulge which he struggled for the necessary courage. At times, again, I was obliged to resolve all into the mere inexplicable vagaries of madness, as I beheld him gazing upon vacancy for long hours, in an attitude of the profoundest attention, as if listening to some imaginary sound. It was no wonder that his condition terrified—that it infected me. I felt creeping upon me, by slow yet certain degrees, the wild influences of his own fantastic yet impressive superstitions.

It was, most especially, upon retiring to bed late in the night of the seventh or eighth day after the placing of the lady Madeline within the donjon, that I experienced the full power of such feelings. Sleep came not near my couch—while the hours waned and waned away. I struggled to reason off the nervousness which had dominion over me. I endeavored to believe that much, if not all of what I felt, was due to the phantasmagoric influence of the gloomy furniture of the room—of the dark and tattered draperies, which, tortured into motion by the breath of a rising tempest, swayed fitfully to and fro upon the walls, and rustled uneasily about the decorations of the bed. But my efforts were fruitless. An irrepressible tremor gradually pervaded my frame; and, at length, there sat upon my very heart an incubus of utterly causeless alarm. Shaking this off with a gasp and a struggle, I uplifted myself upon the pillows, and, peering earnestly within the intense darkness of the chamber, harkened—I know not why, except that an instinctive spirit prompted me—to certain low and indefinite sounds which came, through the pauses of the storm, at long intervals, I knew not whence. Overpowered by an intense sentiment of horror, unaccountable yet unendurable, I threw on my clothes with haste, for I felt that I should sleep no more during the night, and endeavored to arouse myself from the pitiable condition into which I had fallen, by pacing rapidly to and fro through the apartment.

I had taken but few turns in this manner, when a light step on an adjoining staircase arrested my attention. I presently recognized it as that of Usher. In an instant afterwards he rapped, with a gentle touch, at my door, and entered, bearing a lamp.

His countenance was, as usual, cadaverously wan—but there was a species of mad hilarity in his eyes—an evidently restrained hysteria in his whole demeanor. His air appalled me—but anything was preferable to the solitude which I had so long endured, and I even welcomed his presence as a relief.

"And you have not seen it?" he said abruptly, after having stared about him for some moments in silence—"you have not then seen it?—but, stay! you shall." Thus speaking, and having carefully shaded his lamp, he hurried to one of the gigantic casements, and threw it freely open to the storm.

The impetuous fury of the entering gust nearly lifted us from our feet. It was, indeed, a tempestuous yet sternly beautiful night, and one wildly singular in its terror and its beauty. A whirlwind had apparently collected its force in our vicinity; for there were frequent and violent alterations in the direction of the wind; and the exceeding density of the clouds (which hung so low as to press upon the turrets of the house) did not prevent our perceiving the lifelike velocity with which they flew careering from all points against each other, without passing away into the distance. I say that even their exceeding density did not prevent our perceiving this—yet we had no glimpse of the moon or stars—nor was there any flashing forth of the lightning. But the under surfaces of the huge masses of agitated vapor, as well as all terrestrial objects immediately around us, were glowing in the unnatural light of a faintly luminous and distinctly visible gaseous exhalation which hung about and enshrouded the mansion.

"You must not—you shall not behold this!" said I, shudderingly, to Usher, as I led him, with a gentle violence, from the window to a seat. "These appearances, which bewilder you, are merely electrical phenomena not uncommon—or it may be that they have their ghastly origin in the rank miasma of the tarn. Let us close this casement—the air is chilling and dangerous to your frame. Here is one of your favorite romances. I will read, and you shall listen—and so we will pass away this terrible night together."

The antique volume which I had taken up was the "Mad Trist" of Sir Launcelot Canning—but I had called it a favorite of Usher's more in sad jest than in earnest; for, in truth, there is little in its uncouth and unimaginative prolixity which could have had interest for the lofty and spiritual ideality of my friend. It was, however, the only book immediately at hand; and I indulged a vague hope that the excitement which now agitated the hypochondriac might find relief (for the history of mental disorder is full of similar anomalies) even in the extremeness of the folly which I should read. Could I have judged, indeed, by the wild overstrained air of vivacity with which he hearkened, or apparently hearkened, to the words of the tale, I might have well congratulated myself upon the success of my design.

I had arrived at that well-known portion of the story where Ethelred, the hero of the Trist, having sought in vain for peaceable admission into the dwelling of the hermit, proceeds to make good an entrance by force. Here, it will be remembered, the words of the narrative run thus:—

"And Ethelred, who was by nature of a doughty heart, and who was now mighty withal, on account of the powerfulness of the wine which he had drunken, waited no longer to hold parley with the hermit, who, in sooth, was of an obstinate and maliceful turn, but, feeling the rain upon his shoulders, and fearing the rising of the tempest, uplifted his mace outright, and, with blows, made quickly room in the plankings of the door for his gauntleted hand, and now pulling therewith sturdily, he so cracked, and ripped, and tore all asunder, that the noise of the dry and hollow-sounding wood alarummed and reverberated throughout the forest."

At the termination of this sentence I started, and for a moment, paused; for it appeared to me (although I at once concluded that my excited fancy had deceived me)—it appeared to me that, from some very remote portion of the mansion or of its vicinity, there came, indistinctly, to my ears, what might have been, in its exact similarity of character, the echo (but a stifled and dull one certainly) of the very cracking and ripping sound which Sir Launcelot had so particularly described. It was, beyond doubt, the coincidence alone which had arrested my attention; for, amid the rattling of the sashes of the casements, and the ordinary commingled noises of the still increasing storm, the sound, in itself, had nothing, surely, which should have interested or disturbed me. I continued the story.

"But the good champion Ethelred, now entering within the door, was sore enraged and amazed to perceive no signal of the maliceful hermit; but, in the stead thereof, a dragon of a scaly and prodigious demeanor, and of a fiery tongue, which sate in guard before a palace of gold, with a floor of silver; and upon the wall there hung a shield of shining brass with this legend enwritten—

WHO ENTERETH HEREIN, A CONQUEROR HATH BIN,
WHO SLAYETH THE DRAGON THE SHIELD HE SHALL WIN.

And Ethelred uplifted his mace, and struck upon the head of the dragon, which fell before him, and gave up his pesty breath, with a shriek so horrid and harsh, and withal so piercing, that Ethelred had fain to close his ears with his hands against the dreadful noise of it, the like whereof was never before heard."

Here again I paused abruptly, and now with a feeling of wild amazement—for there could be no doubt whatever that, in this instance, I did actually hear (although from what direction it proceeded I found it impossible to say) a low and apparently distant, but harsh, protracted, and most unusual screaming or grating sound—the exact counterpart of what my fancy had already conjured up as the sound of the dragon's unnatural shriek as described by the romancer.

Oppressed, as I certainly was, upon the occurrence of this second and most extraordinary coincidence, by a thousand conflicting sensations, in which wonder and extreme terror were predominant, I still retained sufficient presence of mind to avoid exciting, by any observation, the sensitive nervousness of my companion. I was by no means certain that he had noticed the sounds in question; although, assuredly, a strange alteration had, during the last few minutes, taken place in his demeanor. From a position fronting my own, he had gradually brought round his chair, so as to sit with his face to the door of the chamber, and thus I could but partially perceive his features, although I saw that his lips trembled as if he were murmuring inaudibly. His head had dropped upon his breast—yet I knew that he was not asleep, from the wide and rigid opening of the eye as I caught a glance of it in profile. The motion of his body, too, was at variance with this idea—for he rocked from side to side with a gentle yet constant and uniform sway. Having rapidly taken notice of all this, I resumed the narrative of Sir Launcelot, which thus proceeded:—

"And now, the champion, having escaped from the terrible fury of the dragon, bethinking himself of the brazen shield, and of the breaking up of the enchantment which was upon it, removed the carcass from out of the way before him, and approached valorously over the silver pavement of the castle to where the shield was upon the wall; which in sooth tarried not for his full coming, but fell down at his feet upon the silver floor, with a mighty great and terrible ringing sound."

No sooner had these syllables passed my lips, than—as if a shield of brass had indeed, at the moment, fallen heavily upon a floor of silver—I became aware of a distinct, hollow, metallic, and clangorous, yet apparently muffled reverberation.

Completely unnerved, I started convulsively to my feet; but the measured rocking movement of Usher was undisturbed. I rushed to the chair in which he sat. His eyes were bent fixedly before him, and throughout his whole countenance there reigned a more than stony rigidity. But, as I laid my hand upon his shoulder, there came a strong shudder over his frame; a sickly smile quivered about his lips; and I saw that he spoke in a low, hurried, and gibbering murmur, as if unconscious of my presence. Bending closely over his person, I at length drank in the hideous import of his words.

"Not hear it?—yes, I hear it, and *have* heard it. Long—long—long—many minutes, many hours, many days, have I heard it—yet I dared not—oh, pity me, miserable wretch that I am!—I dared not—I *dared* not speak! We *have put her living in the tomb!* Said I not that my senses were acute? I *now* tell you that I heard her first feeble movements in the hollow coffin. I heard them—many, many days ago—yet I dared not—*I dared not speak!* And now—to-night—Ethelred—ha! ha!—the breaking of the hermit's door, and the death-cry of the dragon, and the clangor of the shield—say, rather, the rending of the coffin, and the grating of the iron hinges, and her struggles within the coppered archway of the vault! Oh whither shall I fly? Will she not be here anon? Is she not hurrying to upbraid me for my haste? Have I not heard her footsteps on the stair? Do I not distinguish that heavy and horrible beating of her heart? Madman!"—here he sprung violently to his feet, and shrieked out his syllables, as if in the effort he were giving up his soul—"Madman! *I tell you that she now stands without the door!*"

As if in the superhuman energy of his utterance there had been found the potency of a spell—the huge antique panels to which the speaker pointed, threw slowly back, upon the instant, their ponderous and ebony jaws. It was the work of the rushing gust—but then without those doors there *did* stand the lofty and enshrouded figure of the lady Madeline of Usher. There was blood upon her white robes, and the evidence of some bitter struggle upon every portion of her emaciated frame. For a moment she remained trembling and reeling to and fro upon the threshold—then, with a low moaning cry, fell heavily inward upon the person of her brother, and in her horrible and now final death-agonies, bore him to the floor a corpse, and a victim to the terrors he had dreaded.

From that chamber, and from that mansion, I fled aghast. The storm was still abroad in all its wrath as I found myself crossing the old causeway. Suddenly there shot along the path a wild light, and I turned to see whence a gleam so unusual could have issued—for the vast house and its shadows were alone behind me. The radiance was that of the full, setting, and blood-red moon, which now shone vividly through that once barely discernible fissure, of which I have before spoken, as extending from the roof of the building, in a zigzag direction to the base. While I gazed, this fissure rapidly widened—there came a fierce breath of the whirlwind—the entire orb of the satellite burst at once upon my sight—my brain reeled as I saw the mighty walls rushing asunder—there was a long tumultuous shouting sound like the voice of a thousand waters—and the deep and dank tarn at my feet closed sullenly and silently over the fragments of the *"House of Usher."*

VIII

F. MARION CRAWFORD

The Screaming Skull

1908

I have often heard it scream. No, I am not nervous, I am not imaginative, and I never believed in ghosts, unless that thing is one. Whatever it is, it hates me almost as much as it hated Luke Pratt, and it screams at me.

If I were you, I would never tell ugly stories about ingenious ways of killing people, for you never can tell but that some one at the table may be tired of his or her nearest and dearest. I have always blamed myself for Mrs. Pratt's death, and I suppose I was responsible for it in a way, though heaven knows I never wished her anything but long life and happiness. If I had not told that story she might be alive yet. That is why the thing screams at me, I fancy.

She was a good little woman, with a sweet temper, all things considered, and a nice gentle voice; but I remember hearing her shriek once when she thought her little boy was killed by a pistol that went off, though every one was sure that it was not loaded. It was the same scream; exactly the same, with a sort of rising quaver at the end; do you know what I mean? Unmistakable.

The truth is, I had not realized that the doctor and his wife were not on good terms. They used to bicker a bit now and then when I was here, and I often noticed that little Mrs. Pratt got very red and bit her lip hard to keep her temper, while Luke grew pale and said the most offensive things. He was that sort when he was in the nursery, I remember, and afterward at school. He was my cousin, you know; that is how I came by this house; after he died, and his boy Charley was killed in South Africa, there were no relations left. Yes, it's a pretty little property, just the sort of thing for an old sailor like me who has taken to gardening.

One always remembers one's mistakes much more vividly than one's cleverest things, doesn't one? I've often noticed it. I was dining with the Pratts one night, when I told them the story that afterwards made so much difference. It was a wet night in November, and the sea was moaning. Hush!—if you don't speak you will hear it now....

Do you hear the tide? Gloomy sound, isn't it? Sometimes, about this time of year—hallo!—there it is! Don't be frightened, man—it won't eat you—it's only a noise, after all! But I'm glad you've heard it, because there are always people who think it's the wind, or my imagination, or something. You won't hear it again to-night, I fancy, for it doesn't often come more than once. Yes—that's right. Put another stick on the fire, and a little more stuff into that weak mixture you're so fond of. Do you remember old Blauklot the carpenter, on that German ship that picked us up when the *Clontarf* went to the bottom? We were hove to in a howling gale one night, as snug as you please, with no land within five hundred miles, and the ship coming up and falling off as regularly as clockwork—"Biddy te boor beebles ashore tis night, poys!" old Blauklot sang out, as he went off to his quarters with the sail-maker. I often think of that, now that I'm ashore for good and all.

Yes, it was on a night like this, when I was at home for a spell, waiting to take the *Olympia* out on her first trip—it was on the next voyage that she broke the record, you remember—but that dates it. Ninety-two was the year, early in November.

The weather was dirty, Pratt was out of temper, and the dinner was bad, very bad indeed, which didn't improve matters, and cold, which made it worse. The poor little lady was very unhappy about it, and insisted on making a Welsh rarebit on the table to counteract the raw turnips and the half-boiled mutton. Pratt must have had a hard day. Perhaps he had lost a patient. At all events, he was in a nasty temper.

"My wife is trying to poison me, you see!" he said. "She'll succeed some day." I saw that she was hurt, and I made believe to laugh, and said that Mrs. Pratt was much too clever to get rid of her husband in such a simple way; and then I began to tell them about Japanese tricks with spun glass and chopped horsehair and the like.

Pratt was a doctor, and knew a lot more than I did about such things, but that only put me on my mettle, and I told a story about a woman in Ireland who did for three husbands before any one suspected foul play.

Did you never hear that tale? The fourth husband managed to keep awake and caught her, and she was hanged. How did she do it? She drugged them, and poured melted lead into their ears through a little horn funnel when they were asleep.... No—that's the wind whistling. It's backing up to the southward again. I can tell by the sound. Besides, the other thing doesn't often come more than once in an evening even at this time of year—when it happened. Yes, it was in November. Poor Mrs. Pratt died suddenly in her bed not long after I dined here. I can fix the date, because I got the news in New York by the steamer that followed the *Olympia* when I took her out on her first trip. You had the *Leofric* the same year? Yes, I remember. What a pair of old buffers we are coming to be, you and I. Nearly fifty years since we were apprentices together on the *Clontarf*. Shall you ever forget old Blauklot? "Biddy te boor beebles ashore, poys!" Ha, ha! Take a little more, with all that water. It's the old Hulstkamp I found in the cellar when this house came to me, the same I brought Luke from Amsterdam five-and-twenty years ago. He had never touched a drop of it. Perhaps he's sorry now, poor fellow.

Where did I leave off? I told you that Mrs. Pratt died suddenly—yes. Luke must have been lonely here after she was dead, I should think; I came to see him now and then, and he looked worn and nervous, and told me that his practice was growing too heavy for him, though he wouldn't take an assistant on any account. Years went on, and his son was killed in South Africa, and after that he began to be queer. There was something about him not like other people. I believe he kept his senses in his profession to the end; there was no complaint of his having made bad mistakes in cases, or anything of that sort, but he had a look about him——

Luke was a red-headed man with a pale face when he was young, and he was never stout; in middle age he turned a sandy gray, and after his son died he grew thinner and thinner, till his head looked like a skull with parchment stretched over it very tight, and his eyes had a sort of glare in them that was very disagreeable to look at.

He had an old dog that poor Mrs. Pratt had been fond of, and that used to follow her everywhere. He was a bull-dog, and the sweetest tempered beast you ever saw, though he had a way of hitching his upper lip behind one of his fangs that frightened strangers a good deal. Sometimes, of an evening, Pratt and Bumble—that was the dog's name—used to sit and look at each other a long time, thinking about old times, I suppose, when Luke's wife used to sit in that chair you've got. That was always her place, and this was the doctor's, where I'm sitting. Bumble used to climb up by the footstool—he was old and fat by that time, and could not jump much, and his teeth were getting shaky. He would look steadily at Luke, and Luke looked steadily at the dog, his face growing more and more like a skull with two little coals for eyes; and after about five minutes or so, though it may have been less, old Bumble would suddenly begin to shake all over, and all on a sudden he would set up an awful howl, as if he had been shot, and tumble out of the easy-chair and trot away, and hide himself under the sideboard, and lie there making odd noises.

Considering Pratt's looks in those last months, the thing is not surprising, you know. I'm not nervous or imaginative, but I can quite believe he might have sent a sensitive woman into hysterics—his head looked so much like a skull in parchment.

At last I came down one day before Christmas, when my ship was in dock and I had three weeks off. Bumble was not about, and I said casually that I supposed the old dog was dead.

"Yes," Pratt answered, and I thought there was something odd in his tone even before he went on after a little pause. "I killed him," he said presently. "I could not stand it any longer."

I asked what it was that Luke could not stand, though I guessed well enough.

"He had a way of sitting in her chair and glaring at me, and then howling." Luke shivered a little. "He didn't suffer at all, poor old Bumble," he went on in a hurry, as if he thought I might imagine he had been cruel. "I put dionin into his drink to make him sleep soundly, and then I chloroformed him gradually, so that he could not have felt suffocated even if he was dreaming. It's been quieter since then."

I wondered what he meant, for the words slipped out as if he could not help saying them. I've understood since. He meant that he did not hear that noise so often after the dog was out of the way. Perhaps he thought at first that it was old Bumble in the yard howling at the moon, though it's not that kind of noise, is it? Besides, I know what it is, if Luke didn't. It's only a noise, after all, and a noise never hurt anybody yet. But he was much more imaginative than I am. No doubt there really is something about this place that I don't understand; but when I don't understand a thing, I call it a phenomenon, and I don't take it for granted that it's going to kill me, as he did. I don't understand everything, by long odds, nor do you, nor does any man who has been to sea. We used to talk of tidal waves, for instance, and we could not account for them; now we account for them by calling them submarine earthquakes, and we branch off into fifty theories, any one of which might make earthquakes quite comprehensible if we only knew what they are. I fell in with one of them once, and the inkstand flew straight up from the table against the ceiling of my cabin. The same thing happened to Captain Lecky—I dare say you've read about it in his "Wrinkles." Very good. If that sort of thing took place ashore, in this room for instance, a nervous person would talk about spirits and levitation and fifty things that mean nothing, instead of just quietly setting it down as a "phenomenon" that has not been explained yet. My view of that voice, you see.

Besides, what is there to prove that Luke killed his wife? I would not even suggest such a thing to any one but you. After all, there was nothing but the coincidence that poor little Mrs. Pratt died suddenly in her bed a few days after I told that story at dinner. She was not the only woman who ever died like that. Luke got the doctor over from the next parish, and they agreed that she had died of something the matter with her heart. Why not? It's common enough.

Of course, there was the ladle. I never told anybody about that, and it made me start when I found it in the cupboard in the bedroom. It was new, too—a little tinned iron ladle that had not been in the fire more than once or twice, and there was some lead in it that had been melted, and stuck to the bottom of the bowl, all gray, with hardened dross on it. But that proves nothing. A country doctor is generally a handy man, who does everything for himself, and Luke may have had a dozen reasons for melting a little lead in a ladle. He was fond of sea-fishing, for instance, and he may have cast a sinker for a night-line; perhaps it was a weight for the hall clock, or something like that. All the same, when I found it I had a rather queer sensation, because it looked so much like the thing I had described when I told them the story. Do you understand? It affected me unpleasantly, and I threw it away; it's at the bottom of the sea a mile from the Spit, and it will be jolly well rusted beyond recognizing if it's ever washed up by the tide.

You see, Luke must have bought it in the village, years ago, for the man sells just such ladles still. I suppose they are used in cooking. In any case, there was no reason why an inquisitive housemaid should find such a thing lying about, with lead in it, and wonder what it was, and perhaps talk to the maid who heard me tell the story at dinner—for that girl married the plumber's son in the village, and may remember the whole thing.

You understand me, don't you? Now that Luke Pratt is dead and gone, and lies buried beside his wife, with an honest man's tombstone at his head, I should not care to stir up anything that could hurt his memory. They are both dead, and their son, too. There was trouble enough about Luke's death, as it was.

How? He was found dead on the beach one morning, and there was a coroner's inquest. There were marks on his throat, but he had not been robbed. The verdict was that he had come to his end "by the hands or teeth of some person or animal unknown," for half the jury thought it might have been a big dog that had thrown him down and gripped his windpipe, though the skin of his throat was not broken. No one knew at what time he had gone out, nor where he had been. He was found lying on his back above high-water mark, and an old cardboard bandbox that had belonged to his wife lay under his hand, open. The lid had fallen off. He seemed to have been carrying home a skull in the box—doctors are fond of collecting such things. It had rolled out and lay near his head, and it was a remarkably fine skull, rather small, beautifully shaped and very white, with perfect teeth. That is to say, the upper jaw was perfect, but there was no lower one at all, when I first saw it.

Yes, I found it here when I came. You see, it was very white and polished, like a thing meant to be kept under a glass case, and the people did not know where it came from, nor what to do with it; so they put it back into the bandbox and set it on the shelf of the cupboard in the best bedroom, and of course they showed it to me when I took possession. I was taken down to the beach, too, to be shown the place where Luke was found, and the old fisherman explained just how he was lying, and the skull beside him. The only point he could not explain was why the skull had rolled up the sloping sand toward Luke's head instead of rolling downhill to his feet. It did not seem odd to me at the time, but I have often thought of it since, for the place is rather steep. I'll take you there to-morrow if you like—I made a sort of cairn of stones there afterward.

When he fell down, or was thrown down—whichever happened—the bandbox struck the sand, and the lid came off, and the thing came out and ought to have rolled down. But it didn't. It was close to his head, almost touching it, and turned with the face toward it. I say it didn't strike me as odd when the man told me; but I could not help thinking about it afterward, again and again, till I saw a picture of it all when I closed my eyes; and then I began to ask myself why the plaguey thing had rolled up instead of down, and why it had stopped near Luke's head instead of anywhere else, a yard away, for instance.

You naturally want to know what conclusion I reached, don't you? None that at all explained the rolling, at all events. But I got something else into my head, after a time, that made me feel downright uncomfortable.

Oh, I don't mean as to anything supernatural! There may be ghosts, or there may not be. If there are, I'm not inclined to believe that they can hurt living people except by frightening them, and, for my part, I would rather face any shape of ghost than a fog in the Channel when it's crowded. No. What bothered me was just a foolish idea, that's all, and I cannot tell how it began, nor what made it grow till it turned into a certainty.

I was thinking about Luke and his poor wife one evening over my pipe and a dull book, when it occurred to me that the skull might possibly be hers, and I have never got rid of the thought since. You'll tell me there's no sense in it, no doubt; that Mrs. Pratt was buried like a Christian and is lying in the churchyard where they put her, and that it's perfectly monstrous to suppose her husband kept her skull in her old bandbox in his bedroom. All the same, in the face of reason, and common sense, and probability, I'm convinced that he did. Doctors do all sorts of queer things that would make men like you and me feel creepy, and those are just the things that don't seem probable, nor logical, nor sensible to us.

Then, don't you see?—if it really was her skull, poor woman, the only way of accounting for his having it is that he really killed her, and did it in that way, as the woman killed her husbands in the story, and that he was afraid there might be an examination some day which would betray him. You see, I told that too, and I believe it had really happened some fifty or sixty years ago. They dug up the three skulls, you know, and there was a small lump of lead rattling about in each one. That was what hanged the woman. Luke remembered that, I'm sure. I don't want to know what he did when he thought of it; my taste never ran in the direction of horrors, and I don't fancy you care for them either, do you? No. If you did, you might supply what is wanting to the story.

It must have been rather grim, eh? I wish I did not see the whole thing so distinctly, just as everything must have happened. He took it the night before she was buried, I'm sure, after the coffin had been shut, and when the servant girl was asleep. I would bet anything, that when he'd got it, he put something under the sheet in its place, to fill up and look like it. What do you suppose he put there, under the sheet?

I don't wonder you take me up on what I'm saying! First I tell you that I don't want to know what happened, and that I hate to think about horrors, and then I describe the whole thing to you as if I had seen it. I'm quite sure that it was her work-bag that he put there. I remember the bag very well, for she always used it of an evening; it was made of brown plush, and when it was stuffed full it was about the size of—you understand. Yes, there I am, at it again! You may laugh at me, but you don't live here alone, where it was done, and you didn't tell Luke the story about the melted lead. I'm not nervous, I tell you, but sometimes I begin to feel that I understand why some people are. I dwell on all this when I'm alone, and I dream of it, and when that thing screams—well, frankly, I don't like the noise any more than you do, though I should be used to it by this time.

I ought not to be nervous. I've sailed in a haunted ship. There was a Man in the Top, and two-thirds of the crew died of the West Coast fever inside of ten days after we anchored; but I was all right, then and afterward. I have seen some ugly sights, too, just as you have, and all the rest of us. But nothing ever stuck in my head in the way this does.

You see, I've tried to get rid of the thing, but it doesn't like that. It wants to be there in its place, in Mrs. Pratt's bandbox in the cupboard in the best bedroom. It's not happy anywhere else. How do I know that? Because I've tried it. You don't suppose that I've not tried, do you? As long as it's there it only screams now and then, generally at this time of year, but if I put it out of the house it goes on all night, and no servant will stay here twenty-four hours. As it is, I've often been left alone and have been obliged to shift for myself for a fortnight at a time. No one from the village would ever pass a night under the roof now, and as for selling the place, or even letting it, that's out of the question. The old women say that if I stay here I shall come to a bad end myself before long.

I'm not afraid of that. You smile at the mere idea that any one could take such nonsense seriously. Quite right. It's utterly blatant nonsense, I agree with you. Didn't I tell you that it's only a noise after all when you started and looked round as if you expected to see a ghost standing behind your chair?

I may be all wrong about the skull, and I like to think that I am—when I can. It may be just a fine specimen which Luke got somewhere long ago, and what rattles about inside when you shake it may be nothing but a pebble, or a bit of hard clay, or anything. Skulls that have lain long in the ground generally have something inside them that rattles, don't they? No, I've never tried to get it out, whatever it is; I'm afraid it might be lead, don't you see? And if it is, I don't want to know the fact, for I'd much rather not be sure. If it really is lead, I killed her quite as much as if I had done the deed myself. Anybody must see that, I should think. As long as

I don't know for certain, I have the consolation of saying that it's all utterly ridiculous nonsense, that Mrs. Pratt died a natural death and that the beautiful skull belonged to Luke when he was a student in London. But if I were quite sure, I believe I should have to leave the house; indeed I do, most certainly. As it is, I had to give up trying to sleep in the best bedroom where the cupboard is.

You ask me why I don't throw it into the pond—yes, but please don't call it a "confounded bugbear"—it doesn't like being called names.

There! Lord, what a shriek! I told you so! You're quite pale, man. Fill up your pipe and draw your chair nearer to the fire, and take some more drink. Old Hollands never hurt anybody yet. I've seen a Dutchman in Java drink half a jug of Hulstkamp in a morning without turning a hair. I don't take much rum myself, because it doesn't agree with my rheumatism, but you are not rheumatic and it won't damage you. Besides, it's a very damp night outside. The wind is howling again, and it will soon be in the southwest; do you hear how the windows rattle? The tide must have turned too, by the moaning.

We should not have heard the thing again if you had not said that. I'm pretty sure we should not. Oh yes, if you choose to describe it as a coincidence, you are quite welcome, but I would rather that you should not call the thing names again, if you don't mind. It may be that the poor little woman hears, and perhaps it hurts her, don't you know? Ghost? No! You don't call anything a ghost that you can take in your hands and look at in broad daylight, and that rattles when you shake it. Do you, now? But it's something that hears and understands; there's no doubt about that.

I tried sleeping in the best bedroom when I first came to the house, just because it was the best and the most comfortable, but I had to give it up. It was their room, and there's the big bed she died in, and the cupboard is in the thickness of the wall, near the head, on the left. That's where it likes to be kept, in its bandbox. I only used the room for a fortnight after I came, and then I turned out and took the little room downstairs, next to the surgery, where Luke used to sleep when he expected to be called to a patient during the night.

I was always a good sleeper ashore; eight hours is my dose, eleven to seven when I'm alone, twelve to eight when I have a friend with me. But I could not sleep after three o'clock in the morning in that room—a quarter past, to be accurate—as a matter of fact, I timed it with my old pocket chronometer, which still keeps good time, and it was always at exactly seventeen minutes past three. I wonder whether that was the hour when she died?

It was not what you have heard. If it had been that I could not have stood it two nights. It was just a start and a moan and hard breathing for a few seconds in the cupboard, and it could never have waked me under ordinary circumstances, I'm sure. I suppose you are like me in that, and we are just like other people who have been to sea. No natural sounds disturb us at all, not all the racket of a square-rigger hove to in a heavy gale, or rolling on her beam ends before the wind. But if a lead pencil gets adrift and rattles in the drawer of your cabin table you are awake in a moment. Just so—you always understand. Very well, the noise in the cupboard was no louder than that, but it waked me instantly.

I said it was like a "start." I know what I mean, but it's hard to explain without seeming to talk nonsense. Of course you cannot exactly "hear" a person "start"; at the most, you might hear the quick drawing of the breath between the parted lips and closed teeth, and the almost imperceptible sound of clothing that moved suddenly though very slightly. It was like that.

You know how one feels what a sailing vessel is going to do, two or three seconds before she does it, when one has the wheel. Riders say the same of a horse, but that's less strange, because the horse is a live animal with feelings of its own, and only poets and landsmen talk about a ship being alive, and all that. But I have always felt somehow that besides being a steaming machine or a sailing machine for carrying weights, a vessel at sea is a sensitive instrument, and a means of communication between nature and man, and most particularly the man at the wheel, if she is steered by hand. She takes her impressions directly from wind and sea, tide and stream, and transmits them to the man's hand, just as the wireless telegraph picks up the interrupted currents aloft and turns them out below in the form of a message.

You see what I am driving at; I felt that something started in the cupboard, and I felt it so vividly that I heard it, though there may have been nothing to hear, and the sound inside my head waked me suddenly. But I really heard the other noise. It was as if it were muffled inside a box, as far away as if it came through a long-distance telephone; and yet I knew that it was inside the cupboard near the head of my bed. My hair did not bristle and my blood did not run cold that time. I simply resented being waked up by something that had no business to make a noise, any more than a pencil should rattle in the drawer of my cabin table on board ship.

For I did not understand; I just supposed that the cupboard had some communication with the outside air, and that the wind had got in and was moaning through it with a sort of very faint screech. I struck a light and looked at my watch, and it was seventeen minutes past three. Then I turned over and went to sleep on my right ear. That's my good one; I'm pretty deaf with the other, for I struck the water with it when I was a lad in diving from the foretopsail yard. Silly thing to do, it was, but the result is very convenient when I want to go to sleep when there's a noise.

That was the first night, and the same thing happened again and several times afterward, but not regularly, though it was always at the same time, to a second; perhaps I was sometimes sleeping on my good ear, and sometimes not. I overhauled the cupboard and there was no way by which the wind could get in, or anything else, for the door makes a good fit, having been meant to keep out moths, I suppose; Mrs. Pratt must have kept her winter things in it, for it still smells of camphor and turpentine.

After about a fortnight I had had enough of the noises. So far I had said to myself that it would be silly to yield to it and take the skull out of the room. Things always look differently by daylight, don't they? But the voice grew louder—I suppose one may call it a voice—and it got inside my deaf ear, too, one night. I realized that when I was wide awake, for my good ear was jammed down on the pillow, and I ought not to have heard a fog-horn in that position. But I heard that, and it made me lose my temper, unless it scared me, for sometimes the two are not far apart. I struck a light and got up, and I opened the cupboard, grabbed the bandbox and threw it out of the window, as far as I could.

Then my hair stood on end. The thing screamed in the air, like a shell from a twelve-inch gun. It fell on the other side of the road. The night was very dark, and I could not see it fall, but I know it fell beyond the road. The window is just over the front door, it's fifteen yards to the fence, more or less, and the road is ten yards wide. There's a quickset hedge beyond, along the glebe that belongs to the vicarage.

I did not sleep much more that night. It was not more than half an hour after I had thrown the bandbox out when I heard a shriek outside—like what we've had to-night, but worse, more despairing, I should call it; and it may have been my imagination, but I could have sworn that the screams came nearer and nearer each time. I lit a pipe, and walked up and down for a bit, and then took a book and sat up reading, but I'll be hanged if I can remember what I read nor even what the book was, for every now and then a shriek came up that would have made a dead man turn in his coffin.

A little before dawn some one knocked at the front door. There was no mistaking that for anything else, and I opened my window and looked down, for I guessed that some one wanted the doctor, supposing that the new man had taken Luke's house. It was rather a relief to hear a human knock after that awful noise.

You cannot see the door from above, owing to the little porch. The knocking came again, and I called out, asking who was there, but nobody answered, though the knock was repeated. I sang out again, and said that the doctor did not live here any longer. There was no answer, but it occurred to me that it might be some old countryman who was stone deaf. So I took my candle and went down to open the door. Upon my word, I was not thinking of the thing yet, and I had almost forgotten the other noises. I went down convinced that I should find somebody outside, on the doorstep, with a message. I set the candle on the hall table, so that the wind should not blow it out when I opened. While I was drawing the old-fashioned bolt I heard the knocking again. It was not loud, and it had a queer, hollow sound, now that I was close to it, I remember, but I certainly thought it was made by some person who wanted to get in.

It wasn't. There was nobody there, but as I opened the door inward, standing a little on one side, so as to see out at once, something rolled across the threshold and stopped against my foot.

I drew back as I felt it, for I knew what it was before I looked down. I cannot tell you how I knew, and it seemed unreasonable, for I am still quite sure that I had thrown it across the road. It's a French window, that opens wide, and I got a good swing when I flung it out. Besides, when I went out early in the morning, I found the bandbox beyond the thickset hedge.

You may think it opened when I threw it, and that the skull dropped out; but that's impossible, for nobody could throw an empty cardboard box so far. It's out of the question; you might as well try to fling a ball of paper twenty-five yards, or a blown bird's egg.

To go back, I shut and bolted the hall door, picked the thing up carefully, and put it on the table beside the candle. I did that mechanically, as one instinctively does the right thing in danger without thinking at all—unless one does the opposite. It may seem odd, but I believe my first thought had been that somebody might come and find me there on the threshold while it was resting against my foot, lying a little on its side, and turning one hollow eye up at my face, as if it meant to accuse me. And the light and shadow from the candle played in the hollows of the eyes as it stood on the table, so that they seemed to open and shut at me. Then the candle went out quite unexpectedly, though the door was fastened and there was not the least draft; and I used up at least half a dozen matches before it would burn again.

I sat down rather suddenly, without quite knowing why. Probably I had been badly frightened, and perhaps you will admit there was no great shame in being scared. The thing had come home, and it wanted to go upstairs, back to its cupboard. I sat still and stared at it for a bit, till I began to feel very cold; then I took it and carried it up and set it in its place, and I remember that I spoke to it, and promised that it should have its bandbox again in the morning.

You want to know whether I stayed in the room till daybreak? Yes, but I kept a light burning, and sat up smoking and reading, most likely out of fright; plain, undeniable fear, and you need not call it cowardice either, for that's not the same thing. I could not have stayed alone with that thing in the cupboard; I should have been scared to death, though I'm not more timid than other people. Confound it all, man, it had crossed the road alone, and had got up the doorstep and had knocked to be let in.

When the dawn came, I put on my boots and went out to find the bandbox. I had to go a good way round, by the gate near the highroad, and I found the box open and hanging on the other side of the hedge. It had caught on the twigs by the string, and the lid had fallen off and was lying on the ground below it. That shows that it did not open till it was well over; and if it had not opened as soon as it left my hand, what was inside it must have gone beyond the road too.

That's all. I took the box upstairs to the cupboard, and put the skull back and locked it up. When the girl brought me my breakfast she said she was sorry, but that she must go, and she did not care if she lost her month's wages. I looked at her, and her face was a sort of greenish, yellowish white. I pretended to be surprised, and asked what was the matter; but that was of no use, for she just turned on me and wanted to know whether I meant to stay in a haunted house, and how long I expected to live if I did, for though she noticed I was sometimes a little hard of hearing, she did not believe that even I could sleep through those screams again—and if I could, why had I been moving about the house and opening and shutting the front door, between three and four in the morning? There was no answering that, since she had heard me, so off she went, and I was left to myself. I went down to the village during the morning and found a woman who was willing to come and do the little work there is and cook my dinner, on condition that she might go home every night. As for me, I moved downstairs that day, and I have never tried to sleep in the best bedroom since. After a little while I got a brace of middle-aged Scotch servants from London, and things were quiet enough for a long time. I began by telling them that the house was in a very exposed position, and that the wind whistled round it a good deal in the autumn and winter, which had given it a bad name in the village, the Cornish people being inclined to superstition and telling ghost stories. The two hard-faced, sandy-haired sisters almost smiled, and they answered with great contempt that they had no great opinion of any Southern bogey whatever, having been in service in two English haunted houses, where they had never seen so much as the Boy in Gray, whom they reckoned no very particular rarity in Forfarshire.

They stayed with me several months, and while they were in the house we had peace and quiet. One of them is here again now, but she went away with her sister within the year. This one—she was the cook—married the sexton, who works in my garden. That's the way of it. It's a small village and he has not much to do, and he knows enough about flowers to help me nicely, besides doing most of the hard work; for though I'm fond of exercise, I'm getting a little stiff in the hinges. He's a sober, silent sort of fellow, who minds his own business, and he was a widower when I came here—Trehearn is his name, James Trehearn. The Scotch sisters would not admit that there was anything wrong about the house, but when November came they gave me warning that they were going, on the ground that the chapel was such a long walk from here, being in the next parish, and that they could not possibly go to our church. But the younger one came back in the spring, and as soon as the banns could be published she was married to James Trehearn by the vicar, and she seems to have had no scruples about hearing him preach since then. I'm quite satisfied, if she is! The couple live in a small cottage that looks over the churchyard.

I suppose you are wondering what all this has to do with what I was talking about. I'm alone so much that when an old friend comes to see me, I sometimes go on talking just for the sake of hearing my own voice. But in this case there is really a connection of ideas. It was James Trehearn who buried poor Mrs. Pratt, and her husband after her in the same grave, and it's not far from the back of his cottage. That's the connection in my mind, you see. It's plain enough. He knows something; I'm quite sure that he does, by his manner, though he's such a reticent beggar.

Yes, I'm alone in the house at night now, for Mrs. Trehearn does everything herself, and when I have a friend the sexton's niece comes in to wait on the table. He takes his wife home every evening in winter, but in summer, when there's light, she goes by herself. She's not a nervous woman, but she's less sure than she used to be that there are no bogies in England worth a Scotchwoman's notice. Isn't it amusing, the idea that Scotland has a monopoly of the supernatural? Odd sort of national pride, I call that, don't you?

That's a good fire, isn't it? When driftwood gets started at last there's nothing like it, I think. Yes, we get lots of it, for I'm sorry to say there are still a great many wrecks about here. It's a lonely coast, and you may have all the wood you want for the trouble of bringing it in. Trehearn and I borrow a cart now and then, and load it between here and the Spit. I hate a coal fire when I can get wood of any sort. A log is company, even if it's only a piece of a deck-beam or timber sawn off, and the salt in it makes pretty sparks. See how they fly, like Japanese hand-fireworks! Upon my word, with an old friend and a good fire and a pipe, one forgets all about that thing upstairs, especially now that the wind has moderated. It's only a lull, though, and it will blow a gale before morning.

You think you would like to see the skull? I've no objection. There's no reason why you shouldn't have a look at it, and you never saw a more perfect one in your life, except that there are two front teeth missing in the lower jaw.

Oh yes—I had not told you about the jaw yet. Trehearn found it in the garden last spring when he was digging a pit for a new asparagus bed. You know we make asparagus beds six or eight feet deep here. Yes, yes—I had forgotten to tell you that. He was digging straight down, just as he digs a grave; if you want a good asparagus bed made, I advise you to get a sexton to make it for you. Those fellows have a wonderful knack at that sort of digging.

Trehearn had got down about three feet when he cut into a mass of white lime in the side of the trench. He had noticed that the earth was a little looser there, though he says it had not been disturbed for a number of years. I suppose he thought that even old lime might not be good for asparagus, so he broke it out and threw it up. It was pretty hard, he says, in biggish lumps, and out of sheer force of habit he cracked the lumps with his spade as they lay outside the pit beside him; the jawbone of a skull dropped out of one of the pieces. He thinks he must have knocked out the two front teeth in breaking up the lime, but he did not see them anywhere. He's a very experienced man in such things, as you may imagine, and he said at once that the jaw had probably belonged to a young woman, and that the teeth had been complete when she died. He brought it to me, and asked me if I wanted to keep it; if I did not, he said he would drop it into the next grave he made in the churchyard, as he supposed it was a Christian jaw, and ought to have decent burial, wherever the rest of the body might be. I told him that doctors often put bones into quicklime to whiten them nicely, and that I supposed Dr. Pratt had once had a little lime pit in the garden for that purpose, and had forgotten the jaw. Trehearn looked at me quietly.

"Maybe it fitted that skull that used to be in the cupboard upstairs, sir," he said. "Maybe Dr. Pratt had put the skull into the lime to clean it, or something, and when he took it out he left the lower jaw behind. There's some human hair sticking in the lime, sir."

I saw there was, and that was what Trehearn said. If he did not suspect something, why in the world should he have suggested that the jaw might fit the skull? Besides, it did. That's proof that he knows more than he cares to tell. Do you suppose he looked before she was buried? Or perhaps—when he buried Luke in the same grave——

Well, well, it's of no use to go over that, is it? I said I would keep the jaw with the skull, and I took it upstairs and fitted it into its place. There's not the slightest doubt about the two belonging together, and together they are.

Trehearn knows several things. We were talking about plastering the kitchen a while ago, and he happened to remember that it had not been done since the very week when Mrs. Pratt died. He did not say that the mason must have left some lime on the place, but he thought it, and that it was the very same lime he had found in the asparagus pit. He knows a lot. Trehearn is one of your silent beggars who can put two and two together. That grave is very near the back of his cottage, too, and he's one of the quickest men with a spade I ever saw. If he wanted to know the truth, he could, and no one else would ever be the wiser unless he chose to tell. In a quiet village like ours, people don't go and spend the night in the churchyard to see whether the sexton potters about by himself between ten o'clock and daylight.

What is awful to think of, is Luke's deliberation, if he did it; his cool certainty that no one would find him out; above all, his nerve, for that must have been extraordinary. I sometimes think it's bad enough to live in the place where it was done, if it really was done. I always put in the condition, you see, for the sake of his memory, and a little bit for my own sake, too.

I'll go upstairs and fetch the box in a minute. Let me light my pipe; there's no hurry! We had supper early, and it's only half-past nine o'clock. I never let a friend go to bed before twelve, or with less than three glasses—you may have as many more as you like, but you shan't have less, for the sake of old times.

It's breezing up again, do you hear? That was only a lull just now, and we are going to have a bad night.

A thing happened that made me start a little when I found that the jaw fitted exactly. I'm not very easily startled in that way myself, but I have seen people make a quick movement, drawing their breath sharply, when they had thought they were alone and suddenly turned and saw some one very near them. Nobody can call that fear. You wouldn't, would you? No. Well, just when I had set the jaw in its place under the skull, the teeth closed sharply on my finger. It felt exactly as if it were biting me hard, and I confess that I jumped before I realized that I had been pressing the jaw and the skull together with my other hand. I assure you I was not at all nervous. It was broad daylight, too, and a fine day, and the sun was streaming into the best bedroom. It would have been absurd to be nervous, and it was only a quick mistaken impression, but it really made me feel queer. Somehow it made me think of the funny verdict of the coroner's jury on Luke's death, "by the hand or teeth of some person or animal unknown." Ever since that I've wished I had seen those marks on his throat, though the lower jaw was missing then.

I have often seen a man do insane things with his hands that he does not realize at all. I once saw a man hanging on by an old awning stop with one hand, leaning backward, outboard, with all his weight on it, and he was just cutting the stop with the knife in his other hand when I got my arms round him. We were in mid-ocean, going twenty knots. He had not the smallest idea what he was doing; neither had I when I managed to pinch my finger between the teeth of that thing. I can feel it now. It was exactly as if it were alive and were trying to bite me. It would if it could, for I know it hates me, poor thing! Do you suppose that what rattles about inside is really a bit of lead? Well, I'll get the box down presently, and if whatever it is happens to drop out into your hands that's your affair. If it's only a clod of earth or a pebble, the whole matter would be off my mind, and I don't believe I should ever think of the skull again; but somehow I cannot bring myself to shake out the bit of hard stuff myself. The mere idea that it may be lead makes me confoundedly uncomfortable, yet I've got the conviction that I shall know before long. I shall certainly know. I'm sure Trehearn knows, but he's such a silent beggar.

I'll go upstairs now and get it. What? You had better go with me? Ha, ha! do you think I'm afraid of a bandbox and a noise? Nonsense!

Bother the candle, it won't light! As if the ridiculous thing understood what it's wanted for! Look at that—the third match. They light fast enough for my pipe. There, do you see? It's a fresh box, just out of the tin safe where I keep the supply on account of the dampness. Oh, you think the wick of the candle may be damp, do you? All right, I'll light the beastly thing in the fire. That won't go out, at all events. Yes, it sputters a bit, but it will keep lighted now. It burns just like any other candle, doesn't it? The fact is, candles are not very good about here. I don't know where they come from, but they have a way of burning low occasionally, with a greenish flame that spits tiny sparks, and I'm often annoyed by their going out of themselves. It cannot be helped, for it will be long before we have electricity in our village. It really is rather a poor light, isn't it?

You think I had better leave you the candle and take the lamp, do you? I don't like to carry lamps about, that's the truth. I never dropped one in my life, but I have always thought I might, and it's so confoundedly dangerous if you do. Besides, I am pretty well used to these rotten candles by this time.

You may as well finish that glass while I'm getting it, for I don't mean to let you off with less than three before you go to bed. You won't have to go upstairs, either, for I've put you in the old study next to the surgery—that's where I live myself. The fact is, I never ask a friend to sleep upstairs now. The last man who did was Crackenthorpe, and he said he was kept awake all night. You remember old Crack, don't you? He stuck to the Service, and they've just made him an admiral. Yes, I'm off now—unless the candle goes out. I couldn't help asking if you remembered Crackenthorpe. If any one had told us that the skinny little idiot he used to be was to turn out the most successful of the lot of us, we should have laughed at the idea, shouldn't we? You and I did not do badly, it's true—but I'm really going now. I don't mean to let you think that I've been putting it off by talking! As if there were anything to be afraid of! If I were scared, I should tell you so quite frankly, and get you to go upstairs with me.

Here's the box. I brought it down very carefully, so as not to disturb it, poor thing. You see, if it were shaken, the jaw might get separated from it again, and I'm sure it wouldn't like that. Yes, the candle went out as I was coming downstairs, but that was the draft from the leaky window on the landing. Did you hear anything? Yes, there was another scream. Am I pale, do you say? That's nothing. My heart is a little queer sometimes, and I went upstairs too fast. In fact, that's one reason why I really prefer to live altogether on the ground floor.

Wherever that shriek came from, it was not from the skull, for I had the box in my hand when I heard the noise, and here it is now; so we have proved definitely that the screams are produced by something else. I've no doubt I shall find out some day what makes them. Some crevice in the wall, of course, or a crack in a chimney, or a chink in the frame of a window. That's the way all ghost stories end in real life. Do you know, I'm jolly glad I thought of going up and bringing it down for you to see, for that last shriek settles the question. To think that I should have been so weak as to fancy that the poor skull could really cry out like a living thing!

Now I'll open the box, and we'll take it out and look at it under the bright light. It's rather awful to think that the poor lady used to sit there, in your chair, evening after evening, in just the same light, isn't it? But then—I've made up my mind that it's all rubbish from beginning to end, and that it's just an old skull that Luke had when he was a student; and perhaps he put it into the lime merely to whiten it, and could not find the jaw.

I made a seal on the string, you see, after I had put the jaw in its place, and I wrote on the cover. There's the old white label on it still, from the milliner's, addressed to Mrs. Pratt when the hat was sent to her, and as there was room I wrote on the edge: "A skull, once the property of the late Luke Pratt, M.D." I don't quite know why I wrote that, unless it was with the idea of explaining how the thing happened to be in my possession. I cannot help wondering sometimes what sort of hat it was that came in the bandbox. What color was it, do you think? Was it a gay spring hat with a bobbing feather and pretty ribands? Strange that the very same box should hold the head that wore the finery—perhaps. No—we made up our minds that it just came from the hospital in London where Luke did his time. It's far better to look at it in that light, isn't it? There's no more connection between that skull and poor Mrs. Pratt than there was between my story about the lead and—

Good Lord! Take the lamp—don't let it go out, if you can help it—I'll have the window fastened again in a second—I say, what a gale! There, it's out! I told you so! Never mind, there's the firelight—I've got the window shut—the bolt was only half down. Was the box blown off the table? Where the deuce is it? There! That won't open again, for I've put up the bar. Good dodge, an old-fashioned bar—there's nothing like it. Now, you find the bandbox while I light the lamp. Confound those wretched matches! Yes, a pipe spill is better—it must light in the fire—I hadn't thought of it—thank you—there we are again. Now, where's the box? Yes, put it back on the table, and we'll open it.

That's the first time I have ever known the wind to burst that window open; but it was partly carelessness on my part when I last shut it. Yes, of course I heard the scream. It seemed to go all round the house before it broke in at the window. That proves that it's always been the wind and nothing else, doesn't it? When it was not the wind, it was my imagination. I've always been a very imaginative man: I must have been, though I did not know it. As we grow older we understand ourselves better, don't you know?

I'll have a drop of the Hulstkamp neat, by way of an exception, since you are filling up your glass. That damp gust chilled me, and with my rheumatic tendency I'm very much afraid of a chill, for the cold sometimes seems to stick in my joints all winter when it once gets in.

By George, that's good stuff! I'll just light a fresh pipe, now that everything is snug again, and then we'll open the box. I'm so glad we heard that last scream together, with the skull here on the table between us, for a thing cannot possibly be in two places at the same time, and the noise most certainly came from outside, as any noise the wind makes must. You thought you heard it scream through the room after the window was burst open? Oh yes, so did I, but that was natural enough when everything was open. Of course we heard the wind. What could one expect?

Look here, please. I want you to see that the seal is intact before we open the box together. Will you take my glasses? No, you have your own. All right. The seal is sound, you see, and you can read the words of the motto easily. "Sweet and low"—that's it—because the poem goes on "Wind of the Western sea," and says, "blow him again to me," and all that. Here is the seal on my watch-chain, where it's hung for more than forty years. My poor little wife gave it to me when I was courting, and I never had any other. It was just like her to think of those words—she was always fond of Tennyson.

It's of no use to cut the string, for it's fastened to the box, so I'll just break the wax and untie the knot, and afterward we'll seal it up again. You see, I like to feel that the thing is safe in its place, and that nobody can take it out. Not that I should suspect Trehearn of meddling with it, but I always feel that he knows a lot more than he tells.

You see, I've managed it without breaking the string, though when I fastened it I never expected to open the bandbox again. The lid comes off easily enough. There! Now look!

What? Nothing in it? Empty? It's gone, man, the skull is gone!

No, there's nothing the matter with me. I'm only trying to collect my thoughts. It's so strange. I'm positively certain that it was inside when I put on the seal last spring. I can't have imagined that: it's utterly impossible. If I ever took a stiff glass with a friend now and then, I would admit that I might have made some idiotic mistake when I had taken too much. But I don't, and I never did. A pint of ale at supper and half a go of rum at bedtime was the most I ever took in my good days. I believe it's always we sober fellows who get rheumatism and gout! Yet there was my seal, and there is the empty bandbox. That's plain enough.

I say, I don't half like this. It's not right. There's something wrong about it, in my opinion. You needn't talk to me about supernatural manifestations, for I don't believe in them, not a little bit! Somebody must have tampered with the seal and stolen the skull. Sometimes, when I go out to work in the garden in summer, I leave my watch and chain on the table. Trehearn must have taken the seal then, and used it, for he would be quite sure that I should not come in for at least an hour.

If it was not Trehearn—oh, don't talk to me about the possibility that the thing has got out by itself! If it has, it must be somewhere about the house, in some out-of-the-way corner, waiting. We may come upon it anywhere, waiting for us, don't you know?—just waiting in the dark. Then it will scream at me; it will shriek at me in the dark, for it hates me, I tell you!

The bandbox is quite empty. We are not dreaming, either of us. There, I turn it upside down.

What's that? Something fell out as I turned it over. It's on the floor, it's near your feet, I know it is, and we must find it. Help me to find it, man. Have you got it? For God's sake, give it to me, quickly!

Lead! I knew it when I heard it fall. I knew it couldn't be anything else by the little thud it made on the hearth-rug. So it was lead after all, and Luke did it.

I feel a little bit shaken up—not exactly nervous, you know, but badly shaken up, that's the fact. Anybody would, I should think. After all, you cannot say that it's fear of the thing, for I went up and brought it down—at least, I believed I was bringing it down, and that's the same thing, and by George, rather than give in to such silly nonsense, I'll take the box upstairs again and put it back in its place. It's not that. It's the certainty that the poor little woman came to her end in that way, by my fault, because I told the story. That's what is so dreadful. Somehow, I had always hoped that I should never be quite sure of it, but there is no doubting it now. Look at that!

Look at it! That little lump of lead with no particular shape. Think of what it did, man! Doesn't it make you shiver? He gave her something to make her sleep, of course, but there must have been one moment of awful agony. Think of having boiling lead poured into your brain. Think of it. She was dead before she could scream, but only think of—oh! there it is again—it's just outside—I know it's just outside—I can't keep it out of my head!—oh!—oh!

You thought I had fainted? No, I wish I had, for it would have stopped sooner. It's all very well to say that it's only a noise, and that a noise never hurt anybody—you're as white as a shroud yourself. There's only one thing to be done, if we hope to close an eye to-night. We must find it and put it back into its bandbox and shut it up in the cupboard, where it likes to be. I don't know how it got out, but it wants to get in again. That's why it screams so awfully to-night—it was never so bad as this—never since I first——

Bury it? Yes, if we can find it, we'll bury it, if it takes us all night. We'll bury it six feet deep and ram down the earth over it, so that it shall never get out again, and if it screams, we shall hardly hear it so deep down. Quick, we'll get the lantern and look for it. It cannot be far away; I'm sure it's just outside—it was coming in when I shut the window, I know it.

Yes, you're quite right. I'm losing my senses, and I must get hold of myself. Don't speak to me for a minute or two; I'll sit quite still and keep my eyes shut and repeat something I know. That's the best way.

"Add together the altitude, the latitude, and the polar distance, divide by two and subtract the altitude from the half-sum; then add the logarithm of the secant of the latitude, the cosecant of the polar distance, the cosine of the half-sum and the sine of the half-sum minus the altitude"—there! Don't say that I'm out of my senses, for my memory is all right, isn't it?

Of course, you may say that it's mechanical, and that we never forget the things we learned when we were boys and have used almost every day for a lifetime. But that's the very point. When a man is going crazy, it's the mechanical part of his mind that gets out of order and won't work right; he remembers things that never happened, or he sees things that aren't real, or he hears noises when there is perfect silence. That's not what is the matter with either of us, is it?

Come, we'll get the lantern and go round the house. It's not raining—only blowing like old boots, as we used to say. The lantern is in the cupboard under the stairs in the hall, and I always keep it trimmed in case of a wreck.

No use to look for the thing? I don't see how you can say that. It was nonsense to talk of burying it, of course, for it doesn't want to be buried; it wants to go back into its bandbox and be taken upstairs, poor thing! Trehearn took it out, I know, and made the seal over again. Perhaps he took it to the churchyard, and he may have meant well. I daresay he thought that it would not scream any more if it were quietly laid in consecrated ground, near where it belongs. But it has come home. Yes, that's it. He's not half a bad fellow, Trehearn, and rather religiously inclined, I think. Does not that sound natural, and reasonable, and well meant? He supposed it screamed because it was not decently buried—with the rest. But he was wrong. How should he know that it screams at me because it hates me, and because it's my fault that there was that little lump of lead in it?

No use to look for it, anyhow? Nonsense! I tell you it wants to be found—Hark! what's that knocking? Do you hear it? Knock—knock—knock—three times, then a pause, and then again. It has a hollow sound, hasn't it?

It has come home. I've heard that knock before. It wants to come in and be taken upstairs, in its box. It's at the front door.

Will you come with me? We'll take it in. Yes, I own that I don't like to go alone and open the door. The thing will roll in and stop against my foot, just as it did before, and the light will go out. I'm a good deal shaken by finding that bit of lead, and, besides, my heart isn't quite right—too much strong tobacco, perhaps. Besides, I'm quite willing to own that I'm a bit nervous to-night, if I never was before in my life.

That's right, come along! I'll take the box with me, so as not to come back. Do you hear the knocking? It's not like any other knocking I ever heard. If you will hold this door open, I can find the lantern under the stairs by the light from this room without bringing the lamp into the hall—it would only go out.

The thing knows we are coming—hark! It's impatient to get in. Don't shut the door till the lantern is ready, whatever you do. There will be the usual trouble with the matches, I suppose—no, the first one, by Jove! I tell you it wants to get in, so there's no trouble. All right with that door now; shut it, please. Now come and hold the lantern, for it's blowing so hard outside that I shall have to use both hands. That's it, hold the light low. Do you hear the knocking still? Here goes—I'll open just enough with my foot against the bottom of the door—now!

Catch it! it's only the wind that blows it across the floor, that's all—there's half a hurricane outside, I tell you! Have you got it? The bandbox is on the table. One minute, and I'll have the bar up. There!

Why did you throw it into the box so roughly? It doesn't like that, you know.

What do you say? Bitten your hand? Nonsense, man! You did just what I did. You pressed the jaws together with your other hand and pinched yourself. Let me see. You don't mean to say you have drawn blood? You must have squeezed hard, by Jove, for the skin is certainly torn. I'll give you some carbolic solution for it before we go to bed, for they say a scratch from a skull's tooth may go bad and give trouble.

Come inside again and let me see it by the lamp. I'll bring the bandbox—never mind the lantern, it may just as well burn in the hall, for I shall need it presently when I go up the stairs. Yes, shut the door if you will; it makes it more cheerful and bright. Is your finger still bleeding? I'll get you the carbolic in an instant; just let me see the thing.

Ugh! There's a drop of blood on the upper jaw. It's on the eye-tooth. Ghastly, isn't it? When I saw it running along the floor of the hall, the strength almost went out of my hands, and I felt my knees bending; then I understood that it was the gale, driving it over the smooth boards. You don't blame me? No, I should think not! We were boys together, and we've seen a thing or two, and we may just as well own to each other that we were both in a beastly funk when it slid across the floor at you. No wonder you pinched your finger picking it up, after that, if I did the same thing out of sheer nervousness, in broad daylight, with the sun streaming in on me.

Strange that the jaw should stick to it so closely, isn't it? I suppose it's the dampness, for it shuts like a vice—I have wiped off the drop of blood, for it was not nice to look at. I'm not going to try to open the jaws, don't be afraid! I shall not play any tricks with the poor thing, but I'll just seal the box again, and we'll take it upstairs and put it away where it wants to be. The wax is on the writing-table by the window. Thank you. It will be long before I leave my seal lying about again, for Trehearn to use, I can tell you. Explain? I don't explain natural phenomena, but if you choose to think that Trehearn had hidden it somewhere in the bushes, and that the gale blew it to the house against the door, and made it knock, as if it wanted to be let in, you're not thinking the impossible, and I'm quite ready to agree with you.

Do you see that? You can swear that you've actually seen me seal it this time, in case anything of the kind should occur again. The wax fastens the strings to the lid, which cannot possibly be lifted, even enough to get in one finger. You're quite satisfied, aren't you? Yes. Besides, I shall lock the cupboard and keep the key in my pocket hereafter.

Now we can take the lantern and go upstairs. Do you know? I'm very much inclined to agree with your theory that the wind blew it against the house. I'll go ahead, for I know the stairs; just hold the lantern near my feet as we go up. How the wind howls and whistles! Did you feel the sand on the floor under your shoes as we crossed the hall?

Yes—this is the door of the best bedroom. Hold up the lantern, please. This side, by the head of the bed. I left the cupboard open when I got the box. Isn't it queer how the faint odor of women's dresses will hang about an old closet for years? This is the shelf. You've seen me set the box there, and now you see me turn the key and put it into my pocket. So that's done!

Good-night. Are you sure you're quite comfortable? It's not much of a room, but I daresay you would as soon sleep here as upstairs to-night. If you want anything, sing out; there's only a lath and plaster partition between us. There's not so much wind on this side by half. There's the Hollands on the table, if you'll have one more nightcap. No? Well, do as you please. Good-night again, and don't dream about that thing, if you can.

The following paragraph appeared in the *Penraddon News*, 23rd November, 1906:

MYSTERIOUS DEATH OF A RETIRED SEA CAPTAIN

The village of Tredcombe is much disturbed by the strange death of Captain Charles Braddock, and all sorts of impossible stories are circulating with regard to the circumstances, which certainly seem difficult of explanation. The retired captain, who had successfully commanded in his time the largest and fastest liners belonging to one of the principal transatlantic steamship companies, was found dead in his bed on Tuesday morning in his own cottage, a quarter of a mile from the village. An examination was made at once by the local practitioner, which revealed the horrible fact that the deceased had been bitten in the throat by a human assailant, with such amazing force as to crush the windpipe and cause death. The marks of the teeth of both jaws were so plainly visible on the skin that they could be counted, but the perpetrator of the deed had evidently lost the two lower middle incisors. It is hoped that this peculiarity may help to identify the murderer, who can only be a dangerous escaped maniac. The deceased, though over sixty-five years of age, is said to have been a hale man of considerable physical strength, and it is remarkable that no signs of any struggle were visible in the room, nor could it be ascertained how the murderer had entered the house. Warning has been sent to all the insane asylums in the United Kingdom, but as yet no information has been received regarding the escape of any dangerous patient.

The coroner's jury returned the somewhat singular verdict that Captain Braddock came to his death "by the hands or teeth of some person unknown." The local surgeon is said to have expressed privately the opinion that the maniac is a woman, a view he deduces from the small size of the jaws, as shown by the marks of the teeth. The whole affair is shrouded in mystery. Captain Braddock was a widower, and lived alone. He leaves no children.

NOTE.—Students of ghost lore and haunted houses will find the foundation of the foregoing story in the legends about a skull which is still preserved in the farmhouse called Bettiscombe Manor, situated, I believe, on the Dorsetshire coast.

IX

EDITH NESBIT

Man-Size IN *Marble*

1887

Although every word of this story is as true as despair, I do not expect people to believe it. Nowadays a "rational explanation" is required before belief is possible. Let me, then, at once offer the "rational explanation" which finds most favor among those who have heard the tale of my life's tragedy. It is held that we were "under a delusion," Laura and I, on that 31st of October; and that this supposition places the whole matter on a satisfactory and believable basis. The reader can judge, when he, too, has heard my story, how far this is an "explanation" and in what sense it is "rational." There were three who took part in this: Laura and I and another man. The other man still lives and can speak to the truth of the least credible part of my story.

I never in my life knew what it was to have as much money as I required to supply the most ordinary needs—good colors, books and cab-fares—and when we were married we knew quite well that we should only be able to live at all by "strict punctuality and attention to business." I used to paint in those days and Laura used to write, and we felt sure we could keep the pot at least simmering. Living in town was out of the question, so we went to look for a cottage in the country, which should be at once sanitary and picturesque. So rarely do these two qualities meet in one cottage that our search was for some time quite fruitless. But when we got away from friends and house-agents, on our honeymoon, our wits grew clear again and we knew a pretty cottage when at last we saw one.

It was at Brenzett—a little village set on a hill over against the southern marshes. We had gone there, from the seaside village where we were staying, to see the church, and two fields from the church we found this cottage. It stood quite by itself, about two miles from the village. It was a long, low building, with rooms sticking out in unexpected places. There was a bit of stonework—ivy-covered and moss-grown, just two old rooms, all that was left of a big house that had once stood there—and round this stonework the house had grown up. Stripped of its roses and jasmine it would have been hideous. As it stood it was charming and after a brief examination we took it. It was absurdly cheap. There was a jolly old-fashioned garden, with grass paths and no end of hollyhocks and sunflowers and big lilies. From the window you could see the marsh-pastures and beyond them the blue, thin line of the sea.

We got a tall old peasant woman to do for us. Her face and figure were good, though her cooking was of the homeliest; but she understood all about gardening and told us all the old names of the coppices and cornfields and the stories of the smugglers and highwaymen and, better still, of the "things that walked" and of the "sights" which met one in lonely glens of a starlit night. We soon came to leave all the domestic business to Mrs. Dorman and to use her legends in little magazine stories which brought in the jingling guinea.

We had three months of married happiness and did not have a single quarrel. One October evening I had been down to smoke a pipe with the doctor—our only neighbor—a pleasant young Irishman. Laura had stayed at home to finish a comic sketch. I left her laughing over her own jokes and came in to find her a crumpled heap of pale muslin, weeping on the window seat.

"Good heavens, my darling, what's the matter?" I cried, taking her in my arms. "What is the matter? Do speak."

"It's Mrs. Dorman," she sobbed.

"What has she done?" I inquired, immensely relieved.

"She says she must go before the end of the month and she says her niece is ill; she's gone down to see her now, but I don't believe that's the reason, because her niece is always ill. I believe someone has been setting her against us. Her manner was so queer——"

"Never mind, Pussy," I said; "whatever you do, don't cry, or I shall have to cry to keep you in countenance and then you'll never respect your man again."

"But you see," she went on, "it is really serious, because these village people are so sheepy and if one won't do a thing you may be quite sure none of the others will. And I shall have to cook the dinners and wash up the hateful greasy plates; and you'll have to carry cans of water about and clean the boots and knives—and we shall never have any time for work or earn any money or anything."

I represented to her that even if we had to perform these duties the day would still present some margin for other toils and recreations. But she refused to see the matter in any but the grayest light.

"I'll speak to Mrs. Dorman when she comes back and see if I can't come to terms with her," I said. "Perhaps she wants a rise in her screw. It will be all right. Let's walk up to the church."

The church was a large and lonely one and we loved to go there, especially upon bright nights. The path skirted a wood, cut through it once, and ran along the crest of the hill through two meadows and round the churchyard wall, over which the old yews loomed in black masses of shadow.

This path, which was partly paved, was called "the bier-walk," for it had long been the way by which the corpses had been carried to burial. The churchyard was richly treed and was shaded by great elms which stood just outside and stretched their majestic arms in benediction of the happy dead. A large, low porch let one into the building by a Norman doorway and a heavy oak door studded with iron. Inside, the arches rose into darkness, and between them the reticulated windows, which stood out white in the moonlight. In the chancel, the windows were of rich glass, which showed in faint light their noble coloring and made the black oak of the choir pews hardly more solid than the shadows. But on each side of the altar lay a gray marble figure of a knight in full plate armor lying upon a low slab, with hands held up in everlasting prayer, and these figures, oddly enough, were always to be seen if there was any glimmer of light in the church. Their names were lost, but the peasants told of them that they had been fierce and wicked men, marauders by land and sea, who had been the scourge of their time and had been guilty of deeds so foul that the house they had lived in—the big house, by the way, that had stood on the site of our cottage—had been stricken by lightning and the vengeance of Heaven. But for all that, the gold of their heirs had bought them a place in the church. Looking at the bad, hard faces reproduced in the marble, this story was easily believed.

The church looked at its best and weirdest on that night, for the shadows of the yew tree fell through the windows upon the floor of the nave and touched the pillars with tattered shade. We sat down together without speaking and watched the solemn beauty of the old church with some of that awe which inspired its early builders. We walked to the chancel and looked at the sleeping warriors. Then we rested some time on the stone seat in the porch, looking out over the stretch of quiet moonlit meadows, feeling in every fiber of our being the peace of the night and of our happy love; and came away at last with a sense that even scrubbing and black-leading were but small troubles at their worst.

Mrs. Dorman had come back from the village and I at once invited her to a tête-a-tête.

"Now, Mrs. Dorman," I said, when I had got her into my painting room, "what's all this about your not staying with us?"

"I should be glad to get away, sir, before the end of the month," she answered, with her usual placid dignity.

"Have you any fault to find, Mrs. Dorman?"

"None at all, sir: you and your lady have always been most kind I'm sure——"

"Well, what is it? Are your wages not high enough?"

"No, sir, I gets quite enough."

"Then why not stay?"

"I'd rather not"—with some hesitation—"my niece is ill."

"But your niece has been ill ever since we came. Can't you stay for another month?"

"No, sir, I'm bound to go by Thursday."

And this was Monday!

"Well, I must say, I think you might have let us know before. There's no time now to get anyone else and your mistress is not fit to do heavy housework. Can't you stay till next week?"

"I might be able to come back next week."

"But why must you go this week?" I persisted. "Come, out with it."

Mrs. Dorman drew the little shawl, which she always wore, tightly across her bosom, as though she were cold. Then she said, with a sort of effort: "They say, sir, as this was a big house in Catholic times and there was many deeds done here."

The nature of the "deeds" might be vaguely inferred from the inflection of Mrs. Dorman's voice—which was enough to make one's blood run cold. I was glad that Laura was not in the room. She was always nervous, as highly strung natures are, and I felt that these tales about our house, told by this old peasant woman, with her impressive manner and contagious credulity, might have made our home less dear to my wife.

"Tell me all about it, Mrs. Dorman," I said; "you needn't mind about telling me. I'm not like the young people who make fun of such things."

Which was partly true.

"Well, sir"—she sank her voice—"you may have seen in the church, beside the altar, two shapes."

"You mean the effigies of the knights in armor," I said cheerfully.

"I mean them two bodies, drawed out man-size in marble," she returned, and I had to admit that her description was a thousand times more graphic than mine, to say nothing of a certain weird force and uncanniness about the phrase "drawed out man-size in marble."

"They do say, as on All Saints' Eve them two bodies sits up on their slabs and gets off them and then walks down the aisle, *in their marble*"—another good phrase, Mrs. Dorman—"and as the church clock strikes eleven they walks out of the church door and over the graves and long the bier-walk and if it's a wet night there's the marks of their feet in the morning."

"And where do they go?" I asked, rather fascinated.

"They comes back here to their home, sir, and if anyone meets them——"

"Well, what then?" I asked.

But no—not another word could I get from her, save that her niece was ill and she must go.

"Whatever you do, sir, lock the door early on All Saints' Eve and make the cross-sign over the doorstep and on the windows."

"But has anyone ever seen these things?" I persisted. "Who was here last year?"

"No one, sir; the lady as owned the house only stayed here in summer and she always went to London a full month afore *the* night. And I'm sorry to inconvenience you and your lady, but my niece is ill and I must go on Thursday."

I could have shaken her for her absurd reiteration of that obvious fiction, after she had told me her real reasons.

I did not tell Laura the legend of the shapes that "walked in their marble," partly because a legend concerning our house might perhaps trouble my wife and partly, I think, from some more occult reason. This was not quite the same to me as any other story, and I did not want to talk about it till the day it was over. I had very soon ceased to think of the legend, however. I was painting a portrait of Laura, against the lattice window, and I could not think of much else. I had got a splendid background of yellow and gray sunset and was working away with enthusiasm at her face.

On Thursday Mrs. Dorman went. She relented, at parting, so far as to say: "Don't you put yourself about too much, ma'am, and if there's any little thing I can do next week I'm sure I shan't mind."

Thursday passed off pretty well. Friday came. It is about what happened on that Friday that this is written.

I got up early, I remember, and lighted the kitchen fire and had just achieved a smoky success when my little wife came running down as sunny and sweet as the clear October morning itself. We prepared breakfast together and found it very good fun. The housework was soon done and when brushes and brooms and pails were quiet again the house was still indeed. It is wonderful what a difference one makes in a house. We really missed Mrs. Dorman, quite apart from considerations concerning pots and pans. We spent the day in dusting our books and putting them straight, and dined gaily on cold steak and coffee. Laura was, if possible, brighter and gayer and sweeter than usual and I began to think that a little domestic toil was really good for her. We had never been so merry since we were married and the walk we had that afternoon was, I think, the happiest time of all my life. When we had watched the deep scarlet clouds slowly pale into leaden gray against a pale green sky and saw the white mists curl up along the hedgerows in the distant marsh we came back to the house hand in hand.

"You are sad, my darling," I said, half-jestingly, as we sat down together in our little parlor. I expected a disclaimer, for my own silence had been the silence of complete happiness.

To my surprise she said: "Yes, I think I am sad, or, rather, I am uneasy. I don't think I'm very well. I have shivered three or four times since we came in; and it is not cold, is it?"

"No," I said, and hoped it was not a chill caught from the treacherous mists that roll up from the marshes in the dying night. No—she said, she did not think so.

Then, after a silence, she spoke suddenly: "Do you ever have presentiments of evil?"

"No," I said, smiling, "and I shouldn't believe in them if I had."

"I do," she went on; "the night my father died I knew it, though he was right away in the north of Scotland." I did not answer in words.

She sat looking at the fire for some time in silence, gently stroking my hand. At last she sprang up, came behind me and, drawing my head back, kissed me.

"There, it's over now," she said. "What a baby I am! Come, light the candles and we'll have some of these new Rubenstein duets."

And we spent a happy hour or two at the piano.

At about half-past ten I began to long for the good-night pipe, but Laura looked so white that I felt it would be brutal of me to fill our sitting-room with the fumes of strong cavendish.

"I'll take my pipe outside," I said.

"Let me come, too."

"No, sweetheart, not tonight; you're much too tired. I shan't be long. Go to bed or I shall have an invalid to nurse tomorrow as well as the boots to clean."

I kissed her and was turning to go when she flung her arms round my neck and held me as if she would never let me go again. I stroked her hair.

"Come, Pussy, you're over-tired. The housework has been too much for you."

She loosened her clasp a little and drew a deep breath.

"No. We've been very happy today, Jack, haven't we? Don't stay out too long."

"I won't, my dearie."

I strolled out of the front door, leaving it unlatched. What a night it was! The jagged masses of heavy dark cloud were rolling at intervals from horizon to horizon and thin white wreaths covered the stars. Through all the rush of the cloud river the moon swam, breasting the waves and disappearing again in the darkness.

I walked up and down, drinking in the beauty of the quiet earth and the changing sky. The night was absolutely silent. Nothing seemed to be abroad. There was no skurrying of rabbits or twitter of the half-asleep birds. And though the clouds went sailing across the sky, the wind that drove them never came low enough to rustle the dead leaves in the woodland paths. Across the meadows I could see the church tower standing out black and gray against the sky. I walked there thinking over our three months of happiness.

I heard a bell-beat from the church. Eleven already! I turned to go in, but the night held me. I could not go back into our little warm rooms yet. I would go up to the church.

I looked in at the low window as I went by. Laura was half-lying on her chair in front of the fire. I could not see her face, only her little head showed dark against the pale blue wall. She was quite still. Asleep, no doubt.

I walked slowly along the edge of the wood. A sound broke the stillness of the night, it was a rustling in the wood. I stopped and listened. The sound stopped too. I went on and now distinctly heard another step than mine answer mine like an echo. It was a poacher or a wood-stealer, most likely, for these were not unknown in our Arcadian neighborhood. But whoever it was, he was a fool not to step more lightly. I turned into the wood and now the footstep seemed to come from the path I had just left. It must be an echo, I thought. The wood looked perfect in the moonlight. The large dying ferns and the brushwood showed where through thinning foliage the pale light came down. The tree trunks stood up like Gothic columns all around me. They reminded me of the church, and I turned into the bier-walk, and passed through the corpse-gate between the graves to the low porch.

I paused for a moment on the stone seat where Laura and I had watched the fading landscape. Then I noticed that the door of the church was open and I blamed myself for having left it unlatched the other night. We were the only people who ever cared to come to the church except on Sundays and I was vexed to think that through our carelessness the damp autumn airs had had a chance of getting in and injuring the old fabric. I went in. It will seem strange, perhaps, that I should have gone halfway up the aisle before I remembered—with a sudden chill, followed by as sudden a rush of self-contempt—that this was the very day and hour when, according to tradition, the "shapes drawed out man-size in marble" began to walk.

Having thus remembered the legend and remembered it with a shiver, of which I was ashamed, I could not do otherwise than walk up towards the altar, just to look at the figures—as I said to myself; really what I wanted was to assure myself, first, that I did not believe the legend and, secondly, that it was not true. I was rather glad that I had come. I thought now I could tell Mrs. Dorman how vain her fancies were and how peacefully the marble figures slept on through the ghastly hour. With my hands in my pockets I passed up the aisle. In the gray dim light the eastern end of the church looked larger than usual and the arches above the two tombs looked larger too. The moon came out and showed me the reason. I stopped short, my heart gave a leap that nearly choked me and then sank sickeningly.

The "bodies drawed out man-size" *were gone!* and their marble slabs lay wide and bare in the vague moonlight that slanted through the east window.

Were they really gone or was I mad? Clenching my nerves, I stooped and passed my hand over the smooth slabs and felt their flat unbroken surface. Had someone taken the things away? Was it some vile practical joke? I would make sure, anyway. In an instant I had made a torch of a newspaper, which happened to be in my pocket and, lighting it, held it high above my head. Its yellow glare illumined the dark arches and those slabs. The figures *were* gone. And I was alone in the church; or was I alone?

And then a horror seized me, a horror indefinable and indescribable—an overwhelming certainty of supreme and accomplished calamity. I flung down the torch and tore along the aisle and out through the porch, biting my lips as I ran to keep myself from shrieking aloud. Oh, was I mad—or what was this that possessed me? I leaped the churchyard wall and took the straight cut across the fields, led by the light from our windows. Just as I got over the first stile a dark figure seemed to spring out of the ground. Mad still with that certainty of misfortune, I made for the thing that stood in my path, shouting, "Get out of the way, can't you!"

But my push met with a more vigorous resistance than I had expected. My arms were caught just above the elbow and held as in a vice and the raw-boned Irish doctor actually shook me.

"Let me go, you fool," I gasped. "The marble figures have gone from the church; I tell you they've gone."

He broke into a ringing laugh. "I'll have to give ye a draft tomorrow, I see. Ye've been smoking too much and listening to old wives' tales."

"I tell you I've seen the bare slabs."

"Well, come back with me. I'm going up to old Palmer's—his daughter's ill; we'll look in at the church and let me see the bare slabs."

"You go, if you like," I said, a little less frantic for his laughter; "I'm going home to my wife."

"Rubbish man," said he; "d'ye think I'll permit that? Are ye to go saying all yer life that ye've seen solid marble endowed with vitality and me to go all me life saying ye were a coward? No, sir—ye shan't do it."

The night air—a human voice—and I think also the physical contact with this six feet of solid common sense, brought me back a little to my ordinary self and the word "coward" was a mental shower-bath.

"Come on, then," I said sullenly, "perhaps you're right."

He still held my arm tightly. We got over the stile and back to the church. All was still as death. The place smelt very damp and earthy. We walked up the aisle. I am not ashamed to confess that I shut my eyes: I knew the figures would not be there. I heard Kelly strike a match.

"Here they are, ye see, right enough; ye've been dreaming or drinking, asking yer pardon for the imputation."

I opened my eyes. By Kelly's expiring vesta I saw two shapes lying "in their marble" on their slabs. I drew a deep breath.

"I'm awfully indebted to you," I said. "It must have been some trick of the light or I have been working rather hard, perhaps that's it. I was quite convinced they were gone."

"I'm aware of that," he answered rather grimly; "ye'll have to be careful of that brain of yours, my friend, I assure ye."

He was leaning over and looking at the right-hand figure, whose stony face was the most villainous and deadly in expression.

"By Jove," he said, "something has been afoot here—this hand is broken."

And so it was. I was certain that it had been perfect the last time Laura and I had been there.

"Perhaps someone has *tried* to remove them," said the young doctor.

"Come along," I said, "or my wife will be getting anxious. You'll come in and have a drop of whisky and drink confusion to ghosts and better sense to me."

"I ought to go up to Palmer's, but it's so late now I'd best leave it till the morning," he replied.

I think he fancied I needed him more than did Palmer's girl, so, discussing how such an illusion could have been possible and deducing from this experience large generalities concerning ghostly apparitions, we walked up to our cottage. We saw, as we walked up the garden path, that bright light streamed out of the front door and presently saw that the parlor door was open, too. Had she gone out?

"Come in," I said, and Dr. Kelly followed me into the parlor. It was all ablaze with candles, not only the wax ones, but at least a dozen guttering, glaring tallow dips, stuck in vases and ornaments in unlikely places. Light, I knew, was Laura's remedy for nervousness. Poor child! Why had I left her? Brute that I was.

We glanced round the room and at first we did not see her. The window was open and the draft set all the candles flaring one way. Her chair was empty and her handkerchief and book lay on the floor. I turned to the window. There, in the recess of the window, I saw her. Oh, my child, my love, had she gone to that window to watch for me? And what had come into the room behind her? To what had she turned with that look of frantic fear and horror? Oh, my little one, had she thought that it was I whose step she heard and turned to meet—what?

She had fallen back across a table in the window and her body lay half on it and half on the window-seat, and her head hung down over the table, the brown hair loosened and fallen to the carpet. Her lips were drawn back and her eyes wide, wide open. They saw nothing now. What had they seen last?

The doctor moved towards her, but I pushed him aside and sprang to her; caught her in my arms and cried: "It's all right, Laura! I've got you safe, wifie."

She fell into my arms in a heap. I clasped her and kissed her and called her by all her pet names, but I think I knew all the time that she was dead. Her hands were tightly clenched. In one of them she held something fast. When I was quite sure that she was dead and that nothing mattered at all any more, I let him open her hand to see what she held.

It was a gray marble finger.

X

WASHINGTON IRVING

The Legend OF *Sleepy Hollow*

1820

Found Among the Papers of the Late Diedrich Knickerbocker.

A pleasing land of drowsy head it was,
Of dreams that wave before the half-shut eye;
And of gay castles in the clouds that pass,
Forever flushing round a summer sky.
CASTLE OF INDOLENCE

In the bosom of one of those spacious coves which indent the eastern shore of the Hudson, at that broad expansion of the river denominated by the ancient Dutch navigators the Tappan Zee, and where they always prudently shortened sail and implored the protection of St. Nicholas when they crossed, there lies a small market town or rural port, which by some is called Greensburgh, but which is more generally and properly known by the name of Tarry Town. This name was given, we are told, in former days, by the good housewives of the adjacent country, from the inveterate propensity of their husbands to linger about the village tavern on market days. Be that as it may, I do not vouch for the fact, but merely advert to it, for the sake of being precise and authentic. Not far from this village, perhaps about two miles, there is a little valley or rather lap of land among high hills, which is one of the quietest places in the whole world. A small brook glides through it, with just murmur enough to lull one to repose; and the occasional whistle of a quail or tapping of a woodpecker is almost the only sound that ever breaks in upon the uniform tranquillity.

I recollect that, when a stripling, my first exploit in squirrel-shooting was in a grove of tall walnut-trees that shades one side of the valley. I had wandered into it at noontime, when all nature is peculiarly quiet, and was startled by the roar of my own gun, as it broke the Sabbath stillness around and was prolonged and reverberated by the angry echoes. If ever I should wish for a retreat whither I might steal from the world and its distractions, and dream quietly away the remnant of a troubled life, I know of none more promising than this little valley.

From the listless repose of the place, and the peculiar character of its inhabitants, who are descendants from the original Dutch settlers, this sequestered glen has long been known by the name of SLEEPY HOLLOW, and its rustic lads are called the Sleepy Hollow Boys throughout all the neighboring country. A drowsy, dreamy influence seems to hang over the land, and to pervade the very atmosphere. Some say that the place was bewitched by a High German doctor, during the early days of the settlement; others, that an old Indian chief, the prophet or wizard of his tribe, held his powwows there before the country was discovered by Master Hendrick Hudson. Certain it is, the place still continues under the sway of some witching power, that holds a spell over the minds of the good people, causing them to walk in a continual reverie. They are given to all kinds of marvelous beliefs, are subject to trances and visions, and frequently see strange sights, and hear music and voices in the air. The whole neighborhood abounds with local tales, haunted spots, and twilight superstitions; stars shoot and meteors glare oftener across the valley than in any other part of the country, and the nightmare, with her whole ninefold, seems to make it the favorite scene of her gambols.

The dominant spirit, however, that haunts this enchanted region, and seems to be commander-in-chief of all the powers of the air, is the apparition of a figure on horseback, without a head. It is said by some to be the ghost of a Hessian trooper, whose head had been carried away by a cannon-ball, in some nameless battle during the Revolutionary War, and who is ever and anon seen by the country folk hurrying along in the gloom of night, as if on the wings of the wind. His haunts are not confined to the valley, but extend at times to the adjacent roads, and especially to the vicinity of a church at no great distance. Indeed, certain of the most authentic historians of those parts, who have been careful in collecting and collating the floating facts concerning this specter, allege that the body of the trooper having been buried in the churchyard, the ghost rides forth to the scene of battle in nightly quest of his head, and that the rushing speed with which he sometimes passes along the hollow, like a midnight blast, is owing to his being belated, and in a hurry to get back to the churchyard before daybreak.

Such is the general purport of this legendary superstition, which has furnished materials for many a wild story in that region of shadows; and the specter is known at all the country firesides, by the name of the Headless Horseman of Sleepy Hollow.

It is remarkable that the visionary propensity I have mentioned is not confined to the native inhabitants of the valley, but is unconsciously imbibed by every one who resides there for a time. However wide awake they may have been before they entered that sleepy region, they are sure, in a little time, to inhale the witching influence of the air, and begin to grow imaginative, to dream dreams, and see apparitions.

I mention this peaceful spot with all possible laud, for it is in such little retired Dutch valleys, found here and there embosomed in the great State of New York, that population, manners, and customs remain fixed, while the great torrent of migration and improvement, which is making such incessant changes in other parts of this restless country, sweeps by them unobserved. They are like those little nooks of still water, which border a rapid stream, where we may see the straw and bubble riding quietly at anchor, or slowly revolving in their mimic harbor, undisturbed by the rush of the passing current. Though many years have elapsed since I trod the drowsy shades of Sleepy Hollow, yet I question whether I should not still find the same trees and the same families vegetating in its sheltered bosom.

In this by-place of nature there abode, in a remote period of American history, that is to say, some thirty years since, a worthy wight of the name of Ichabod Crane, who sojourned, or, as he expressed it, "tarried," in Sleepy Hollow, for the purpose of instructing the children of the vicinity. He was a native of Connecticut, a State which supplies the Union with pioneers for the mind as well as for the forest, and sends forth yearly its legions of frontier woodmen and country schoolmasters. The cognomen of Crane was not inapplicable to his person. He was tall, but exceedingly lank, with narrow shoulders, long arms and legs, hands that dangled a mile out of his sleeves, feet that might have served for shovels, and his whole frame most loosely hung together. His head was small, and flat at top, with huge ears, large green glassy cycs, and a long snipe nose, so that it looked like a weather-cock perched upon his spindle neck to tell which way the wind blew. To see him striding along the profile of a hill on a windy day, with his clothes bagging and fluttering about him, one might have mistaken him for the genius of famine descending upon the earth, or some scarecrow eloped from a cornfield.

His schoolhouse was a low building of one large room, rudely constructed of logs; the windows partly glazed, and partly patched with leaves of old copybooks. It was most ingeniously secured at vacant hours, by a withe twisted in the handle of the door, and stakes set against the window shutters; so that though a thief might get in with perfect ease, he would find some embarrassment in getting out,—an idea most probably borrowed by the architect, Yost Van Houten, from the mystery of an eelpot. The schoolhouse stood in a rather lonely but pleasant situation, just at the foot of a woody hill, with a brook running close by, and a formidable birch-tree growing at one end of it. From hence the low murmur of his pupils' voices, conning over their lessons, might be heard in a drowsy summer's day, like the hum of a beehive; interrupted now and then by the authoritative voice of the master, in the tone of menace or command, or, peradventure, by the appalling sound of the birch, as he urged some tardy loiterer along the flowery path of knowledge. Truth to say, he was a conscientious man, and ever bore in mind the golden maxim, "Spare the rod and spoil the child." Ichabod Crane's scholars certainly were not spoiled.

I would not have it imagined, however, that he was one of those cruel potentates of the school who joy in the smart of their subjects; on the contrary, he administered justice with discrimination rather than severity; taking the burden off the backs of the weak, and laying it on those of the strong. Your mere puny stripling, that winced at the least flourish of the rod, was passed by with indulgence; but the claims of justice were satisfied by inflicting a double portion on some little tough wrong-headed, broad-skirted Dutch urchin, who sulked and swelled and grew dogged and sullen beneath the birch. All this he called "doing his duty by their parents;"and he never inflicted a chastisement without following it by the assurance, so consolatory to the smarting urchin, that "he would remember it and thank him for it the longest day he had to live."

When school hours were over, he was even the companion and playmate of the larger boys; and on holiday afternoons would convoy some of the smaller ones home, who happened to have pretty sisters, or good housewives for mothers, noted for the comforts of the cupboard. Indeed, it behooved him to keep on good terms with his pupils. The revenue arising from his school was small, and would have been scarcely sufficient to furnish him with daily bread, for he was a huge feeder, and, though lank, had the dilating powers of an anaconda; but to help out his maintenance, he was, according to country custom in those parts, boarded and lodged at the houses of the farmers whose children he instructed. With these he lived successively a week at a time, thus going the rounds of the neighborhood, with all his worldly effects tied up in a cotton handkerchief.

That all this might not be too onerous on the purses of his rustic patrons, who are apt to consider the costs of schooling a grievous burden, and schoolmasters as mere drones, he had various ways of rendering himself both useful and agreeable. He assisted the farmers occasionally in the lighter labors of their farms, helped to make hay, mended the fences, took the horses to water, drove the cows from pasture, and cut wood for the winter fire. He laid aside, too, all the dominant dignity and absolute sway with which he lorded it in his little empire, the school, and became wonderfully gentle and ingratiating. He found favor in the eyes of the mothers by petting the children, particularly the youngest; and like the lion bold, which whilom so magnanimously the lamb did hold, he would sit with a child on one knee, and rock a cradle with his foot for whole hours together.

In addition to his other vocations, he was the singing-master of the neighborhood, and picked up many bright shillings by instructing the young folks in psalmody. It was a matter of no little vanity to him on Sundays, to take his station in front of the church gallery, with a band of chosen singers; where, in his own mind, he completely carried away the psalm from the parson. Certain it is, his voice resounded far above all the rest of the congregation; and there are peculiar quavers still to be heard in that church, and which may even be heard half a mile off, quite to the opposite side of the millpond, on a still Sunday morning, which are said to be legitimately descended from the nose of Ichabod Crane. Thus, by divers little makeshifts, in that ingenious way which is commonly denominated "by hook and by crook," the worthy pedagogue got on tolerably enough, and was thought, by all who understood nothing of the labor of headwork, to have a wonderfully easy life of it.

The schoolmaster is generally a man of some importance in the female circle of a rural neighborhood; being considered a kind of idle, gentlemanlike personage, of vastly superior taste and accomplishments to the rough country swains, and, indeed, inferior in learning only to the parson. His appearance, therefore, is apt to occasion some little stir at the tea-table of a farmhouse, and the addition of a supernumerary dish of cakes or sweetmeats, or, peradventure, the parade of a silver teapot. Our man of letters, therefore, was peculiarly happy in the smiles of all the country damsels. How he would figure among them in the churchyard, between services on Sundays; gathering grapes for them from the wild vines that overran the surrounding trees; reciting for their amusement all the epitaphs on the tombstones; or sauntering, with a whole bevy of them, along the banks of the adjacent millpond; while the more bashful country bumpkins hung sheepishly back, envying his superior elegance and address.

From his half-itinerant life, also, he was a kind of traveling gazette, carrying the whole budget of local gossip from house to house, so that his appearance was always greeted with satisfaction. He was, moreover, esteemed by the women as a man of great erudition, for he had read several books quite through, and was a perfect master of Cotton Mather's "History of New England Witchcraft," in which, by the way, he most firmly and potently believed.

He was, in fact, an odd mixture of small shrewdness and simple credulity. His appetite for the marvelous, and his powers of digesting it, were equally extraordinary; and both had been increased by his residence in this spell-bound region. No tale was too gross or monstrous for his capacious swallow. It was often his delight, after his school was dismissed in the afternoon, to stretch himself on the rich bed of clover bordering the little brook that whimpered by his schoolhouse, and there con over old Mather's direful tales, until the gathering dusk of evening made the printed page a mere mist before his eyes. Then, as he wended his way by swamp and stream and awful woodland, to the farmhouse where he happened to be quartered, every sound of nature, at that witching hour, fluttered his excited imagination,—the moan of the whip-poor-will[1] from the hillside, the boding cry of the tree toad, that harbinger of storm, the dreary hooting of the screech owl, or

---

1 The whip-poor-will is a bird which is only heard at night. It receives its name from its note, which is thought to resemble those words.

the sudden rustling in the thicket of birds frightened from their roost. The fireflies, too, which sparkled most vividly in the darkest places, now and then startled him, as one of uncommon brightness would stream across his path; and if, by chance, a huge blockhead of a beetle came winging his blundering flight against him, the poor varlet was ready to give up the ghost, with the idea that he was struck with a witch's token. His only resource on such occasions, either to drown thought or drive away evil spirits, was to sing psalm tunes and the good people of Sleepy Hollow, as they sat by their doors of an evening, were often filled with awe at hearing his nasal melody, "in linked sweetness long drawn out," floating from the distant hill, or along the dusky road.

Another of his sources of fearful pleasure was to pass long winter evenings with the old Dutch wives, as they sat spinning by the fire, with a row of apples roasting and spluttering along the hearth, and listen to their marvelous tales of ghosts and goblins, and haunted fields, and haunted brooks, and haunted bridges, and haunted houses, and particularly of the headless horseman, or Galloping Hessian of the Hollow, as they sometimes called him. He would delight them equally by his anecdotes of witchcraft, and of the direful omens and portentous sights and sounds in the air, which prevailed in the earlier times of Connecticut; and would frighten them woefully with speculations upon comets and shooting stars; and with the alarming fact that the world did absolutely turn round, and that they were half the time topsy-turvy!

But if there was a pleasure in all this, while snugly cuddling in the chimney corner of a chamber that was all of a ruddy glow from the crackling wood fire, and where, of course, no specter dared to show its face, it was dearly purchased by the terrors of his subsequent walk homewards. What fearful shapes and shadows beset his path, amidst the dim and ghastly glare of a snowy night! With what wistful look did he eye every trembling ray of light streaming across the waste fields from some distant window! How often was he appalled by some shrub covered with snow, which, like a sheeted specter, beset his very path! How often did he shrink with curdling awe at the sound of his own steps on the frosty crust beneath his feet; and dread to look over his shoulder, lest he should behold some uncouth being tramping close behind him! And how often was he thrown into complete dismay by some rushing blast, howling among the trees, in the idea that it was the Galloping Hessian on one of his nightly scourings!

All these, however, were mere terrors of the night, phantoms of the mind that walk in darkness; and though he had seen many specters in his time, and been more than once beset by Satan in divers shapes, in his lonely perambulations, yet daylight put an end to all these evils; and he would have passed a pleasant life of it, in despite of the Devil and all his works, if his path had not been crossed by a being that causes more perplexity to mortal man than ghosts, goblins, and the whole race of witches put together, and that was—a woman.

Among the musical disciples who assembled, one evening in each week, to receive his instructions in psalmody, was Katrina Van Tassel, the daughter and only child of a substantial Dutch farmer. She was a blooming lass of fresh eighteen; plump as a partridge; ripe and melting and rosy-cheeked as one of her father's peaches, and universally famed, not merely for her beauty, but her vast expectations. She was withal a little of a coquette, as might be perceived even in her dress, which was a mixture of ancient and modern fashions, as most suited to set off her charms. She wore the ornaments of pure yellow gold, which her great-great-grandmother had brought over from Saardam; the tempting stomacher of the olden time, and withal a provokingly short petticoat, to display the prettiest foot and ankle in the country round.

Ichabod Crane had a soft and foolish heart towards the sex; and it is not to be wondered at that so tempting a morsel soon found favor in his eyes, more especially after he had visited her in her paternal mansion. Old Baltus Van Tassel was a perfect picture of a thriving, contented, liberal-hearted farmer. He seldom, it is true, sent either his eyes or his thoughts beyond the boundaries of his own farm; but within those everything was snug, happy and well-conditioned. He was satisfied with his wealth, but not proud of it; and piqued himself upon the hearty abundance, rather than the style in which he lived. His stronghold was situated on the banks of the Hudson, in one of those green, sheltered, fertile nooks in which the Dutch farmers are so fond of nestling. A great elm tree spread its broad branches over it, at the foot of which bubbled up a spring of the softest and sweetest water, in a little well formed of a barrel; and then stole sparkling away through the grass, to a neighboring brook, that babbled along among alders and dwarf willows. Hard by the farmhouse was a vast barn, that might have served for a church; every window and crevice of which seemed bursting forth with the treasures of the farm; the flail was busily resounding within it from morning to night; swallows and martins skimmed twittering about the eaves; and rows of pigeons, some with one eye turned up, as if watching the weather, some with their heads under their wings or buried in their bosoms, and others swelling, and cooing, and bowing about their dames, were enjoying the sunshine on the roof. Sleek unwieldy porkers were grunting in the repose and abundance of their pens, from whence sallied forth, now and then, troops of suckling pigs, as if to snuff the air. A stately squadron of snowy geese were riding in an adjoining pond, convoying whole fleets of ducks; regiments of turkeys were gobbling through the farmyard, and Guinea fowls fretting about it, like ill-tempered housewives, with their peevish, discontented cry. Before the barn door strutted the gallant cock, that pattern of a husband, a warrior and a fine gentleman, clapping his burnished wings and crowing in the pride and gladness of his heart,—sometimes tearing up the earth with his feet, and then generously calling his ever-hungry family of wives and children to enjoy the rich morsel which he had discovered.

The pedagogue's mouth watered as he looked upon this sumptuous promise of luxurious winter fare. In his devouring mind's eye, he pictured to himself every roasting-pig running about with a pudding in his belly, and an apple in his mouth; the pigeons were snugly put to bed in a comfortable pie, and tucked in with a coverlet of crust; the geese were swimming in their own gravy; and the ducks pairing cozily in dishes, like snug married couples, with a decent competency of onion sauce. In the porkers he saw carved out the future sleek side of bacon, and juicy relishing ham; not a turkey but he beheld daintily trussed up, with its gizzard under its wing, and, peradventure, a necklace of savory sausages; and even bright chanticleer himself lay sprawling on his back, in a side dish, with uplifted claws, as if craving that quarter which his chivalrous spirit disdained to ask while living.

As the enraptured Ichabod fancied all this, and as he rolled his great green eyes over the fat meadow lands, the rich fields of wheat, of rye, of buckwheat, and Indian corn, and the orchards burdened with ruddy fruit, which surrounded the warm tenement of Van Tassel, his heart yearned after the damsel who was to inherit these domains, and his imagination expanded with the idea, how they might be readily turned into cash, and the money invested in immense tracts of wild land, and shingle palaces in the wilderness. Nay, his busy fancy already realized his hopes, and presented to him the blooming Katrina, with a whole family of children, mounted on the top of a wagon loaded with household trumpery, with pots and kettles dangling beneath; and he beheld himself bestriding a pacing mare, with a colt at her heels, setting out for Kentucky, Tennessee,—or the Lord knows where!

When he entered the house, the conquest of his heart was complete. It was one of thosc spacious farmhouses, with high-ridged but lowly sloping roofs, built in the style handed down from the first Dutch settlers; the low projecting eaves forming a piazza along the front, capable of being closed up in bad weather. Under this were hung flails, harness, various utensils of husbandry, and nets for fishing in the neighboring river. Benches were built along the sides for summer use; and a great spinning-wheel at one end, and a churn at the other, showed the various uses to which this important porch might be devoted. From this piazza the wondering Ichabod entered the hall, which formed the center of the mansion, and the place of usual residence. Here rows of resplendent pewter, ranged on a long dresser, dazzled his eyes. In one corner stood a huge bag of wool, ready to be spun; in another, a quantity of linsey-woolsey just from the loom; ears of Indian corn, and strings of dried apples and peaches, hung in gay festoons along the walls, mingled with the gaud of red peppers; and a door left ajar gave him a peep into the best parlor, where the claw-footed chairs and dark mahogany tables shone like mirrors; andirons, with their accompanying shovel and tongs, glistened from their covert of asparagus tops; mock-oranges and conch-shells decorated the mantelpiece; strings of various-colored birds' eggs were suspended above it; a great ostrich egg was hung from the center of the room, and a corner cupboard, knowingly left open, displayed immense treasures of old silver and well-mended china.

From the moment Ichabod laid his eyes upon these regions of delight, the peace of his mind was at an end, and his only study was how to gain the affections of the peerless daughter of Van Tassel. In this enterprise, however, he had more real difficulties than generally fell to the lot of a knight-errant of yore, who seldom had anything but giants, enchanters, fiery dragons, and such like easily conquered adversaries, to contend with and had to make his way merely through gates of iron and brass, and walls of adamant to the castle keep, where the lady of his heart was confined; all which he achieved as easily as a man would carve his way to the center of a Christmas pie; and then the lady gave him her hand as a matter of course. Ichabod, on the contrary, had to win his way to the heart of a country coquette, beset with a labyrinth of whims and caprices, which were forever presenting new difficulties and impediments; and he had to encounter a host of fearful adversaries of real flesh and blood, the numerous rustic admirers, who beset every portal to her heart, keeping a watchful and angry eye upon each other, but ready to fly out in the common cause against any new competitor.

Among these, the most formidable was a burly, roaring, roystering blade, of the name of Abraham, or, according to the Dutch abbreviation, Brom Van Brunt, the hero of the country round, which rang with his feats of strength and hardihood. He was broad-shouldered and double-jointed, with short curly black hair, and a bluff but not unpleasant countenance, having a mingled air of fun and arrogance. From his Herculean frame and great powers of limb he had received the nickname of BROM BONES, by which he was universally known. He was famed for great knowledge and skill in horsemanship, being as dexterous on horseback as a Tartar. He was foremost at all races and cock fights; and, with the ascendancy which bodily strength always acquires in rustic life, was the umpire in all disputes, setting his hat on one side, and giving his decisions with an air and tone that admitted of no gainsay or appeal. He was always ready for either a fight or a frolic; but had more mischief than ill-will in his composition; and with all his overbearing roughness, there was a strong dash of waggish good humor at bottom. He had three or four boon companions, who regarded him as their model, and at the head of whom he scoured the country, attending every scene of feud or merriment for miles round. In cold weather he was distinguished by a fur cap, surmounted with a flaunting fox's tail; and when the folks at a country gathering descried this well-known crest at a distance, whisking about among a squad of hard riders, they always stood by for a squall. Sometimes his crew would be heard dashing along past the farmhouses at midnight, with whoop and halloo, like a troop of Don Cossacks; and the old dames, startled out of their sleep, would listen for a moment till the hurry-scurry had clattered by, and then exclaim, "Ay, there goes Brom Bones and his gang!" The neighbors looked upon him with a mixture of awe, admiration, and good-will; and, when any madcap prank or rustic brawl occurred in the vicinity, always shook their heads, and warranted Brom Bones was at the bottom of it.

This rantipole hero had for some time singled out the blooming Katrina for the object of his uncouth gallantries, and though his amorous toyings were something like the gentle caresses and endearments of a bear, yet it was whispered that she did not altogether discourage his hopes. Certain it is, his advances were signals for rival candidates to retire, who felt no inclination to cross a lion in his amours; insomuch, that when his horse was seen tied to Van Tassel's paling, on a Sunday night, a sure sign that his master was courting, or, as it is termed, "sparking," within, all other suitors passed by in despair, and carried the war into other quarters.

Such was the formidable rival with whom Ichabod Crane had to contend, and, considering all things, a stouter man than he would have shrunk from the competition, and a wiser man would have despaired. He had, however, a happy mixture of pliability and perseverance in his nature; he was in form and spirit like a supple-jack—yielding, but tough; though he bent, he never broke; and though he bowed beneath the slightest pressure, yet, the moment it was away—jerk!—he was as erect, and carried his head as high as ever.

To have taken the field openly against his rival would have been madness; for he was not a man to be thwarted in his amours, any more than that stormy lover, Achilles. Ichabod, therefore, made his advances in a quiet and gently insinuating manner. Under cover of his character of singing-master, he made frequent visits at the farmhouse; not that he had anything to apprehend from the meddlesome interference of parents, which is so often a stumbling-block in the path of lovers. Balt Van Tassel was an easy indulgent soul; he loved his daughter better even than his pipe, and, like a reasonable man and an excellent father, let her have her way in everything. His notable little wife, too, had enough to do to attend to her housekeeping and manage her poultry; for, as she sagely observed, ducks and geese are foolish things, and must be looked after, but girls can take care of themselves. Thus, while the busy dame bustled about the house, or plied her spinning-wheel at one end of the piazza, honest Balt would sit smoking his evening pipe at the other, watching the achievements of a little wooden warrior, who, armed with a sword in each hand, was most valiantly fighting the wind on the pinnacle of the barn. In the mean time, Ichabod would carry on his suit with the daughter by the side of the spring under the great elm, or sauntering along in the twilight, that hour so favorable to the lover's eloquence.

I profess not to know how women's hearts are wooed and won. To me they have always been matters of riddle and admiration. Some seem to have but one vulnerable point, or door of access; while others have a thousand avenues, and may be captured in a thousand different ways. It is a great triumph of skill to gain the former, but a still greater proof of generalship to maintain possession of the latter, for man must battle for his fortress at every door and window. He who wins a thousand common hearts is therefore entitled to some renown; but he who keeps undisputed sway over the heart of a coquette is indeed a hero. Certain it is, this was not the case with the redoubtable Brom Bones; and from the moment Ichabod Crane made his advances, the interests of the former evidently declined: his horse was no longer seen tied to the palings on Sunday nights, and a deadly feud gradually arose between him and the preceptor of Sleepy Hollow.

Brom, who had a degree of rough chivalry in his nature, would fain have carried matters to open warfare and have settled their pretensions to the lady, according to the mode of those most concise and simple reasoners, the knights-errant of yore,—by single combat; but Ichabod was too conscious of the superior might of his adversary to enter the lists against him; he had overheard a boast of Bones, that he would "double the schoolmaster up, and lay him on a shelf of his own schoolhouse;" and he was too wary to give him an opportunity. There was something extremely provoking in this obstinately pacific system; it left Brom no alternative but to draw upon the funds of rustic waggery in his disposition, and to play off boorish practical jokes upon his rival. Ichabod became the object of whimsical persecution to Bones and his gang of rough riders. They harried his hitherto peaceful domains; smoked out his singing school by stopping up the chimney; broke into the schoolhouse at night, in spite of its formidable fastenings of withe and window stakes, and turned everything topsy-turvy, so that the poor schoolmaster began to think all the witches in the country held their meetings there. But what was still more annoying, Brom took all opportunities of turning him into ridicule in presence of his mistress, and had a scoundrel dog whom he taught to whine in the most ludicrous manner, and introduced as a rival of Ichabod's, to instruct her in psalmody.

In this way matters went on for some time, without producing any material effect on the relative situations of the contending powers. On a fine autumnal afternoon, Ichabod, in pensive mood, sat enthroned on the lofty stool from whence he usually watched all the concerns of his little literary realm. In his hand he swayed a ferule, that scepter of despotic power; the birch of justice reposed on three nails behind the throne, a constant terror to evil doers, while on the desk before him might be seen sundry contraband articles and prohibited weapons, detected upon the persons of idle urchins, such as half-munched apples, popguns, whirligigs, fly-cages, and whole legions of rampant little paper gamecocks. Apparently there had been some appalling act of justice recently inflicted, for his scholars were all busily intent upon their books, or slyly whispering behind them with one eye kept upon the master; and a kind of buzzing stillness reigned throughout the schoolroom. It was suddenly interrupted by the appearance of a negro in tow-cloth jacket and trousers, a round-crowned fragment of a hat, like the cap of Mercury, and mounted on the back of a ragged, wild, half-broken colt, which he managed with a rope by way of halter. He came clattering up to the school door with an invitation to Ichabod to attend a merry-making or "quilting frolic," to be held that evening at Mynheer Van Tassel's; and having delivered his message with that air of importance, and effort at fine language, which a negro is apt to display on petty embassies of the kind, he dashed over the brook, and was seen scampering away up the hollow, full of the importance and hurry of his mission.

All was now bustle and hubbub in the late quiet schoolroom. The scholars were hurried through their lessons without stopping at trifles; those who were nimble skipped over half with impunity, and those who were tardy had a smart application now and then in the rear, to quicken their speed or help them over a tall word. Books were flung aside without being put away on the shelves, inkstands were overturned, benches thrown down, and the whole school was turned loose an hour before the usual time, bursting forth like a legion of young imps, yelping and racketing about the green in joy at their early emancipation.

The gallant Ichabod now spent at least an extra half hour at his toilet, brushing and furbishing up his best, and indeed only suit of rusty black, and arranging his locks by a bit of broken looking-glass that hung up in the schoolhouse. That he might make his appearance before his mistress in the true style of a cavalier, he borrowed a horse from the farmer with whom he was domiciliated, a choleric old Dutchman of the name of Hans Van Ripper, and, thus gallantly mounted, issued forth like a knight-errant in quest of adventures. But it is meet I should, in the true spirit of romantic story, give some account of the looks and equipments of my hero and his steed. The animal he bestrode was a broken-down plow-horse, that had outlived almost everything but its viciousness. He was gaunt and shagged, with a ewe neck, and a head like a hammer; his rusty mane and tail were tangled and knotted with burs; one eye had lost its pupil, and was glaring and spectral, but the other had the gleam of a genuine devil in it. Still he must have had fire and mettle in his day, if we may judge from the name he bore of Gunpowder. He had, in fact, been a favorite steed of his master's, the choleric Van Ripper, who was a furious rider, and had infused, very probably, some of his own spirit into the animal; for, old and broken-down as he looked, there was more of the lurking devil in him than in any young filly in the country.

Ichabod was a suitable figure for such a steed. He rode with short stirrups, which brought his knees nearly up to the pommel of the saddle; his sharp elbows stuck out like grasshoppers'; he carried his whip perpendicularly in his hand, like a scepter, and as his horse jogged on, the motion of his arms was not unlike the flapping of a pair of wings. A small wool hat rested on the top of his nose, for so his scanty strip of forehead might be called, and the skirts of his black coat fluttered out almost to the horse's tail. Such was the appearance of Ichabod and his steed as they shambled out of the gate of Hans Van Ripper, and it was altogether such an apparition as is seldom to be met with in broad daylight.

It was, as I have said, a fine autumnal day; the sky was clear and serene, and nature wore that rich and golden livery which we always associate with the idea of abundance. The forests had put on their sober brown and yellow, while some trees of the tenderer kind had been nipped by the frosts into brilliant dyes of orange, purple, and scarlet. Streaming files of wild ducks began to make their appearance high in the air; the bark of the squirrel might be heard from the groves of beech and hickory-nuts, and the pensive whistle of the quail at intervals from the neighboring stubble field.

The small birds were taking their farewell banquets. In the fullness of their revelry, they fluttered, chirping and frolicking from bush to bush, and tree to tree, capricious from the very profusion and variety around them. There was the honest cock robin, the favorite game of stripling sportsmen, with its loud querulous note; and the twittering blackbirds flying in sable clouds; and the golden-winged woodpecker with his crimson crest, his broad black gorget, and splendid plumage; and the cedar bird, with its red-tipt wings and yellow-tipt tail and its little monteiro cap of feathers; and the blue jay, that noisy coxcomb, in his gay light blue coat and white underclothes, screaming and chattering, nodding and bobbing and bowing, and pretending to be on good terms with every songster of the grove.

As Ichabod jogged slowly on his way, his eye, ever open to every symptom of culinary abundance, ranged with delight over the treasures of jolly autumn. On all sides he beheld vast store of apples; some hanging in oppressive opulence on the trees; some gathered into baskets and barrels for the market; others heaped up in rich piles for the cider-press. Farther on he beheld great fields of Indian corn, with its golden ears peeping from their leafy coverts, and holding out the promise of cakes and hasty-pudding; and the yellow pumpkins lying beneath them, turning up their fair round bellies to the sun, and giving ample prospects of the most luxurious of pies; and anon he passed the fragrant buckwheat fields breathing the odor of the beehive, and as he beheld them, soft anticipations stole over his mind of dainty slapjacks, well buttered, and garnished with honey or treacle, by the delicate little dimpled hand of Katrina Van Tassel.

Thus feeding his mind with many sweet thoughts and "sugared suppositions," he journeyed along the sides of a range of hills which look out upon some of the goodliest scenes of the mighty Hudson. The sun gradually wheeled his broad disk down in the west. The wide bosom of the Tappan Zee lay motionless and glassy, excepting that here and there a gentle undulation waved and prolonged the blue shadow of the distant mountain. A few amber clouds floated in the sky, without a breath of air to move them. The horizon was of a fine golden tint, changing gradually into a pure apple green, and from that into the deep blue of the mid-heaven. A slanting ray lingered on the woody crests of the precipices that overhung some parts of the river, giving greater depth to the dark gray and purple of their rocky sides. A sloop was loitering in the distance, dropping slowly down with the tide, her sail hanging uselessly against the mast; and as the reflection of the sky gleamed along the still water, it seemed as if the vessel was suspended in the air.

It was toward evening that Ichabod arrived at the castle of the Heer Van Tassel, which he found thronged with the pride and flower of the adjacent country. Old farmers, a spare leathern-faced race, in homespun coats and breeches, blue stockings, huge shoes, and magnificent pewter buckles. Their brisk, withered little dames, in close-crimped caps, long-waisted short gowns, homespun petticoats, with scissors and pincushions, and gay calico pockets hanging on the outside. Buxom lasses, almost as antiquated as their mothers, excepting where a straw hat, a fine ribbon, or perhaps a white frock, gave symptoms of city innovation. The sons, in short square-skirted coats, with rows of stupendous brass buttons, and their hair generally queued in the fashion of the times, especially if they could procure an eel-skin for the purpose, it being esteemed throughout the country as a potent nourisher and strengthener of the hair.

Brom Bones, however, was the hero of the scene, having come to the gathering on his favorite steed Daredevil, a creature, like himself, full of mettle and mischief, and which no one but himself could manage. He was, in fact, noted for preferring vicious animals, given to all kinds of tricks which kept the rider in constant risk of his neck, for he held a tractable, well-broken horse as unworthy of a lad of spirit.

Fain would I pause to dwell upon the world of charms that burst upon the enraptured gaze of my hero, as he entered the state parlor of Van Tassel's mansion. Not those of the bevy of buxom lasses, with their luxurious display of red and white; but the ample charms of a genuine Dutch country tea-table, in the sumptuous time of autumn. Such heaped up platters of cakes of various and almost indescribable kinds, known only to experienced Dutch housewives! There was the doughty doughnut, the tender olykoek, and the crisp and crumbling cruller; sweet cakes and short cakes, ginger cakes and honey cakes, and the whole family of cakes. And then there were apple pies, and peach pies, and pumpkin pies; besides slices of ham and smoked beef; and moreover delectable dishes of preserved plums, and peaches, and pears, and quinces; not to mention broiled shad and roasted chickens; together with bowls of milk and cream, all mingled higgledy-piggledy, pretty much as I have enumerated them, with the motherly teapot sending up its clouds of vapor from the midst—Heaven bless the mark! I want breath and time to discuss this banquet as it deserves, and am too eager to get on with my story. Happily, Ichabod Crane was not in so great a hurry as his historian, but did ample justice to every dainty.

He was a kind and thankful creature, whose heart dilated in proportion as his skin was filled with good cheer, and whose spirits rose with eating, as some men's do with drink. He could not help, too, rolling his large eyes round him as he ate, and chuckling with the possibility that he might one day be lord of all this scene of almost unimaginable luxury and splendor. Then, he thought, how soon he'd turn his back upon the old schoolhouse; snap his fingers in the face of Hans Van Ripper, and every other niggardly patron, and kick any itinerant pedagogue out of doors that should dare to call him comrade!

Old Baltus Van Tassel moved about among his guests with a face dilated with content and good humor, round and jolly as the harvest moon. His hospitable attentions were brief, but expressive, being confined to a shake of the hand, a slap on the shoulder, a loud laugh, and a pressing invitation to "fall to, and help themselves."

And now the sound of the music from the common room, or hall, summoned to the dance. The musician was an old gray-headed negro, who had been the itinerant orchestra of the neighborhood for more than half a century. His instrument was as old and battered as himself. The greater part of the time he scraped on two or three strings, accompanying every movement of the bow with a motion of the head; bowing almost to the ground, and stamping with his foot whenever a fresh couple were to start.

Ichabod prided himself upon his dancing as much as upon his vocal powers. Not a limb, not a fiber about him was idle; and to have seen his loosely hung frame in full motion, and clattering about the room, you would have thought St. Vitus himself, that blessed patron of the dance, was figuring before you in person. He was the admiration of all the negroes; who, having gathered, of all ages and sizes, from the farm and the neighborhood, stood forming a pyramid of shining black faces at every door and window, gazing with delight at the scene, rolling their white eyeballs, and showing grinning rows of ivory from ear to ear. How could the flogger of urchins be otherwise than animated and joyous? The lady of his heart was his partner in the dance, and smiling graciously in reply to all his amorous oglings; while Brom Bones, sorely smitten with love and jealousy, sat brooding by himself in one corner.

When the dance was at an end, Ichabod was attracted to a knot of the sager folks, who, with Old Van Tassel, sat smoking at one end of the piazza, gossiping over former times, and drawing out long stories about the war.

This neighborhood, at the time of which I am speaking, was one of those highly favored places which abound with chronicle and great men. The British and American line had run near it during the war; it had, therefore, been the scene of marauding and infested with refugees, cowboys, and all kinds of border chivalry. Just sufficient time had elapsed to enable each storyteller to dress up his tale with a little becoming fiction, and, in the indistinctness of his recollection, to make himself the hero of every exploit.

There was the story of Doffue Martling, a large blue-bearded Dutchman, who had nearly taken a British frigate with an old iron nine-pounder from a mud breastwork, only that his gun burst at the sixth discharge. And there was an old gentleman who shall be nameless, being too rich a mynheer to be lightly mentioned, who, in the battle of White Plains, being an excellent master of defense, parried a musket-ball with a small sword, insomuch that he absolutely felt it whiz round the blade, and glance off at the hilt; in proof of which he was ready at any time to show the sword, with the hilt a little bent. There were several more that had been equally great in the field, not one of whom but was persuaded that he had a considerable hand in bringing the war to a happy termination.

But all these were nothing to the tales of ghosts and apparitions that succeeded. The neighborhood is rich in legendary treasures of the kind. Local tales and superstitions thrive best in these sheltered, long-settled retreats; but are trampled under foot by the shifting throng that forms the population of most of our country places. Besides, there is no encouragement for ghosts in most of our villages, for they have scarcely had time to finish their first nap and turn themselves in their graves, before their surviving friends have traveled away from the neighborhood; so that when they turn out at night to walk their rounds, they have no acquaintance left to call upon. This is perhaps the reason why we so seldom hear of ghosts except in our long-established Dutch communities.

The immediate cause, however, of the prevalence of supernatural stories in these parts, was doubtless owing to the vicinity of Sleepy Hollow. There was a contagion in the very air that blew from that haunted region; it breathed forth an atmosphere of dreams and fancies infecting all the land. Several of the Sleepy Hollow people were present at Van Tassel's, and, as usual, were doling out their wild and wonderful legends. Many dismal tales were told about funeral trains, and mourning cries and wailings heard and seen about the great tree where the unfortunate Major André was taken, and which stood in the neighborhood. Some mention was made also of the woman in white, that haunted the dark glen at Raven Rock, and was often heard to shriek on winter nights before a storm, having perished there in the snow. The chief part of the stories, however, turned upon the favorite specter of Sleepy Hollow, the Headless Horseman, who had been heard several times of late, patrolling the country; and, it was said, tethered his horse nightly among the graves in the churchyard.

The sequestered situation of this church seems always to have made it a favorite haunt of troubled spirits. It stands on a knoll, surrounded by locust-trees and lofty elms, from among which its decent, whitewashed walls shine modestly forth, like Christian purity beaming through the shades of retirement. A gentle slope descends from it to a silver sheet of water, bordered by high trees, between which, peeps may be caught at the blue hills of the Hudson. To look upon its grass-grown yard, where the sunbeams seem to sleep so quietly, one would think that there at least the dead might rest in peace. On one side of the church extends a wide woody dell, along which raves a large brook among broken rocks and trunks of fallen trees. Over a deep black part of the stream, not far from the church, was formerly thrown a wooden bridge; the road that led to it, and the bridge itself, were thickly shaded by overhanging trees, which cast a gloom about it, even in the daytime; but occasioned a fearful darkness at night. Such was one of the favorite haunts of the Headless Horseman, and the place where he was most frequently encountered. The tale was told of old Brouwer, a most heretical disbeliever in ghosts, how he met the Horseman returning from his foray into Sleepy Hollow, and was obliged to get up behind him; how they galloped over bush and brake, over hill and swamp, until they reached the bridge; when the Horseman suddenly turned into a skeleton, threw old Brouwer into the brook, and sprang away over the tree-tops with a clap of thunder.

This story was immediately matched by a thrice marvelous adventure of Brom Bones, who made light of the Galloping Hessian as an arrant jockey. He affirmed that on returning one night from the neighboring village of Sing Sing, he had been overtaken by this midnight trooper; that he had offered to race with him for a bowl of punch, and should have won it too, for Daredevil beat the goblin horse all hollow, but just as they came to the church bridge, the Hessian bolted, and vanished in a flash of fire.

All these tales, told in that drowsy undertone with which men talk in the dark, the countenances of the listeners only now and then receiving a casual gleam from the glare of a pipe, sank deep in the mind of Ichabod. He repaid them in kind with large extracts from his invaluable author, Cotton Mather, and added many marvelous events that had taken place in his native State of Connecticut, and fearful sights which he had seen in his nightly walks about Sleepy Hollow.

The revel now gradually broke up. The old farmers gathered together their families in their wagons, and were heard for some time rattling along the hollow roads, and over the distant hills. Some of the damsels mounted on pillions behind their favorite swains, and their light-hearted laughter, mingling with the clatter of hooves, echoed along the silent woodlands, sounding fainter and fainter, until they gradually died away,—and the late scene of noise and frolic was all silent and deserted. Ichabod only lingered behind, according to the custom of country lovers, to have a tête-à-tête with the heiress; fully convinced that he was now on the high road to success. What passed at this interview I will not pretend to say, for in fact I do not know. Something, however, I fear me, must have gone wrong, for he certainly sallied forth, after no very great interval, with an air quite desolate and chapfallen. Oh, these women! these women! Could that girl have been playing off any of her coquettish tricks? Was her encouragement of the poor pedagogue all a mere sham to secure her conquest of his rival? Heaven only knows, not I! Let it suffice to say, Ichabod stole forth with the air of one who had been sacking a hen-roost, rather than a fair lady's heart. Without looking to the right or left to notice the scene of rural wealth, on which he had so often gloated, he went straight to the stable, and with several hearty cuffs and kicks roused his steed most uncourteously from the comfortable quarters in which he was soundly sleeping, dreaming of mountains of corn and oats, and whole valleys of timothy and clover.

It was the very witching time of night that Ichabod, heavy-hearted and crest-fallen, pursued his travels homewards, along the sides of the lofty hills which rise above Tarry Town, and which he had traversed so cheerily in the afternoon. The hour was as dismal as himself. Far below him the Tappan Zee spread its dusky and indistinct waste of waters, with here and there the tall mast of a sloop, riding quietly at anchor under the land. In the dead hush of midnight, he could even hear the barking of the watchdog from the opposite shore of the Hudson; but it was so vague and faint as only to give an idea of his distance from this faithful companion of man. Now and then, too, the long-drawn crowing of a cock, accidentally awakened, would sound far, far off, from some farmhouse away among the hills—but it was like a dreaming sound in his ear. No signs of life occurred near him, but occasionally the melancholy chirp of a cricket, or perhaps the guttural twang of a bullfrog from a neighboring marsh, as if sleeping uncomfortably and turning suddenly in his bed.

All the stories of ghosts and goblins that he had heard in the afternoon now came crowding upon his recollection. The night grew darker and darker; the stars seemed to sink deeper in the sky, and driving clouds occasionally hid them from his sight. He had never felt so lonely and dismal. He was, moreover, approaching the very place where many of the scenes of the ghost stories had been laid. In the center of the road stood an enormous tulip-tree, which towered like a giant above all the other trees of the neighborhood, and formed a kind of landmark. Its limbs were gnarled and fantastic, large enough to form trunks for ordinary trees, twisting down almost to the earth, and rising again into the air. It was connected with the tragical story of the unfortunate André, who had been taken prisoner hard by; and was universally known by the name of Major André's tree. The common people regarded it with a mixture of respect and superstition, partly out of sympathy for the fate of its ill-starred namesake, and partly from the tales of strange sights, and doleful lamentations, told concerning it.

As Ichabod approached this fearful tree, he began to whistle; he thought his whistle was answered; it was but a blast sweeping sharply through the dry branches. As he approached a little nearer, he thought he saw something white, hanging in the midst of the tree: he paused and ceased whistling but, on looking more narrowly, perceived that it was a place where the tree had been scathed by lightning, and the white wood laid bare. Suddenly he heard a groan—his teeth chattered, and his knees smote against the saddle: it was but the rubbing of one huge bough upon another, as they were swayed about by the breeze. He passed the tree in safety, but new perils lay before him.

About two hundred yards from the tree, a small brook crossed the road, and ran into a marshy and thickly wooded glen, known by the name of Wiley's Swamp. A few rough logs, laid side by side, served for a bridge over this stream. On that side of the road where the brook entered the wood, a group of oaks and chestnuts, matted thick with wild grape-vines, threw a cavernous gloom over it. To pass this bridge was the severest trial. It was at this identical spot that the unfortunate André was captured, and under the covert of those chestnuts and vines were the sturdy yeomen concealed who surprised him. This has ever since been considered a haunted stream, and fearful are the feelings of the schoolboy who has to pass it alone after dark.

As he approached the stream, his heart began to thump; he summoned up, however, all his resolution, gave his horse half a score of kicks in the ribs, and attempted to dash briskly across the bridge; but instead of starting forward, the perverse old animal made a lateral movement, and ran broadside against the fence. Ichabod, whose fears increased with the delay, jerked the reins on the other side, and kicked lustily with the contrary foot: it was all in vain; his steed started, it is true, but it was only to plunge to the opposite side of the road into a thicket of brambles and alder bushes. The schoolmaster now bestowed both whip and heel upon the starveling ribs of old Gunpowder, who dashed forward, snuffling and snorting, but came to a stand just by the bridge, with a suddenness that had nearly sent his rider sprawling over his head. Just at this moment a plashy tramp by the side of the bridge caught the sensitive ear of Ichabod. In the dark shadow of the grove, on the margin of the brook, he beheld something huge, misshapen and towering. It stirred not, but seemed gathered up in the gloom, like some gigantic monster ready to spring upon the traveler.

The hair of the affrighted pedagogue rose upon his head with terror. What was to be done? To turn and fly was now too late; and besides, what chance was there of escaping ghost or goblin, if such it was, which could ride upon the wings of the wind? Summoning up, therefore, a show of courage, he demanded in stammering accents, "Who are you?" He received no reply. He repeated his demand in a still more agitated voice. Still there was no answer. Once more he cudgeled the sides of the inflexible Gunpowder, and, shutting his eyes, broke forth with involuntary fervor into a psalm tune. Just then the shadowy object of alarm put itself in motion, and with a scramble and a bound stood at once in the middle of the road. Though the night was dark and dismal, yet the form of the unknown might now in some degree be ascertained. He appeared to be a horseman of large dimensions, and mounted on a black horse of powerful frame. He made no offer of molestation or sociability, but kept aloof on one side of the road, jogging along on the blind side of old Gunpowder, who had now got over his fright and waywardness.

Ichabod, who had no relish for this strange midnight companion, and bethought himself of the adventure of Brom Bones with the Galloping Hessian, now quickened his steed in hopes of leaving him behind. The stranger, however, quickened his horse to an equal pace. Ichabod pulled up, and fell into a walk, thinking to lag behind,—the other did the same. His heart began to sink within him; he endeavored to resume his psalm tune, but his parched tongue clove to the roof of his mouth, and he could not utter a stave. There was something in the moody and dogged silence of this pertinacious companion that was mysterious and appalling. It was soon fearfully accounted for. On mounting a rising ground, which brought the figure of his fellow-traveler in relief against the sky, gigantic in height, and muffled in a cloak, Ichabod was horror-struck on perceiving that he was headless!—but his horror was still more increased on observing that the head, which should have rested on his shoulders, was carried before him on the pommel of his saddle! His terror rose to desperation; he rained a shower of kicks and blows upon Gunpowder, hoping by a sudden movement to give his companion the slip; but the specter started full jump with him. Away, then, they dashed through thick and thin; stones flying and sparks flashing at every bound. Ichabod's flimsy garments fluttered in the air, as he stretched his long lank body away over his horse's head, in the eagerness of his flight.

They had now reached the road which turns off to Sleepy Hollow; but Gunpowder, who seemed possessed with a demon, instead of keeping up it, made an opposite turn, and plunged headlong downhill to the left. This road leads through a sandy hollow shaded by trees for about a quarter of a mile, where it crosses the bridge famous in goblin story; and just beyond swells the green knoll on which stands the whitewashed church.

As yet the panic of the steed had given his unskillful rider an apparent advantage in the chase, but just as he had got half way through the hollow, the girths of the saddle gave way, and he felt it slipping from under him. He seized it by the pommel, and endeavored to hold it firm, but in vain; and had just time to save himself by clasping old Gunpowder round the neck, when the saddle fell to the earth, and he heard it trampled under foot by his pursuer. For a moment the terror of Hans Van Ripper's wrath passed across his mind,—for it was his Sunday saddle; but this was no time for petty fears; the goblin was hard on his haunches; and (unskillful rider that he was!) he had much ado to maintain his seat; sometimes slipping on one side, sometimes on another, and sometimes jolted on the high ridge of his horse's backbone, with a violence that he verily feared would cleave him asunder.

An opening in the trees now cheered him with the hopes that the church bridge was at hand. The wavering reflection of a silver star in the bosom of the brook told him that he was not mistaken. He saw the walls of the church dimly glaring under the trees beyond. He recollected the place where Brom Bones's ghostly competitor had disappeared. "If I can but reach that bridge," thought Ichabod, "I am safe." Just then he heard the black steed panting and blowing close behind him; he even fancied that he felt his hot breath. Another convulsive kick in the ribs, and old Gunpowder sprang upon the bridge; he thundered over the resounding planks; he gained the opposite side; and now Ichabod cast a look behind to see if his pursuer should vanish, according to rule, in a flash of fire and brimstone. Just then he saw the goblin rising in his stirrups, and in the very act of hurling his head at him. Ichabod endeavored to dodge the horrible missile, but too late. It encountered his cranium with a tremendous crash,—he was tumbled headlong into the dust, and Gunpowder, the black steed, and the goblin rider, passed by like a whirlwind.

The next morning the old horse was found without his saddle, and with the bridle under his feet, soberly cropping the grass at his master's gate. Ichabod did not make his appearance at breakfast; dinner-hour came, but no Ichabod. The boys assembled at the schoolhouse, and strolled idly about the banks of the brook; but no schoolmaster. Hans Van Ripper now began to feel some uneasiness about the fate of poor Ichabod, and his saddle. An inquiry was set on foot, and after diligent investigation they came upon his traces. In one part of the road leading to the church was found the saddle trampled in the dirt; the tracks of horses' hooves deeply dented in the road, and evidently at furious speed, were traced to the bridge, beyond which, on the bank of a broad part of the brook, where the water ran deep and black, was found the hat of the unfortunate Ichabod, and close beside it a shattered pumpkin.

The brook was searched, but the body of the schoolmaster was not to be discovered. Hans Van Ripper as executor of his estate, examined the bundle which contained all his worldly effects. They consisted of two shirts and a half; two stocks for the neck; a pair or two of worsted stockings; an old pair of corduroy small-clothes; a rusty razor; a book of psalm tunes full of dog's-ears; and a broken pitch-pipe. As to the books and furniture of the schoolhouse, they belonged to the community, excepting Cotton Mather's "History of Witchcraft," a "New England Almanac," and a book of dreams and fortune-telling; in which last was a sheet of foolscap much scribbled and blotted in several fruitless attempts to make a copy of verses in honor of the heiress of Van Tassel. These magic books and the poetic scrawl were forthwith consigned to the flames by Hans Van Ripper; who, from that time forward, determined to send his children no more to school, observing that he never knew any good come of this same reading and writing. Whatever money the schoolmaster possessed, and he had received his quarter's pay but a day or two before, he must have had about his person at the time of his disappearance.

The mysterious event caused much speculation at the church on the following Sunday. Knots of gazers and gossips were collected in the churchyard, at the bridge, and at the spot where the hat and pumpkin had been found. The stories of Brouwer, of Bones, and a whole budget of others were called to mind; and when they had diligently considered them all, and compared them with the symptoms of the present case, they shook their heads, and came to the conclusion that Ichabod had been carried off by the Galloping Hessian. As he was a bachelor, and in nobody's debt, nobody troubled his head any more about him; the school was removed to a different quarter of the hollow, and another pedagogue reigned in his stead.

It is true, an old farmer, who had been down to New York on a visit several years after, and from whom this account of the ghostly adventure was received, brought home the intelligence that Ichabod Crane was still alive; that he had left the neighborhood partly through fear of the goblin and Hans Van Ripper, and partly in mortification at having been suddenly dismissed by the heiress; that he had changed his quarters to a distant part of the country; had kept school and studied law at the same time; had been admitted to the bar; turned politician; electioneered; written for the newspapers; and finally had been made a justice of the Ten Pound Court. Brom Bones, too, who, shortly after his rival's disappearance conducted the blooming Katrina in triumph to the altar, was observed to look exceedingly knowing whenever the story of Ichabod was related, and always burst into a hearty laugh at the mention of the pumpkin; which led some to suspect that he knew more about the matter than he chose to tell.

The old country wives, however, who are the best judges of these matters, maintain to this day that Ichabod was spirited away by supernatural means; and it is a favorite story often told about the neighborhood round the winter evening fire. The bridge became more than ever an object of superstitious awe; and that may be the reason why the road has been altered of late years, so as to approach the church by the border of the millpond. The schoolhouse being deserted soon fell to decay, and was reported to be haunted by the ghost of the unfortunate pedagogue; and the plowboy, loitering homeward of a still summer evening, has often fancied his voice at a distance, chanting a melancholy psalm tune among the tranquil solitudes of Sleepy Hollow.

POSTSCRIPT.

Found in the Handwriting of Mr. Knickerbocker.

The preceding tale is given almost in the precise words in which I heard it related at a corporation meeting at the ancient city of Manhattoes,[2] at which were present many of its sagest and most illustrious burghers. The narrator was a pleasant, shabby, gentlemanly old fellow, in pepper-and-salt clothes, with a sadly humorous face, and one whom I strongly suspected of being poor—he made such efforts to be entertaining. When his story was concluded, there was much laughter and approbation, particularly from two or three deputy aldermen, who had been asleep the greater part of the time. There was, however, one tall, dry-looking old gentleman, with beetling eyebrows, who maintained a grave and rather severe face throughout, now and then folding his arms, inclining his head, and looking down upon the floor, as if turning a doubt over in his mind. He was one of your wary men, who never laugh but upon good grounds—when they have reason and law on their side. When the mirth of the rest of the company had subsided, and silence was restored, he leaned one arm on the elbow of his chair, and sticking the other akimbo, demanded, with a slight, but exceedingly sage motion of the head, and contraction of the brow, what was the moral of the story, and what it went to prove?

The story-teller, who was just putting a glass of wine to his lips, as a refreshment after his toils, paused for a moment, looked at his inquirer with an air of infinite deference, and, lowering the glass slowly to the table, observed that the story was intended most logically to prove—

"That there is no situation in life but has its advantages and pleasures—provided we will but take a joke as we find it:

"That, therefore, he that runs races with goblin troopers is likely to have rough riding of it.

---

2 New York

"Ergo, for a country schoolmaster to be refused the hand of a Dutch heiress is a certain step to high preferment in the state."

The cautious old gentleman knit his brows tenfold closer after this explanation, being sorely puzzled by the ratiocination of the syllogism, whilc, mcthought, the one in pepper-and-salt eyed him with something of a triumphant leer. At length he observed that all this was very well, but still he thought the story a little on the extravagant—there were one or two points on which he had his doubts.

"Faith, sir," replied the story-teller, "as to that matter, I don't believe one-half of it myself." D. K.

THE END.

XI

ELIZABETH STUART PHELPS

Since I Died

1873

How very still you sit!

If the shadow of an eyelash stirred upon your cheek; if that gray line about your mouth should snap its tension at this quivering end; if the pallor of your profile warmed a little; if that tiny muscle on your forehead, just at the left eyebrow's curve, should start and twitch; if you would but grow a trifle restless, sitting there beneath my steady gaze; if you moved a finger of your folded hands; if you should turn and look behind your chair, or lift your face, half lingering and half longing, half loving and half loth, to ponder on the annoyed and thwarted cry which the wind is making, where I stand between it and yourself, against the half-closed window—Ah, there! You sigh and stir, I think. You lift your head. The little muscle is a captive still; the line about your mouth is tense and hard; the deepening hollow in your cheek has no warmer tint, I see, than the great Doric column which the moonlight builds against the wall. I lean against it; I hold out my arms.

You lift your head and look me in the eye.

If a shudder crept across your figure; if your arms, laid out upon the table, leaped but once above your head; if you named my name; if you held your breath with terror, or sobbed aloud for love, or sprang, or cried—

But you only lift your head and look me in the eye.

If I dared step near, or nearer; if it were Permitted that I should cross the current of your living breath; if it were Willed that I should feel the leap of human blood within your veins; if I should touch your hands, your cheeks, your lips; if I dropped an arm as lightly as a snow-flake round your shoulder—

The fear which no heart has fathomed, the fate which no fancy has faced, the riddle which no soul has read, steps between your substance and my soul.

I drop my arms. I sink into the heart of the pillared light upon the wall. I will not wonder what would happen if my outline were defined upon it to your view. I will not think of that which could be, would be, if I struck across your vision, face to face.

Ah me, how still she sits! With what a fixed, incurious stare she looks me in the eye!

The wind, now that I stand no longer between it and yourself, comes enviously in. It lifts the curtain, and whirls about the room. It bruises the surface of the great pearled pillar where I lean. I am caught within it. Speech and language struggle over me. Mute articulations fill the air. Tears and laughter, and the sounding of soft lips, and the falling of low cries, possess me. Will she listen? Will she bend her head? Will her lips part in recognition? Is there an alphabet between us? Or have the winds of night a vocabulary to lift before her holden eyes?

We sat many times together, and talked of this. Do you remember, dear? You held my hand. Tears that I could not see, fell on it; we sat by the great hall-window up-stairs, where the maple shadow goes to sleep, face down across the floor, upon a lighted night; the old green curtain waved its hands upon us like a mesmerist, I thought; like a priest, you said.

"When we are parted, you shall go," you said; and when I shook my head you smiled—you always smiled when you said that, but you said it always quite the same.

I think I hardly understood you then. Now that I hold your eyes in mine, and you see me not; now when I stretch my hand and you touch me not; now that I cry your name, and you hear it not,—I comprehend you, tender one! A wisdom not of earth was in your words. "To live, is dying; I will die. To die is life, and you shall live."

Now when the fever turned, I thought of this.

That must have been—ah! how long ago? I miss the conception of that for which *how long* stands index.

Yet I perfectly remember that I perfectly understood it to be at three o'clock on a rainy Sunday morning that I died. Your little watch stood in its case of olive-wood upon the table, and drops were on the window. I noticed both, though you did not know it. I see the watch now, in your pocket; I cannot tell if the hands move, or only pulsate like a heart-throb, to and fro; they stand and point, mute golden fingers, paralyzed and pleading, forever at the hour of three. At this I wonder.

When first you said I "was sinking fast," the words sounded as old and familiar as a nursery tale. I heard you in the hall. The doctor had just left, and you went to mother and took her face in your two arms, and laid your hand across her mouth, as if it were she who had spoken. She cried out and threw up her thin old hands; but you stood as still as Eternity. Then I thought again: "It is she who dies; I shall live."

So often and so anxiously we have talked of this thing called death, that now that it is all over between us, I cannot understand why we found in it such a source of distress. It bewilders me. I am often bewildered here. Things and the fancies of things possess a relation which as yet is new and strange to me. Here is a mystery.

Now, in truth, it seems a simple matter for me to tell you how it has been with me since your lips last touched me, and your arms held me to the vanishing air.

Oh, drawn, pale lips! Nerveless, dropping arms! I told you I would come. Did ever promise fail I spoke to you? "Come and show me Death," you said. I have come to show you Death. I could show you the fairest sight and sweetest, that ever blessed your eyes. Why, look! Is it not fair? Am I terrible? Do you shrink or shiver? Would you turn from me, or hide your strained, expectant face?

Would she? Does she? Will she?—

Ah, how the room widened! I could tell you that. It grew great and luminous day by day. At night the walls throbbed; lights of rose ran round them, and blue fire, and a tracery as of the shadows of little leaves. As the walls expanded, the air fled. But I tried to tell you how little pain I knew or feared. Your haggard face bent over me. I could not speak; when I would, I struggled, and you said "She suffers!" Dear, it was so very little!

Listen, till I tell you how that night came on. The sun fell, and the dew slid down. It seemed to me that it slid into my heart, but still I felt no pain. Where the walls pulsed and receded, the hills came in. Where the old bureau stood, above the glass, I saw a single mountain with a face of fire, and purple hair. I tried to tell you this, but you said: "She wanders." I laughed in my heart at that, for it was such a blessed wandering! As the night locked the sun below the mountain's solemn, watching face, the Gates of Space were lifted up before me; the everlasting doors of Matter swung for me upon their rusty hinges, and the King of Glories entered in and out. All the kingdoms of the earth, and the power of them, beckoned to me, across the mist my failing senses made,—ruins and roses, and the brows of Jura and the singing of the Rhine; a shaft of red light on the Sphinx's smile, and caravans in sand-storms, and an icy wind at sea, and gold in mines that no man knew, and mothers sitting at their doors in valleys singing babes to sleep, and women in dank cellars selling souls for bread, and the whir of wheels in giant factories, and a single prayer somewhere in a den of death,—I could not find it, though I searched,—and the smoke of battle, and broken music, and a sense of lilies alone beside a stream at the rising of the sun—and, at last, your face, dear, all alone.

I discovered then, that the walls and roof of the room had vanished quite. The night-wind blew in. The maple in the yard almost brushed my cheek. Stars were about me, and I thought the rain had stopped, yet seemed to hear it, upon the seeming of a window which I could not find.

One thing only hung between me and immensity. It was your single, awful, haggard face. I looked my last into your eyes. Stronger than death, they held and claimed my soul. I feebly raised my hand to find your own. More cruel than the grave, your wild grasp chained me. Then I struggled, and you cried out, and your face slipped, and I stood free.

I stood upon the floor, beside the bed. That which had been I, lay there at rest, but terrible, before me. You hid your face, and I saw you slide upon your knees. I laid my hand upon your head; you did not stir; I spoke to you: "Dear, look around a minute!" but you knelt quite still. I walked to and fro about the room, and meeting my mother, touched her on the elbow; she only said, "She's gone!" and sobbed aloud. "I have not *gone!*" I cried; but she sat sobbing on.

The walls of the room had settled now, and the ceiling stood in its solid place. The window was shut, but the door stood open. Suddenly I was restless, and I ran.

I brushed you in hurrying by, and hit the little lightstand where the tumblers stood; I looked to see if it would fall, but it only shivered as if a breath of wind had struck it once.

But I was restless, and I ran. In the hall I met the doctor. This amused me, and I stopped to think it over. "Ah, Doctor," said I, "you need not trouble yourself to go up. I'm quite well to-night, you see." But he made me no answer; he gave me no glance; he hung up his hat, and laid his hand upon the banister against which I leaned, and went ponderously up.

It was not until he had nearly reached the landing that it occurred to me, still leaning on the banister, that his heavy arm must have swept against and *through* me, where I stood against the oaken moldings which he grasped.

I saw his feet fall on the stairs above me; but they made no sound which reached my ear. "You'll not disturb me *now* with your big boots, sir," said I, nodding; "never fear!"

But he disappeared from sight above me, and still I heard no sound.

Now the doctor had left the front door unlatched.

As I touched it, it blew open wide, and solemnly. I passed out and down the steps. I could see that it was chilly, yet I felt no chill. Frost was on the grass, and in the east a pallid streak, like the cheek of one who had watched all night. The flowers in the little square plots hung their heads and drew their shoulders up; there was a lonely, late lily which I broke and gathered to my heart, where I breathed upon it, and it warmed and looked me kindly in the eye. This, I remember, gave me pleasure. I wandered in and out about the garden in the scattering rain; my feet left no trace upon the dripping grass, and I saw with interest that the garment which I wore, gathered no moisture and no cold. I sat musing for a while upon the piazza, in the garden-chair, not caring to go in. It was so many months since I had felt able to sit upon the piazza in the open air. "By and by," I thought, I would go in and upstairs to see you once again. The curtains were drawn from the parlor windows and I passed and repassed, looking in.

All this while the cheek of the east was warming, and the air gathering faint heats and lights about me. I remembered, presently, the old arbor at the garden-foot, where, before I was sick, we sat so much together; and thinking, "She will be surprised to know that I have been down alone." I was restless, and I ran again.

I meant to come back and see you, dear, once more. I saw the lights in the room where I had lain sick, overhead; and your shadow on the curtain; and I blessed it with all the love of life and death, as I bounded by.

The air was thick with sweetness from the dying flowers. The birds woke, and the zenith lighted, and the leap of health was in my limbs. The old arbor held out its soft arms to me—but I was restless, and I ran.

The field opened before me, and meadows with broad bosoms, and a river flashed before me like a scimitar, and woods interlocked their hands to stay me—but being restless, on I ran.

The house dwindled behind me; and the light in my sick-room, and your shadow on the curtain. But yet I was restless, and I ran.

In the twinkling of an eye I fell into a solitary place. Sand and rocks were in it, and a falling wind. I paused, and knelt upon the sand, and mused a little in this place. I mused of you, and life and death, and love and agony;—but these had departed from me, as dim and distant as the fainting wind. A sense of solemn expectation filled the air. A tremor and a trouble wrapped my soul.

"I must be dead!" I said aloud. I had no sooner spoken than I learned that I was not alone.

The sun had risen, and on a ledge of ancient rock, weather-stained and red, there had fallen over against me the outline of a Presence lifted up against the sky; and turning suddenly, I saw. . . .

Lawful to utter, but utterance has fled! Lawful to utter, but a greater than Law restrains me! Am I blotted from your desolate fixed eyes? Lips that my mortal lips have pressed, can you not quiver when I cry? Soul that my eternal soul has loved, can you stand enveloped in my presence, and not spring like a fountain to me? Would you not know how it has been with me since your perishable eyes beheld my perished face? What my eyes have seen, or my ears have heard, or my heart conceived without you? If I have missed or mourned for you? If I have watched or longed for you? Marked your solitary days and sleepless nights, and tearless eyes, and monotonous slow echo of my unanswering name? Would you not know?

Alas! would she? Would she not? My soul misgives me with a matchless, solitary fear. I am called, and I slip from her. I am beckoned, and I lose her.

Her face dims, and her folded, lonely hands fade from my sight.

Time to tell her a guarded thing! Time to whisper a treasured word! A moment to tell her that *Death is dumb, for Life is deaf!* A moment to tell her——

XII

MARY ELIZABETH BRADDON

The Shadow IN THE *Corner*

1879

Wildheath Grange stood a little way back from the road, with a barren stretch of heath behind it, and a few tall fir-trees, with straggling wind-tossed heads, for its only shelter. It was a lonely house on a lonely road, little better than a lane, leading across a desolate waste of sandy fields to the sea-shore; and it was a house that bore a bad name among the natives of the village of Holcroft, which was the nearest place where humanity might be found.

It was a good old house, nevertheless, substantially built in the days when there was no stint of stone and timber—a good old gray stone house, with many gables, deep window seats, and a wide staircase, long dark passages, hidden doors in queer corners, closets as large as some modern rooms, and cellars in which a company of soldiers might have lain perdu.

This spacious old mansion was given over to rats and mice, loneliness, echoes, and the occupation of three elderly people; Michael Bascom, whose forbears had been landowners of importance in the neighborhood, and his two servants, Daniel Skegg and his wife, who had served the owner of that grim old house ever since he left the university, where he had lived fifteen years of his life—five as student, and ten as professor of natural science.

At three-and-thirty Michael Bascom had seemed a middle-aged man; at fifty-six he looked and moved and spoke like on old man. During that interval of twenty-three years he had lived alone in Wildheath Grange, and the country people told each other that the house had made him what he was. This was a fanciful and superstitious notion on their part, doubtless; yet it would not have been difficult to have traced a certain affinity between the dull gray building and the man who lived in it. Both seemed alike remote from the common cares and interests of humanity; both had an air of settled melancholy, engendered by perpetual solitude; both had the same faded complexion, the same look of slow decay.

Yet lonely as Michael Bascom's life was at Wildheath Grange, he would not for any consideration have altered its tenor. He had been glad to exchange the comparative seclusion of college rooms for the unbroken solitude of Wildheath. He was a fanatic in his love of scientific research, and his quiet days were filled to the brim with labors that seldom failed to interest and satisfy him. There were periods of depression, occasional hours of doubt, when the goal towards which he strove seemed unattainable, and his spirit fainted within him. Happily such times were rare with him. He had a dogged power of continuity which ought to have carried him to the highest pinnacle of achievement, and which perhaps might ultimately have won for him a grand name and a world-wide renown, but for a catastrophe which burdened the declining years of his harmless life with an unconquerable remorse.

One autumn morning—when he had lived just three-and-twenty years at Wildheath, and had only lately begun to perceive that his faithful butler and body servant, who was middle-aged when he first employed him, was actually getting old—Mr. Bascom's breakfast meditations over the latest treatise on the atomic theory were interrupted by an abrupt demand from that very Daniel Skegg. The man was accustomed to wait upon his master in the most absolute silence, and his sudden breaking out into speech was almost as startling as if the bust of Socrates above the bookcase had burst into human language.

"It's no use," said Daniel; "my missus must have a girl!"

"A what?" demanded Mr. Bascom, without taking his eyes from the line he had been reading.

"A girl—a girl to trot about and wash up, and help the old lady. She's getting weak on her legs, poor soul. We've none of us grown younger in the last twenty years."

"Twenty years!" echoed Michael Bascom scornfully. "What is twenty years in the formation of a stratum—what even in the growth of an oak—the cooling of a volcano!"

"Not much, perhaps, but it's apt to tell upon the bones of a human being."

"The manganese staining to be seen upon some skulls would certainly indicate—" began the scientist dreamily.

"I wish my bones were only as free from rheumatics as they were twenty years ago," pursued Daniel testily; "and then perhaps *I* should make light of twenty years. Howsoever, the long and the short of it is, my missus must have a girl. She can't go on trotting up and down these everlasting passages, and standing in that stony scullery year after year, just as if she was a young woman. She must have a girl to help."

"Let her have twenty girls," said Mr. Bascom, going back to his book.

"What's the use of talking like that, sir? Twenty girls, indeed! We shall have rare work to get one."

"Because the neighborhood is sparsely populated?" interrogated Mr. Bascom, still reading.

"No, sir. Because this house is known to be haunted."

Michael Bascom laid down his book, and turned a look of grave reproach upon his servant.

"Skegg," he said in a severe voice, "I thought you had lived long enough with me to be superior to any folly of that kind."

"I don't say that *I* believe in ghosts," answered Daniel with a semi-apologetic air; "but the country people do. There's not a mortal among 'em that will venture across our threshold after nightfall."

"Merely because Anthony Bascom, who led a wild life in London, and lost his money and land, came home here broken-hearted, and is supposed to have destroyed himself in this house—the only remnant of property that was left him out of a fine estate."

"Supposed to have destroyed himself!" cried Skegg; "why the fact is as well known as the death of Queen Elizabeth, or the great fire of London. Why, wasn't he buried at the cross-roads between here and Holcroft?"

"An idle tradition, for which you could produce no substantial proof," retorted Mr. Bascom.

"I don't know about proof: but the country people believe it as firmly as they believe their Gospel."

"If their faith in the Gospel was a little stronger they need not trouble themselves about Anthony Bascom."

"Well," grumbled Daniel, as he began to clear the table, a girl of some kind we must get, but she'll have to be a foreigner, or a girl that's hard driven for a place."

When Daniel Skegg said a foreigner, he did not mean the native of some distant land, but a girl who had not been born and bred at Holcroft. Daniel had been raised and reared in that insignificant hamlet, and, small and dull as the spot was, he considered it the center of the earth, and the world beyond it only margin.

Michael Bascom was too deep in the atomic theory to give a second thought to the necessities of an old servant. Mrs. Skegg was an individual with whom he rarely came in contact. She lived for the most part in a gloomy region at the north end of the house, where she ruled over the solitude of a kitchen, that looked almost as big as a cathedral, and numerous offices of the scullery, larder, and pantry class, where she carried on a perpetual warfare with spiders and beetles, and wore her old life out in the labor of sweeping and scrubbing. She was a woman of severe aspect, dogmatic piety, and a bitter tongue. She was a good plain cook, and ministered diligently to her master's wants. He was not an epicure, but liked his life to be smooth and easy, and the equilibrium of his mental power would have been disturbed by a bad dinner.

He heard no more about the proposed addition to his household for a space of ten days, when Daniel Skegg again startled him amidst his studious repose by the abrupt announcement—

"I've got a girl!"

"Oh," said Michael Bascom; "have you?" and he went on with his book.

This time he was reading an essay on phosphorus and its functions in relation to the human brain.

"Yes," pursued Daniel in his usual grumbling tone; "she was a waif and stray, or I shouldn't have got her. If she'd been a native she'd never have come to us."

"I hope she's respectable," said Michael.

"Respectable! That's the only fault she has, poor thing. She's too good for the place. She's never been in service before, but she says she's willing to work, and I daresay my old woman will be able to break her in. Her father was a small tradesman at Yarmouth. He died a month ago, and left this poor thing homeless. Mrs. Midge, at Holcroft, is her aunt, and she said to the girl, Come and stay with me till you get a place; and the girl has been staying with Mrs. Midge for the last three weeks, trying to hear of a place. When Mrs. Midge heard that my missus wanted a girl to help, she thought it would be the very thing for her niece Maria. Luckily Maria had heard nothing about this house, so the poor innocent dropped me a curtsy, and said she'd be thankful to come, and would do her best to learn her duty. She'd had an easy time of it with her father, who had educated her above her station, like a fool as he was," growled Daniel.

"By your own account I'm afraid you've made a bad bargain," said Michael. "You don't want a young lady to clean kettles and pans."

"If she was a young duchess my old woman would make her work," retorted Skegg decisively.

"And pray where are you going to put this girl?" asked Mr. Bascom, rather irritably; "I can't have a strange young woman tramping up and down the passages outside my room. You know what a wretched sleeper I am, Skegg. A mouse behind the wainscot is enough to wake me."

"I've thought of that," answered the butler, with his look of ineffable wisdom. "I'm not going to put her on your floor. She's to sleep in the attics."

"Which room?"

"The big one at the north end of the house. That's the only ceiling that doesn't let water. She might as well sleep in a shower-bath as in any of the other attics."

"The room at the north end," repeated Mr. Bascom thoughtfully; "isn't that—?"

"Of course it is," snapped Skegg; "but she doesn't know anything about it."

Mr. Bascom went back to his books, and forgot all about the orphan from Yarmouth, until one morning on entering his study he was startled by the appearance of a strange girl, in a neat black and white cotton gown, busy dusting the volumes which were stacked in blocks upon his spacious writing-table—and doing it with such deft and careful hands that he had no inclination to be angry at this unwonted liberty. Old Mrs. Skegg had religiously refrained from all such dusting, on the plea that she did not wish to interfere with the master's ways. One of the master's ways, therefore, had been to inhale a good deal of dust in the course of his studies.

The girl was a slim little thing, with a pale and somewhat old-fashioned face, flaxen hair, braided under a neat muslin cap, a very fair complexion, and light blue eyes. They were the lightest blue eyes Michael Bascom had ever seen, but there was a sweetness and gentleness in their expression which atoned for their insipid color.

"I hope you do not object to my dusting your books, sir," she said, dropping a curtsy.

She spoke with a quaint precision which struck Michael Bascom as a pretty thing in its way.

"No; I don't object to cleanliness, so long as my books and papers are not disturbed. If you take a volume off my desk, replace it on the spot you took it from. That's all I ask."

"I will be very careful, sir."

"When did you come here?"

"Only this morning, sir."

The student seated himself at his desk, and the girl withdrew, drifting out of the room as noiselessly as a flower blown across the threshold. Michael Bascom looked after her curiously. He had seen very little of youthful womanhood in his dry-as-dust career, and he wondered at this girl as at a creature of a species hitherto unknown to him. How fairly and delicately she was fashioned; what a translucent skin; what soft and pleasing accents issued from those rose-tinted lips. A pretty thing, assuredly, this kitchen wench! A pity that in all this busy world there could be no better work found for her than the scouring of pots and pans.

Absorbed in considerations about dry bones, Mr. Bascom thought no more of the pale-faced handmaiden. He saw her no more about his rooms. Whatever work she did there was done early in the morning, before the scholar's breakfast.

She had been a week in the house, when he met her one day in the hall. He was struck by the change in her appearance.

The girlish lips had lost their rose-bud hue; the pale blue eyes had a frightened look, and there were dark rings round them, as in one whose nights had been sleepless, or troubled by evil dreams.

Michael Bascom was so startled by an undefinable look in the girl's face that, reserved as he was by habit and nature, he expanded so far as to ask her what ailed her.

"There is something amiss, I am sure," he said. "What is it?"

"Nothing, sir," she faltered, looking still more scared at his question. "Indeed, it is nothing; or nothing worth troubling you about."

"Nonsense. Do you suppose, because I live among books, I have no sympathy with my fellow-creatures? Tell me what is wrong with you, child. You have been grieving about the father you have lately lost, I suppose."

"No, sir; it is not that. I shall never leave off being sorry for that. It is a grief which will last me all my life."

"What, there is something else then?" asked Michael impatiently. "I see; you are not happy here. Hard work does not suit you. I thought as much."

"Oh, sir, please don't think that," cried the girl, very earnestly. "Indeed I am glad to work—glad to be in service; it is only——"

She faltered and broke down, the tears rolling slowly from her sorrowful eyes, despite her effort to keep them back.

"Only what?" cried Michael, growing angry. "The girl is full of secrets and mysteries. What do you mean, wench?"

"I—I know it is very foolish, sir; but I am afraid of the room where I sleep."

"Afraid! Why?"

"Shall I tell you the truth, sir? Will you promise not to be angry?"

"I will not be angry if you will only speak plainly; but you provoke me by these hesitations and suppressions."

"And please, sir, do not tell Mrs. Skegg that I have told you. She would scold me, or perhaps even send me away."

"Mrs. Skegg shall not scold you. Go on, child."

"You may not know the room where I sleep, sir; it is a large room at one end of the house, looking towards the sea. I can see the dark line of water from the window, and I wonder sometimes to think that it is the same ocean I used to see when I was a child at Yarmouth. It is very lonely, sir, at the top of the house. Mr. and Mrs. Skegg sleep in a little room near the kitchen, you know, sir, and I am quite alone on the top floor."

"Skegg told me you had been educated in advance of your position in life, Maria. I should have thought the first effect of a good education would have been to make you superior to any foolish fancies about empty rooms."

"Oh, pray sir, do not think it is any fault in my education. Father took such pains with me; he spared no expense in giving me as good an education as a tradesman's daughter need wish for. And he was a religious man, sir. He did not believe"—here she paused with a suppressed shudder—"in the spirits of the dead appearing to the living since the days of miracles, when the ghost of Samuel appeared to Saul. He never put any foolish ideas into my head, sir. I hadn't a thought of fear when I first lay down to rest in the big lonely room upstairs."

"Well, what then?"

"But on the very first night," the girl went on breathlessly, "I felt weighed down in my sleep as if there were some heavy burden laid upon my chest. It was not a bad dream, but it was a sense of trouble that followed me all through my sleep; and just at daybreak—it begins to be light a little after six—I woke suddenly, with the cold perspiration pouring down my face, and knew that there was something dreadful in the room."

"What do you mean by something dreadful. Did you see anything?"

"Not much, sir; but it froze the blood in my veins, and I knew it was this that had been following me and weighing upon me all through my sleep. In the corner between the fire-place and the wardrobe, I saw a shadow—a dim, shapeless shadow——"

"Produced by an angle of the wardrobe, I daresay."

"No, sir. I could see the shadow of the wardrobe, distinct and sharp, as if it had been painted on the wall. This shadow was in the corner—a strange, shapeless mass; or, if it had any shape at all, it seemed——"

"What?" asked Michael eagerly.

"The shape of a dead body hanging against the wall!"

Michael Bascom grew strangely pale, yet he affected utter incredulity.

"Poor child," he said kindly; "you have been fretting about your father until your nerves are in a weak state, and you are full of fancies. A shadow in the corner, indeed; why, at daybreak, every corner is full of shadows. My old coat, flung upon a chair, will make you as good a ghost as you need care to see."

"Oh, sir, I have tried to think it is my fancy. But I have had the same burden weighing me down every night. I have seen the same shadow every morning."

"But when broad daylight comes, can you not see what stuff your shadow is made of?"

"No, sir; the shadow goes before it is broad daylight."

"Of course, just like other shadows. Come, come, get these silly notions out of your head, or you will never do for the work-a-day world. I could easily speak to Mrs. Skegg, and make her give you another room, if I wanted to encourage you in your folly. But that would be about the worst thing I could do for you. Besides, she tells me that all the other rooms on that floor are damp; and, no doubt, if she shifted you into one of them, you would discover another shadow in another corner, and get rheumatism into the bargain. No, my good girl, you must try to prove yourself the better for a superior education."

"I will do my best, sir," Maria answered meekly, dropping a curtsy.

Maria went back to the kitchen sorely depressed. It was a dreary life she led at Wildheath Grange—dreary by day, awful by night; for the vague burden and the shapeless shadow, which seemed so slight a matter to the elderly scholar, were unspeakably terrible to her. Nobody had told her that the house was haunted; yet she walked about those echoing passages wrapped round with a cloud of fear. She had no pity from Daniel Skegg and his wife. Those two pious souls had made up their minds that the character of the house should be upheld, so far as Maria went. To her, as a foreigner, the Grange should be maintained to be an immaculate dwelling, tainted by no sulphurous blast from the under world. A willing, biddable girl had become a necessary element in the existence of Mrs. Skegg. That girl had been found and that girl must be kept. Any fancies of a supernatural character must be put down with a high hand.

"Ghosts, indeed!" cried the amiable Skegg. "Read your Bible, Maria, and don't talk no more about ghosts."

"There are ghosts in the Bible," said Maria, with a shiver at the recollection of certain awful passages in the Scripture she knew so well.

"Ah, they was in their right place, or they wouldn't ha' been there," retorted Mrs. Skegg. "You ain't agoin' to pick holes in your Bible, I hope, Maria, at your time of life."

Maria sat down quietly in her corner by the kitchen fire, and turned over the leaves of her dead father's Bible till she came to the chapters they two had loved best and oftenest read together. He had been a simple-minded, straightforward man, the Yarmouth cabinet-maker—a man full of aspirations after good, innately refined, instinctively religious. He and his motherless girl had spent their lives alone together, in the neat little home, which Maria had so soon learnt to cherish and beautify; and they had loved each other with an almost romantic love.

They had had the same tastes, the same ideas. Very little had sufficed to make them happy. But inexorable death parted father and daughter, in one of those sharp sudden partings which are like the shock of an earthquake—instantaneous ruin, desolation and despair.

Maria's fragile form had bent before the tempest. She had lived through a trouble that might have crushed a stronger nature. Her deep religious convictions, and her belief that this cruel parting would not be for ever, had sustained her. She faced life, and its cares and duties, with a gentle patience which was the noblest form of courage.

Michael Bascom told himself that the servant-girl's foolish fancy about the room that had been given her was not a matter for serious consideration. Yet the idea dwelt in his mind unpleasantly, and disturbed him at his labors. The exact sciences require the complete power of a man's brain, his undistracted attention; and on this particular evening Michael found that he was only giving his work a part of his attention. The girl's pale face, the girl's tremulous tones, thrust themselves into the foreground of his thoughts.

He closed his book with a fretful sigh, wheeled his large arm-chair round to the fire, and gave himself up to contemplation. To attempt study with so disturbed a mind was useless. It was a dull gray evening, early in November; the student's reading-lamp was lighted, but the shutters were not yet shut, nor the curtains drawn. He could see the leaden sky outside his windows, the fir-tree tops tossing in the angry wind. He could hear the wintry blast whistling amidst the gables, before it rushed off seaward with a savage howl that sounded like a war-whoop.

Michael Bascom shivered, and drew nearer the fire.

"It's childish, foolish nonsense," he said to himself, "yet it's strange she should have that fancy about the shadow; for they say Anthony Bascom destroyed himself in that room. I remember hearing it when I was a boy, from an old servant whose mother was housekeeper at the great house in Anthony's time. I never heard how he died, poor fellow—whether he poisoned himself, or shot himself, or cut his throat; but I've been told that was the room. Old Skegg has heard it too. I could see that by his manner when he told me the girl was to sleep there."

He sat for a long time, till the gray of evening outside his study windows changed to the black of night, and the war-whoop of the wind died away to a low complaining murmur. He sat looking into the fire, and letting his thoughts wander back to the past and the traditions he had heard in his boyhood.

That was a sad, foolish story of his great-uncle, Anthony Bascom: the pitiful story of a wasted fortune and a wasted life. A riotous collegiate career at Cambridge, a racing-stable at Newmarket, an imprudent marriage, a dissipated life in London, a runaway wife, an estate forfeited to Jew money-lenders, and then the fatal end.

Michael had often heard that dismal story; how, when Anthony Bascom's fair false wife had left him, when his credit was exhausted, and his friends had grown tired of him, and all was gone except Wildheath Grange, Anthony, the broken-down man of fashion, had come to that lonely house unexpectedly one night, and had ordered his bed to be got ready for him in the room where he used to sleep when he came to the place for the wild duck shooting, in his boyhood. His old blunderbuss was still hanging over the mantelpiece, where he had left it when he came into the property, and could afford to buy the newest thing in fowling-pieces. He had not been to Wildheath for fifteen years; nay, for a good many of those years he had almost forgotten that the dreary old house belonged to him.

The woman who had been housekeeper at Bascom Park, till house and lands had passed into the hands of the Jews, was at this time the sole occupant of Wildheath. She cooked some supper for her master, and made him as comfortable as she could in the long untenanted dining-room; but she was distressed to find, when she cleared the table after he had gone upstairs to bed, that he had eaten hardly anything.

Next morning she got his breakfast ready in the same room, which she managed to make brighter and cheerier than it had looked overnight. Brooms, dusting-brushes, and a good fire did much to improve the aspect of things. But the morning wore on to noon, and the old housekeeper listened in vain for her master's footfall on the stairs. Noon waned to late afternoon. She had made no attempt to disturb him, thinking that he had worn himself out by a tedious journey on horseback, and that he was sleeping the sleep of exhaustion. But when the brief November day clouded with the first shadows of twilight, the old woman grew seriously alarmed, and went upstairs to her master's door, where she waited in vain for any reply to her repeated calls and knockings.

The door was locked on the inside, and the housekeeper was not strong enough to break it open. She rushed downstairs again full of fear, and ran bare-headed out into the lonely road. There was no habitation nearer than the turnpike on the old coach road, from which this side road branched off to the sea. There was scanty hope of a chance passer-by. The old woman ran along the road, hardly knowing whither she was going or what she was going to do, but with a vague idea that she must get somebody to help her.

Chance favored her. A cart, laden with sea-weed, came lumbering slowly along from the level line of sands yonder where the land melted into water. A heavy lumbering farm-laborer walked beside the cart.

"For God's sake, come in and burst open my master's door!" she entreated, seizing the man by the arm. "He's lying dead, or in a fit, and I can't get to help him."

"All right, missus," answered the man, as if such an invitation were a matter of daily occurrence. "Whoa, Dobbin; stond still, horse, and be donged to thee."

Dobbin was glad enough to be brought to anchor on the patch of waste grass in front of the Grange garden. His master followed the housekeeper upstairs, and shattered the old-fashioned box-lock with one blow of his ponderous fist.

The old woman's worst fear was realized. Anthony Bascom was dead. But the mode and manner of his death Michael had never been able to learn. The housekeeper's daughter, who told him the story, was an old woman when he was a boy. She had only shaken her head, and looked unutterable things, when he questioned her too closely. She had never even admitted that the old squire had committed suicide. Yet the tradition of his self-destruction was rooted in the minds of the natives of Holcroft: and there was a settled belief that his ghost, at certain times and seasons, haunted Wildheath Grange.

Now Michael Bascom was a stern materialist. For him the universe, with all its inhabitants, was but a stupendous machine, governed by inexorable laws. To such a man the idea of a ghost was simply absurd—as absurd as the assertion that two and two make five, or that a circle can be formed of a straight line. Yet he had a kind of dilettante interest in the idea of a mind which could believe in ghosts. The subject offered a curious psychological study. This poor little pale girl, now, had evidently got some supernatural terror into her head, which could only be conquered by rational treatment.

"I know what I ought to do," Michael Bascom said to himself suddenly. "I'll occupy that room myself to-night, and demonstrate to this foolish girl that her notion about the shadow is nothing more than a silly fancy, bred of timidity and low spirits. An ounce of proof is better than a pound of argument. If I can prove to her that I have spent a night in the room, and seen no such shadow, she will understand what an idle thing superstition is."

Daniel came in presently to shut the shutters.

"Tell your wife to make up my bed in the room where Maria has been sleeping, and to put her into one of the rooms on the first floor for to-night, Skegg," said Mr. Bascom.

"Sir?"

Mr. Bascom repeated his order.

"That silly wench has been complaining to you about her room," Skegg exclaimed indignantly. "She doesn't deserve to be well fed and cared for in a comfortable home. She ought to go to the workhouse."

"Don't be angry with the poor girl, Skegg. She has taken a foolish fancy into her head, and I want to show her how silly she is," said Mr. Bascom.

"And you want to sleep in his—in that room yourself," said the butler.

"Precisely."

"Well," mused Skegg, "if he does walk—which I don't believe—he was your own flesh and blood; and I don't suppose he'll do you any hurt."

When Daniel Skegg went back to the kitchen he railed mercilessly at poor Maria, who sat pale and silent in her corner by the hearth, darning old Mrs. Skegg's gray worsted stockings, which were the roughest and harshest covering that ever human foot clothed itself withal. "Was there ever such a whimsical, fine, lady-like miss," demanded Daniel, "to come into a gentleman's house, and drive him out of his own bedroom to sleep in an attic, with her nonsenses and vagaries." If this was the result of being educated above one's station, Daniel declared that he was thankful he had never got so far in his schooling as to read words of two syllables without spelling. Education might be hanged, for him, if this was all it led to.

"I am very sorry," faltered Maria, weeping silently over her work. "Indeed, Mr. Skegg, I made no complaint. My master questioned me, and I told him the truth. That was all."

"All!" exclaimed Mr. Skegg irately; "all, indeed! I should think it was enough."

Poor Maria held her peace. Her mind, fluttered by Daniel's unkindness, had wandered away from that bleak big kitchen to the lost home of the past—the snug little parlor where she and her father had sat beside the cozy hearth on such a night as this; she with her smart work-box and her plain sewing, he with the newspaper he loved to read; the petted cat purring on the rug, the kettle singing on the bright brass trivet, the tea tray pleasantly suggestive of the most comfortable meal in the day.

Oh, those happy nights, that dear companionship! Were they really gone for ever, leaving nothing behind them but unkindness and servitude?

Michael Bascom retired later than usual that night. He was in the habit of sitting at his books long after every other lamp but his own had been extinguished. The Skeggs had subsided into silence and darkness in their dreary ground-floor bed-chamber. To-night his studies were of a peculiarly interesting kind, and belonged to the order of recreative reading rather than of hard work. He was deep in the history of that mysterious people who had their dwelling-place in the Swiss lakes, and was much exercised by certain speculations and theories about them.

The old eight-day clock on the stairs was striking two as Michael slowly ascended, candle in hand, to the hitherto unknown region of the attics. At the top of the staircase he found himself facing a dark narrow passage which led northwards, a passage that was in itself sufficient to strike terror to a superstitious mind, so black and uncanny did it look.

"Poor child," mused Mr. Bascom, thinking of Maria; "this attic floor is rather dreary, and for a young mind prone to fancies——"

He had opened the door of the north room by this time, and stood looking about him.

It was a large room, with a ceiling that sloped on one side, but was fairly lofty upon the other; an old-fashioned room, full of old-fashioned furniture—big, ponderous, clumsy—associated with a day that was gone and people that were dead. A walnut-wood wardrobe stared him in the face—a wardrobe with brass handles, which gleamed out of the darkness like diabolical eyes. There was a tall four-post bed-stead, which had been cut down on one side to accommodate the slope of the ceiling, and which had a misshapen and deformed aspect in consequence. There was an old mahogany bureau, that smelt of secrets. There were some heavy old chairs with rush bottoms, moldy with age, and much worn. There was a corner washstand, with a big basin and a small jug—the odds and ends of past years. Carpet there was none, save a narrow strip beside the bed.

"It is a dismal room," mused Michael, with the same touch of pity for Maria's weakness which he had felt on the landing just now.

To him it mattered nothing where he slept; but having let himself down to a lower level by his interest in the Swiss lake-people, he was in a manner humanized by the lightness of his evening's reading, and was even inclined to compassionate the feebleness of a foolish girl.

He went to bed, determined to sleep his soundest. The bed was comfortable, well supplied with blankets, rather luxurious than otherwise, and the scholar had that agreeable sense of fatigue which promises profound and restful slumber.

He dropped off to sleep quickly, but woke with a start ten minutes afterwards. What was this consciousness of a burden of care that had awakened him—this sense of all-pervading trouble that weighed upon his spirits and oppressed his heart—this icy horror of some terrible crisis in life through which he must inevitably pass? To him these feelings were as novel as they were painful. His life had flowed on with smooth and sluggish tide, unbroken by so much as a ripple of sorrow. Yet to-night he felt all the pangs of unavailing remorse; the agonizing memory of a life wasted; the stings of humiliation and disgrace, shame, ruin; the foreshadowing of a hideous death, which he had doomed himself to die by his own hand. These were the horrors that pressed him round and weighed him down as he lay in Anthony Bascom's room.

Yes, even he, the man who could recognize nothing in nature, or in nature's God, better or higher than an irresponsible and invariable machine governed by mechanical laws, was fain to admit that here he found himself face to face with a psychological mystery. This trouble, which came between him and sleep, was the trouble that had pursued Anthony Bascom on the last night of his life. So had the suicide felt as he lay in that lonely room, perhaps striving to rest his wearied brain with one last earthly sleep before he passed to the unknown intermediate land where all is darkness and slumber. And that troubled mind had haunted the room ever since. It was not the ghost of the man's body that returned to the spot where he had suffered and perished, but the ghost of his mind—his very self; no meaningless simulacrum of the clothes he wore, and the figure that filled them.

Michael Bascom was not the man to abandon his high ground of sceptical philosophy without a struggle. He tried his hardest to conquer this oppression that weighed upon mind and sense. Again and again he succeeded in composing himself to sleep, but only to wake again and again to the same torturing thoughts, the same remorse, the same despair. So the night passed in unutterable weariness; for though he told himself that the trouble was not his trouble, that there was no reality in the burden, no reason for the remorse, these vivid fancies were as painful as realities, and took as strong a hold upon him.

The first streak of light crept in at the window—dim, and cold, and gray; then came twilight, and he looked at the corner between the wardrobe and the door.

Yes; there was the shadow: not the shadow of the wardrobe only—that was clear enough, but a vague and shapeless something which darkened the dull brown wall; so faint, so shadowy, that he could form no conjecture as to its nature, or the thing it represented. He determined to watch this shadow till broad daylight; but the weariness of the night had exhausted him, and before the first dimness of dawn had passed away he had fallen fast asleep, and was tasting the blessed balm of undisturbed slumber. When he woke the winter sun was shining in at the lattice, and the room had lost its gloomy aspect. It looked old-fashioned, and gray, and brown, and shabby; but the depth of its gloom had fled with the shadows and the darkness of night.

Mr. Bascom rose refreshed by a sound sleep, which had lasted nearly three hours. He remembered the wretched feelings which had gone before that renovating slumber; but he recalled his strange sensations only to despise them, and he despised himself for having attached any importance to them.

"Indigestion very likely," he told himself; "or perhaps mere fancy, engendered of that foolish girl's story. The wisest of us is more under the dominion of imagination than he would care to confess. Well, Maria shall not sleep in this room any more. There is no particular reason why she should, and she shall not be made unhappy to please old Skegg and his wife."

When he had dressed himself in his usual leisurely way, Mr. Bascom walked up to the corner where he had seen or imagined the shadow, and examined the spot carefully.

At first sight he could discover nothing of a mysterious character. There was no door in the papered wall, no trace of a door that had been there in the past. There was no trap-door in the worm-eaten boards. There was no dark ineradicable stain to hint at murder. There was not the faintest suggestion of a secret or a mystery.

He looked up at the ceiling. That was sound enough, save for a dirty patch here and there where the rain had blistered it.

Yes; there was something—an insignificant thing, yet with a suggestion of grimness which startled him.

About a foot below the ceiling he saw a large iron hook projecting from the wall, just above the spot where he had seen the shadow of a vaguely defined form. He mounted on a chair the better to examine this hook, and to understand, if he could, the purpose for which it had been put there.

It was old and rusty. It must have been there for many years. Who could have placed it there, and why? It was not the kind of hook upon which one would hang a picture or one's garments. It was placed in an obscure corner. Had Anthony Bascom put it there on the night he died, or did he find it there ready for a fatal use?

"If I were a superstitious man," thought Michael; "I should be inclined to believe that Anthony Bascom hung himself from that rusty old hook."

"Sleep well, sir?" asked Daniel, as he waited upon his master at breakfast.

"Admirably," answered Michael, determined not to gratify the man's curiosity. He had always resented the idea that Wildheath Grange was haunted.

"Oh, indeed, sir. You were so late that I fancied——"

"Late, yes! I slept so well that I overshot my usual hour for waking. But, by-the-way, Skegg, as that poor girl objects to the room, let her sleep somewhere else. It can't make any difference to us, and it may make some difference to her."

"Humph!" muttered Daniel in his grumpy way; "you didn't see anything queer up there, did you?"

"See anything? Of course not."

"Well, then, why should she see things? It's all her silly fiddle-faddle."

"Never mind, let her sleep in another room."

"There ain't another room on the top floor that's dry."

"Then let her sleep on the floor below. She creeps about quietly enough, poor little timid thing. She won't disturb me."

Daniel grunted, and his master understood the grunt to mean obedient assent; but here Mr. Bascom was unhappily mistaken. The proverbial obstinacy of the pig family is as nothing compared with the obstinacy of a cross-grained old man, whose narrow mind has never been illuminated by education. Daniel was beginning to feel jealous of his master's compassionate interest in the orphan girl. She was a sort of gentle clinging thing that might creep into an elderly bachelor's heart unawares, and make herself a comfortable nest there.

"We shall have fine carryings-on, and me and my old woman will be nowhere, if I don't put down my heel pretty strong upon this nonsense," Daniel muttered to himself, as he carried the breakfast-tray to the pantry.

Maria met him in the passage.

"Well, Mr. Skegg, what did my master say?" she asked breathlessly. "Did he see anything strange in the room?"

"No, girl. What should he see? He said you were a fool."

"Nothing disturbed him? And he slept there peacefully?" faltered Maria.

"Never slept better in his life. Now don't you begin to feel ashamed of yourself?"

"Yes," she answered meekly; "I am ashamed of being so full of fancies. I will go back to my room to-night, Mr. Skegg, if you like and I will never complain of it again."

"I hope you won't," snapped Skegg; "you've given us trouble enough already."

Maria sighed, and went about her work in saddest silence. The day wore slowly on, like all other days in that lifeless old house. The scholar sat in his study; Maria moved softly from room to room, sweeping and dusting in the cheerless solitude. The mid-day sun faded into the gray of afternoon, and evening came down like a blight upon the dull old house.

Throughout that day Maria and her master never met. Anyone who had been so far interested in the girl as to observe her appearance would have seen that she was unusually pale, and that her eyes had a resolute look, as of one who was resolved to face a painful ordeal. She ate hardly anything all day. She was curiously silent. Skegg and his wife put down both these symptoms to temper.

"She won't eat and she won't talk," said Daniel to the partner of his joys. "That means sulkiness, and I never allowed sulkiness to master me when I was a young man, and you tried it on as a young woman, and I'm not going to be conquered by sulkiness in my old age."

Bed-time came, and Maria bade the Skeggs a civil goodnight, and went up to her lonely garret without a murmur.

The next morning came, and Mrs. Skegg looked in vain for her patient handmaiden, when she wanted Maria's services in preparing the breakfast.

"The wench sleeps sound enough this morning," said the old woman. "Go and call her, Daniel. My poor legs can't stand them stairs."

"Your poor legs are getting uncommon useless," muttered Daniel testily, as he went to do his wife's behest.

He knocked at the door, and called Maria—once, twice, thrice, many times; but there was no reply. He tried the door, and found it locked. He shook the door violently, cold with fear.

Then he told himself that the girl had played him a trick. She had stolen away before daybreak, and left the door locked to frighten him. But, no; this could not be, for he could see the key in the lock when he knelt down and put his eye to the keyhole. The key prevented his seeing into the room.

"She's in there, laughing in her sleeve at me," he told himself; "but I'll soon be even with her."

There was a heavy bar on the staircase, which was intended to secure the shutters of the window that lighted the stairs. It was a detached bar, and always stood in a corner near the window, which it was but rarely employed to fasten. Daniel ran down to the landing, and seized upon this massive iron bar, and then ran back to the garret door.

One blow from the heavy bar shattered the old lock, which was the same lock the carter had broken with his strong fist seventy years before. The door flew open, and Daniel went into the attic which he had chosen for the stranger's bed-chamber.

Maria was hanging from the hook in the wall. She had contrived to cover her face decently with her handkerchief. She had hanged herself deliberately about an hour before Daniel found her, in the early gray of morning. The doctor, who was summoned from Holcroft, was able to declare the time at which she had slain herself, but there was no one who could say what sudden access of terror had impelled her to the desperate act, or under what slow torture of nervous apprehension her mind had given way. The coroner's jury returned the customary merciful verdict of "Temporary insanity."

The girl's melancholy fate darkened the rest of Michael Bascom's life. He fled from Wildheath Grange as from an accursed spot, and from the Skeggs as from the murderers of a harmless innocent girl. He ended his days at Oxford, where he found the society of congenial minds, and the books he loved. But the memory of Maria's sad face, and sadder death, was his abiding sorrow. Out of that deep shadow his soul was never lifted.

XIII

AMELIA B. EDWARDS

The Phantom Coach

1864

The circumstances I am about to relate to you have truth to recommend them. They happened to myself and my recollection of them is as vivid as if they had taken place only yesterday. Twenty years, however, have gone by since that night. During those twenty years I have told the story to but one other person. I tell it now with a reluctance which I find it difficult to overcome. All I entreat, meanwhile, is that you will abstain from forcing your own conclusions upon me. I want nothing explained away. I desire no arguments. My mind on this subject is quite made up and, having the testimony of my own senses to rely upon, I prefer to abide by it.

Well! It was just twenty years ago and within a day or two of the end of the grouse season. I had been out all day with my gun and had had no sport to speak of. The wind was due east; the month, December; the place, a bleak wide moor in the far north of England. And I had lost my way. It was not a pleasant place in which to lose one's way, with the first feathery flakes of a coming snowstorm just fluttering down upon the heather and the leaden evening closing in all around. I shaded my eyes with my hand and stared anxiously into the gathering darkness, where the purple moorland melted into a range of low hills, some ten or twelve miles distant. Not the faintest smoke-wreath, not the tiniest cultivated patch or fence or sheep-track, met my eyes in any direction. There was nothing for it but to walk on and take my chance of finding what shelter I could, by the way. So I shouldered my gun again and pushed wearily forward; for I had been on foot since an hour after day-break and had eaten nothing since breakfast.

Meanwhile, the snow began to come down with ominous steadiness and the wind fell. After this, the cold became more intense and the night came rapidly up. As for me, my prospects darkened with the darkening sky and my heart grew heavy as I thought how my young wife was already watching for me through the window of our little inn parlor and thought of all the suffering in store for her throughout this weary night. We had been married four months and, having spent our autumn in the Highlands, were now lodging in a remote little village situated just on the verge of the great English moorlands. We were very much in love and, of course, very happy. This morning, when we parted, she had implored me to return before dusk and I had promised her that I would. What would I not have given to have kept my word!

Even now, weary as I was, I felt that with a supper, an hour's rest, and a guide, I might still get back to her before midnight, if only guide and shelter could be found.

And all this time, the snow fell and the night thickened. I stopped and shouted every now and then, but my shouts seemed only to make the silence deeper. Then a vague sense of uneasiness came upon me and I began to remember stories of travelers who had walked on and on in the falling snow until, wearied out, they were fain to lie down and sleep their lives away. Would it be possible, I asked myself, to keep on thus through all the long dark night? Would there not come a time when my limbs must fail and my resolution give way? When I, too, must sleep the sleep of death. Death! I shuddered. How hard to die just now, when life lay all so bright before me! How hard for my darling, whose whole loving heart—but that thought was not to be borne! To banish it, I shouted again, louder and longer, and then listened eagerly. Was my shout answered, or did I only fancy that I heard a far-off cry? I halloed again and again the echo followed. Then a wavering speck of light came suddenly out of the dark, shifting, disappearing, growing momentarily nearer and brighter. Running towards it at full speed, I found myself, to my great joy, face to face with an old man and a lantern.

"Thank God!" was the exclamation that burst involuntarily from my lips.

Blinking and frowning, he lifted his lantern and peered into my face.

"What for?" growled he, sulkily.

"Well—for you. I began to fear I should be lost in the snow."

"Eh, then, folks do get cast away hereabouts fra' time to time, an' what's to hinder you from bein' cast away likewise, if the Lord's so minded?"

"If the Lord is so minded that you and I shall be lost together, friend, we must submit," I replied; "but I don't mean to be lost without you. How far am I now from Dwolding?"

"A gude twenty mile, more or less."

"And the nearest village?"

"The nearest village is Wyke, an' that's twelve mile t'other side."

"Where do you live, then?"

"Out yonder," said he, with a vague jerk of the lantern.

"You're going home, I presume?"

"Maybe I am."

"Then I'm going with you."

The old man shook his head and rubbed his nose reflectively with the handle of the lantern.

"It ain't o' no use," growled he. "He 'ont let you in—not he."

"We'll see about that," I replied, briskly. "Who is He?"

"The master."

"Who is the master?"

"That's nowt to you," was the unceremonious reply.

"Well, well; you lead the way and I'll engage that the master shall give me shelter and a supper tonight."

"Eh you can try him!" muttered my reluctant guide; and, still shaking his head, he hobbled, gnome-like, away through the falling snow. A large mass loomed up presently out of the darkness, and a huge dog rushed out, barking furiously.

"Is this the house?" I asked.

"Ay, it's the house. Down, Bey!" And he fumbled in his pocket for the key.

I drew up close behind him, prepared to lose no chance of entrance, and saw in the little circle of light shed by the lantern that the door was heavily studded with iron nails, like the door of a prison. In another minute he had turned the key and I had pushed past him into the house.

Once inside, I looked round with curiosity and found myself in a great raftered hall, which served, apparently, a variety of uses. One end was piled to the roof with corn, like a barn. The other was stored with flour-sacks, agricultural implements, casks and all kinds of miscellaneous lumber; while from the beams overhead hung rows of hams, flitches and bunches of dried herbs for winter use. In the center of the floor stood some huge object gauntly dressed in a dingy wrapping-cloth, and reaching half way to the rafters. Lifting a corner of this cloth I saw, to my surprise, a telescope of very considerable size, mounted on a rude movable platform, with four small wheels. The tube was made of painted wood, bound round with bands of metal rudely fashioned; the speculum, so far as I could estimate its size in the dim light, measured at least fifteen inches in diameter. While I was yet examining the instrument and asking myself whether it was not the work of some self-taught optician, a bell rang sharply.

"That's for you," said my guide, with a malicious grin. "Yonder's his room."

He pointed to a low black door at the opposite side of the hall. I crossed over, rapped somewhat loudly and went in, without waiting for an invitation. A huge, white-haired old man rose from a table covered with books and papers and confronted me sternly.

"Who are you?" said he. "How came you here? What do you want?"

"James Murray, barrister-at-law. On foot across the moor. Meat, drink and sleep."

He bent his bushy brows into a portentous frown.

"Mine is not a house of entertainment," he said, haughtily. "Jacob, how dared you admit this stranger?"

"I didn't admit him," grumbled the old man. "He followed me over the muir and shouldered his way in before me. I'm no match for six foot two."

"And pray, sir, by what right have you forced an entrance into my house?"

"The same by which I should have clung to your boat, if I were drowning. The right of self-preservation."

"Self-preservation?"

"There's an inch of snow on the ground already," I replied, briefly; "and it would be deep enough to cover my body before daybreak."

He strode to the window, pulled aside a heavy black curtain and looked out.

"It is true," he said. "You can stay, if you choose, till morning. Jacob, serve the supper."

With this he waved me to a seat, resumed his own and became at once absorbed in the studies from which I had disturbed him.

I placed my gun in a corner, drew a chair to the hearth and examined my quarters at leisure. Smaller and less incongruous in its arrangements than the hall, this room contained, nevertheless, much to awaken my curiosity. The floor was carpetless. The whitewashed walls were in parts scrawled over with strange diagrams and in others covered with shelves crowded with philosophical instruments, the uses of many of which were unknown to me. On one side of the fireplace, stood a bookcase filled with dingy folios; on the other, a small organ, fantastically decorated with painted carvings of medieval saints and devils. Through the half-opened door of a cupboard at the further end of the room, I saw a long array of geological specimens, surgical preparations, crucibles, retorts, and jars of chemicals; while on the mantel-shelf beside me, amid a number of small objects, stood a model of the solar system, a small galvanic battery and a microscope. Every chair had its burden. Every corner was heaped high with books. The very floor was littered over with maps, casts, papers, tracings and learned lumber of all conceivable kinds.

I stared about me with an amazement increased by every fresh object upon which my eyes chanced to rest. So strange a room I had never seen; yet seemed it stranger still, to find such a room in a lone farmhouse amid those wild and solitary moors! Over and over again, I looked from my host to his surroundings and from his surroundings back to my host, asking myself who and what he could be? His head was singularly fine; but it was more the head of a poet than of a philosopher. Broad in the temples, prominent over the eyes and clothed with a rough profusion of perfectly white hair, it had all the ideality and much of the ruggedness that characterizes the head of Ludwig van Beethoven. There were the same deep lines about the mouth and the same stern furrows in the brow. There was the same concentration of expression. While I was yet observing him, the door opened and Jacob brought in the supper. His master then closed his book, rose and with more courtesy of manner than he had yet shown, invited me to the table.

A dish of ham and eggs, a loaf of brown bread and a bottle of admirable sherry, were placed before me.

"I have but the homeliest farmhouse fare to offer you, sir," said my entertainer. "Your appetite, I trust, will make up for the deficiencies of our larder."

I had already fallen upon the viands and now protested, with the enthusiasm of a starving sportsman, that I had never eaten anything so delicious.

He bowed stiffly and sat down to his own supper, which consisted, primitively, of a jug of milk and a basin of porridge. We ate in silence and, when we had done, Jacob removed the tray. I then drew my chair back to the fireside. My host, somewhat to my surprise, did the same and turning abruptly towards me, said: "Sir, I have lived here in strict retirement for three-and-twenty years. During that time, I have not seen as many strange faces and I have not read a single newspaper. You are the first stranger who has crossed my threshold for more than four years. Will you favor me with a few words of information respecting that outer world from which I have parted company so long?"

"Pray interrogate me," I replied. "I am heartily at your service."

He bent his head in acknowledgment; leaned forward, with his elbows resting on his knees and his chin supported in the palms of his hands; stared fixedly into the fire; and proceeded to question me.

His enquiries related chiefly to scientific matters, with the later progress of which, as applied to the practical purposes of life, he was almost wholly unacquainted. No student of science myself, I replied as well as my slight information permitted; but the task was far from easy and I was much relieved when, passing from interrogation to discussion, he began pouring forth his own conclusions upon the facts which I had been attempting to place before him. He talked and I listened spellbound. He talked till I believe he almost forgot my presence and only thought aloud. I had never heard anything like it then; I have never heard anything like it since. Familiar with all systems of all philosophies, subtle in analysis, bold in generalization, he poured forth his thoughts in an uninterrupted stream and, still leaning forward in the same moody attitude with his eyes fixed upon the fire, wandered from topic to topic, from speculation to speculation, like an inspired dreamer. From practical science to mental philosophy; from electricity in the wire to electricity in the nerve; from Watts to Mesmer, from Mesmer to Reichenbach, from Reichenbach to Swedenborg, Spinoza, Condillac, Descartes, Berkeley, Aristotle, Plato, and the Magi and mystics of the East, were transitions which, however bewildering in their variety and scope, seemed easy and harmonious upon his lips as sequences in music. By and by—I forget now by what link of conjecture or illustration—he passed on to that field which lies beyond the boundary line of even conjectural philosophy and reaches no man knows whither. He spoke of the soul and its aspirations; of the spirit and its powers; of second sight; of prophecy; of those phenomena which, under the names of ghosts, specters and supernatural appearances, have been denied by the sceptics and attested by the credulous, of all ages.

"The world," he said, "grows hourly more and more sceptical of all that lies beyond its own narrow radius; and our men of science foster the fatal tendency. They condemn as fable all that resists experiment. They reject as false all that cannot be brought to the test of the laboratory or the dissecting-room. Against what superstition have they waged so long and obstinate a war, as against the belief in apparitions? And yet what superstition has maintained its hold upon the minds of men so long and so firmly? Show me any fact in physics, in history, in archaeology, which is supported by testimony so wide and so various. Attested by all races of men, in all ages and in all climates, by the soberest sages of antiquity, by the rudest savage of today, by the Christian, the Pagan, the Pantheist, the Materialist, this phenomenon is treated as a nursery tale by the philosophers of our century. Circumstantial evidence weighs with them as a feather in the balance. The comparison of causes with effects, however valuable in physical science, is put aside as worthless and unreliable. The evidence of competent witnesses, however conclusive in a court of justice, counts for nothing. He who pauses before he pronounces, is condemned as a trifler. He who believes, is a dreamer or a fool."

He spoke with bitterness and, having said thus, relapsed for some minutes into silence. Presently he raised his head from his hands and added, with an altered voice and manner: "I, sir, paused, investigated, believed, and was not ashamed to state my convictions to the world. I, too, was branded as a visionary, held up to ridicule by my contemporaries, and hooted from that field of science in which I had labored with honor during all the best years of my life. These things happened just three-and-twenty years ago. Since then, I have lived as you see me living now and the world has forgotten me, as I have forgotten the world. You have my history."

"It is a very sad one," I murmured, scarcely knowing what to answer.

"It is a very common one," he replied. "I have only suffered for the truth, as many a better and wiser man has suffered before me."

He rose, as if desirous of ending the conversation, and went over to the window.

"It has ceased snowing," he observed, as he dropped the curtain, and came back to the fireside.

"Ceased!" I exclaimed, starting eagerly to my feet. "Oh, if it were only possible—but no! it is hopeless. Even if I could find my way across the moor, I could not walk twenty miles tonight."

"Walk twenty miles tonight!" repeated my host. "What are you thinking of?"

"Of my wife," I replied, impatiently. "Of my young wife, who does not know that I have lost my way and who is at this moment breaking her heart with suspense and terror."

"Where is she?"

"At Dwolding, twenty miles away."

"At Dwolding," he echoed, thoughtfully. "Yes, the distance, it is true, is twenty miles; but—are you so very anxious to save the next six or eight hours?"

"So very, very anxious, that I would give ten guineas at this moment for a guide and a horse."

"Your wish can be gratified at a less costly rate," said he, smiling. "The night mail from the north, which changes horses at Dwolding, passes within five miles of this spot and will be due at a certain crossroad in about an hour and a quarter. If Jacob were to go with you across the moor and put you into the old coach-road, you could find your way, I suppose, to where it joins the new one?"

"Easily—gladly."

He smiled again, rang the bell, gave the old servant his directions and, taking a bottle of whisky and a wineglass from the cupboard in which he kept his chemicals, said: "The snow lies deep and it will be difficult walking tonight on the moor. A glass of usquebaugh before you start?"

I would have declined the spirit, but he pressed it on me and I drank it. It went down my throat like liquid flame and almost took my breath away.

"It is strong," he said; "but it will help to keep out the cold. And now you have no moments to spare. Good-night!"

I thanked him for his hospitality and would have shaken hands but that he had turned away before I could finish my sentence. In another minute I had traversed the hall, Jacob had locked the outer door behind me and we were out on the wide white moor.

Although the wind had fallen, it was still bitterly cold. Not a star glimmered in the black vault overhead. Not a sound, save the rapid crunching of the snow beneath our feet, disturbed the heavy stillness of the night. Jacob, not too well pleased with his mission, shambled on before in sullen silence, his lantern in his hand and his shadow at his feet. I followed, with my gun over my shoulder, as little inclined for conversation as himself. My thoughts were full of my late host. His voice yet rang in my ears. His eloquence yet held my imagination captive. I remember to this day, with surprise, how my over-excited brain retained whole sentences and parts of sentences, troops of brilliant images and fragments of splendid reasoning, in the very words in which he had uttered them. Musing thus over what I had heard, and striving to recall a lost link here and there, I strode on at the heels of my guide, absorbed and unobservant.

Presently—at the end, as it seemed to me, of only a few minutes—he came to a sudden halt and said: "Yon's your road. Keep the stone fence to your right hand and you can't fail of the way."

"This, then, is the old coach-road?"

"Ay, 'tis the old coach-road."

"And how far do I go, before I reach the crossroads?"

"Nigh upon three mile."

I pulled out my purse, and he became more communicative.

"The road's a fair road enough," said he, "for foot passengers; but 'twas over steep and narrow for the northern traffic. You'll mind where the parapet's broken away, close again the signpost. It's never been mended since the accident."

"What accident?"

"Eh, the night mail pitched right over into the valley below—a gude fifty feet an' more—just at the worst bit o' road in the whole county."

"Horrible! Were many lives lost?"

"All. Four were found dead and t'other two died next morning."

"How long is it since this happened?"

"Just nine year."

"Near the signpost, you say? I will bear it in mind. Good-night."

"Gude night, sir, and thankee." Jacob pocketed his half-crown, made a faint pretense of touching his hat and trudged back by the way he had come.

I watched the light of his lantern till it quite disappeared and then turned to pursue my way alone. This was no longer matter of the slightest difficulty, for, despite the dead darkness overhead, the line of stone fence showed distinctly enough against the pale gleam of the snow. How silent it seemed now, with only my footsteps to listen to; how silent and how solitary! A strange disagreeable sense of loneliness stole over me. I walked faster. I hummed a fragment of a tune. I cast up enormous sums in my head and accumulated them at compound interest. I did my best, in short, to forget the startling speculations to which I had but just been listening and, to some extent, I succeeded.

Meanwhile the night air seemed to become colder and colder and though I walked fast I found it impossible to keep myself warm. My feet were like ice. I lost sensation in my hands and grasped my gun mechanically. I even breathed with difficulty, as though, instead of traversing a quiet north country highway, I were scaling the uppermost heights of some gigantic Alp. This last symptom became presently so distressing, that I was forced to stop for a few minutes and lean against the stone fence. As I did so, I chanced to look back up the road and there, to my infinite relief, I saw a distant point of light, like the gleam of an approaching lantern.

I at first concluded that Jacob had retraced his steps and followed me; but even as the conjecture presented itself, a second light flashed into sight—a light evidently parallel with the first, and approaching at the same rate of motion. It needed no second thought to show me that these must be the carriage-lamps of some private vehicle, though it seemed strange that any private vehicle should take a road professedly disused and dangerous.

There could be no doubt, however, of the fact, for the lamps grew larger and brighter every moment, and I even fancied I could already see the dark outline of the carriage between them. It was coming up very fast, and quite noiselessly, the snow being nearly a foot deep under the wheels.

And now the body of the vehicle became distinctly visible behind the lamps. It looked strangely lofty. A sudden suspicion flashed upon me. Was it possible that I had passed the crossroads in the dark without observing the signpost, and could this be the very coach which I had come to meet? No need to ask myself that question a second time, for here it came round the bend of the road, guard and driver, one outside passenger, and four steaming grays, all wrapped in a soft haze of light, through which the lamps blazed out, like a pair of fiery meteors.

I jumped forward, waved my hat and shouted. The mail came down at full speed, and passed me. For a moment I feared that I had not been seen or heard, but it was only for a moment. The coachman pulled up; the guard, muffled to the eyes in capes and comforters, and apparently sound asleep in the rumble, neither answered my hail nor made the slightest effort to dismount; the outside passenger did not even turn his head. I opened the door for myself, and looked in. There were but three travelers inside, so I stepped in, shut the door, slipped into the vacant corner, and congratulated myself on my good fortune.

The atmosphere of the coach seemed, if possible, colder than that of the outer air, and was pervaded by a singularly damp and disagreeable smell. I looked round at my fellow-passengers. They were, all three, men, and all silent. They did not seem to be asleep, but each leaned back in his corner of the vehicle, as if absorbed in his own reflections. I attempted to open a conversation.

"How intensely cold it is tonight," I said, addressing my opposite neighbor.

He lifted his head, looked at me, but made no reply.

"The winter," I added, "seems to have begun in earnest."

Although the corner in which he sat was so dim that I could distinguish none of his features very clearly, I saw that his eyes were still turned full upon me. And yet he answered never a word.

At any other time I should have felt and perhaps expressed, some annoyance, but at the moment I felt too ill to do either. The icy coldness of the night air had struck a chill to my very marrow, and the strange smell inside the coach was affecting me with an intolerable nausea. I shivered from head to foot and, turning to my left-hand neighbor, asked if he had any objection to an open window?

He neither spoke nor stirred.

I repeated the question somewhat more loudly, but with the same result. Then I lost patience, and let the sash down. As I did so the leather strap broke in my hand, and I observed that the glass was covered with a thick coat of mildew, the accumulation, apparently of years. My attention being thus drawn to the condition of the coach, I examined it more narrowly, and saw by the uncertain light of the outer lamps that it was in the last stage of dilapidation. Every part of it was not only out of repair, but in a condition of decay. The sashes splintered at a touch. The leather fittings were crusted over with mold, and literally rotting from the woodwork. The floor was almost breaking away beneath my feet. The whole machine, in short, was foul with damp, and had evidently been dragged from some outhouse, in which it had been moldering away for years, to do another day or two of duty on the road.

I turned to the third passenger, whom I had not yet addressed, and hazarded one more remark.

"This coach," I said, "is in a deplorable condition. The regular mail, I suppose, is under repair?"

He moved his head slowly, and looked me in the face, without speaking a word. I shall never forget that look while I live. I turned cold at heart under it. I turn cold at heart even now when I recall it. His eyes glowed with a fiery unnatural luster. His face was livid as the face of a corpse. His bloodless lips were drawn back as if in the agony of death, and showed the gleaming teeth between.

The words that I was about to utter died upon my lips, and a strange horror—a dreadful horror—came upon me. My sight had by this time become used to the gloom of the coach, and I could see with tolerable distinctness. I turned to my opposite neighbor. He, too, was looking at me, with the same startling pallor in his face and the same stony glitter in his eyes. I passed my hand across my brow. I turned to the passenger on the seat beside my own and saw—oh Heaven! how shall

I describe what I saw? I saw that he was no living man—that none of them were living men, like myself! A pale phosphorescent light—the light of putrefaction—played upon their awful faces; upon their hair, dank with the dews of the grave; upon their clothes, earth-stained and dropping to pieces; upon their hands, which were as the hands of corpses long buried. Only their eyes, their terrible eyes, were living; and those eyes were all turned menacingly upon me!

A shriek of terror, a wild unintelligible cry for help and mercy, burst from my lips as I flung myself against the door and strove in vain to open it.

In that single instant, brief and vivid as a landscape beheld in the flash of summer lightning, I saw the moon shining down through a rift of stormy cloud—the ghastly signpost rearing its warning finger by the wayside—the broken parapet—the plunging horses—the black gulf below. Then, the coach reeled like a ship at sea. Then, came a mighty crash—a sense of crushing pain—and then, darkness.

It seemed as if years had gone by when I awoke one morning from a deep sleep and found my wife watching by my bedside. I will pass over the scene that ensued and give you, in half a dozen words, the tale she told me with tears of thanksgiving. I had fallen over a precipice, close against the junction of the old coach-road and the new, and had only been saved from certain death by lighting upon a deep snowdrift that had accumulated at the foot of the rock beneath. In this snowdrift I was discovered at daybreak by a couple of shepherds, who carried me to the nearest shelter and brought a surgeon to my aid. The surgeon found me in a state of raving delirium, with a broken arm and a compound fracture of the skull. The letters in my pocket-book showed my name and address; my wife was summoned to nurse me; and, thanks to youth and a fine constitution, I came out of danger at last. The place of my fall, I need scarcely say, was precisely that at which a frightful accident had happened to the north mail nine years before.

I never told my wife the fearful events which I have just related to you. I told the surgeon who attended me; but he treated the whole adventure as a mere dream born of the fever in my brain. We discussed the question over and over again, until we found that we could discuss it with temper no longer and then we dropped it. Others may form what conclusions they please—I *know* that twenty years ago I was the fourth inside passenger in that Phantom Coach.

EPILOGUE

PAUL LAURENCE DUNBAR

The Haunted Oak

1900

Pray why are you so bare, so bare,
  Oh, bough of the old oak-tree;
And why, when I go through the shade you throw,
  Runs a shudder over me?

My leaves were green as the best, I trow,
  And sap ran free in my veins,
But I saw in the moonlight dim and weird
  A guiltless victim's pains.

I bent me down to hear his sigh;
  I shook with his gurgling moan,
And I trembled sore when they rode away,
  And left him here alone.

They'd charged him with the old, old crime,
  And set him fast in jail:
Oh, why does the dog howl all night long,
  And why does the night wind wail?

He prayed his prayer and he swore his oath,
  And he raised his hand to the sky;
But the beat of hooves smote on his ear,
  And the steady tread drew nigh.

Who is it rides by night, by night,
  Over the moonlit road?
And what is the spur that keeps the pace,
  What is the galling goad?

And now they beat at the prison door,
  "Ho, keeper, do not stay!
We are friends of him whom you hold within,
  And we fain would take him away

"From those who ride fast on our heels
  With mind to do him wrong;
They have no care for his innocence,
  And the rope they bear is long."

They have fooled the jailer with lying words,
  They have fooled the man with lies;
The bolts unbar, the locks are drawn,
  And the great door open flies.

Now they have taken him from the jail,
  And hard and fast they ride,
And the leader laughs low down in his throat,
  As they halt my trunk beside.

Oh, the judge, he wore a mask of black,
  And the doctor one of white,
And the minister, with his oldest son,
  Was curiously bedight.

Oh, foolish man, why weep you now?
  'Tis but a little space,
And the time will come when these shall dread
  The mem'ry of your face.

I feel the rope against my bark,
  And the weight of him in my grain,
I feel in the throe of his final woe
  The touch of my own last pain.

And never more shall leaves come forth
  On a bough that bears the ban;
I am burned with dread, I am dried and dead,
  From the curse of a guiltless man.

And ever the judge rides by, rides by,
  And goes to hunt the deer,
And ever another rides his soul
  In the guise of a mortal fear.

And ever the man he rides me hard,
  And never a night stays he;
For I feel his curse as a haunted bough,
  On the trunk of a haunted tree.

BIOGRAPHIES

JOHN A. RICE, the illustrator of this volume, is an award-winning actor, writer, and artist specializing in oil pastels. His work has been sold in over thirty-five countries, and he runs J.A.R. Studio, NYC, out of his workspace in Astoria, NY. He is the creator of the internationally popular *Mindscapes Tarot* and most recently illustrated Charles Dickens's *A Christmas Carol* (Abbeville). Rice's mission is "to foster healing, introspection, and creativity through otherworldly art—empowering the internal world so that we can enrich our outer world."

NATHANIEL HAWTHORNE (1804–1864) was an American writer from Salem, Massachusetts, and was best known for *The Scarlet Letter* and *The House of the Seven Gables*. Deeply influenced by his Puritan ancestry, Hawthorne often explored sin, shame, and inherited guilt through allegorical tales with supernatural overtones, such as "Young Goodman Brown" and "The Minister's Black Veil."

WILKIE COLLINS (1824–1889) was born in London and was a close friend of Charles Dickens. A major figure in Victorian literature, he helped pioneer the sensation novel with *The Woman in White* and *The Moonstone*, and his interest in psychology, dreams, and identity carried into many of his frequently anthologized supernatural tales, including the *The Dream Woman* and "Miss Jéromette and the Clergyman."

SIR ARTHUR CONAN DOYLE (1859–1930) was a Scottish physician and author best known for creating Sherlock Holmes. A devout spiritualist in later life, Doyle was deeply influenced by the paranormal, which resulted in his supernatural fiction including "The Captain of the *Pole-Star*" and other ghost stories collected in *Tales of Terror and Mystery*.

LOUISA BALDWIN (1845–1925) was an English writer and member of the MacDonald literary family, as well as the mother of Prime Minister Stanley Baldwin. In addition to publishing novels and poetry, she is best remembered for her ghost stories, which reflect Victorian anxieties around domestic spaces, grief, and madness—particularly those in her collection *The Shadow on the Blind*.

W. W. JACOBS (1863–1943) was a British author best known for comic maritime stories, but he achieved enduring fame with "The Monkey's Paw," one of the most iconic horror tales in English. Though his supernatural output was small, his tightly constructed stories like "The Well" and "Jerry Bundler" are known for their quiet tension and psychological unease.

AMBROSE BIERCE (1842–c. 1914) was an American journalist, satirist, and Civil War veteran who became known for his biting wit and pessimistic worldview, most famously in *The Devil's Dictionary*. His supernatural fiction, much of it collected in *Can Such Things Be?*, is stark and surreal, often shaped by trauma, battlefield death, and philosophical unease.

EDGAR ALLAN POE (1809–1849) was an American writer, editor, and critic widely considered one of the foundational figures in the development of modern horror and Gothic literature. Known for "The Raven," "The Tell-Tale Heart," and "The Fall of the House of Usher," his work is steeped in themes of madness, grief, and the macabre—fertile ground for the horror and ghost story genres he helped define.

F. MARION CRAWFORD (1854–1909) was an American expatriate who spent most of his life in Italy and achieved success with both historical novels and supernatural fiction. His ghost stories, including "The Upper Berth," "The Screaming Skull," and "The Doll's Ghost," are known for their realism, atmospheric buildup, and psychological intensity.

EDITH NESBIT (1858–1924) was a British writer and cofounder of the socialist Fabian Society, best remembered for children's books like *The Railway Children* and *Five Children and It*. She also wrote supernatural fiction for adults, which placed ghostly phenomena and uncanny elements into familiar domestic settings, with stories like "Man-Size in Marble," "The Ebony Frame," and "John Charrington's Wedding."

WASHINGTON IRVING (1783–1859), often called the "Father of American Literature," was a prominent author, essayist, historian, and diplomat born in New York City. One of the first American authors to gain international fame with works like "Rip Van Winkle" and "The Legend of Sleepy Hollow," he blended European folklore with early American settings, laying the groundwork for the country's supernatural literary tradition.

ELIZABETH STUART PHELPS (1844–1911) was an early feminist American author from Massachusetts and the daughter of a minister. A pioneering voice in nineteenth-century literature, she challenged traditional Christian doctrine and gender roles in works like her bestselling spiritualist novel *The Gates Ajar*, which explores grief, the soul, and emotional bonds that continue beyond death.

MARY ELIZABETH BRADDON (1835–1915) was an English actress-turned-author who became famous for her sensational novel *Lady Audley's Secret*. Alongside her crime fiction, she wrote several ghost stories—such as "The Cold Embrace," "The Shadow in the Corner," and "Eveline's Visitant"—that explore themes of gender roles, social mobility, and domestic unease, often centering on women whose fates unfold with grim inevitability.

AMELIA B. EDWARDS (1831–1892) was a British novelist, journalist, and pioneering Egyptologist who cofounded the Egypt Exploration Fund. Her supernatural stories—such as "The Phantom Coach," "The Four-Fifteen Express," and "A Night on the Borders of the Black Forest"—are known for their vivid sense of place, isolation, and suspense rooted in travel and unfamiliar terrain.

PAUL LAURENCE DUNBAR (1872–1906) was a pioneering Black poet and novelist from Ohio, and one of the first to gain national literary recognition in both dialect and standard English with works like *Lyrics of Lowly Life*. His writing explores themes of injustice, spiritual reckoning, and ancestral memory, often drawing on Black oral and folkloric traditions, as seen in "The Haunted Oak."

A NOTE ON THE TYPE

This book is set in a digital version of types acquired in Europe and bequeathed to the University of Oxford by Bishop John Fell in 1686, collectively known as the Fell types. They come from a time when printers were not overly concerned with the stylistic integrity of their types and unabashedly combined French Renaissance italics cut by Robert Granjon with Baroque Dutch romans cut by Christoffel van Dijck some one hundred years later—a pairing that is indeed encountered in some weights of the Fell types. This eclectic and imperfect, but influential, collection of imports from the continent planted the seed for the flowering of original British typography under Caslon and Baskerville that followed in the eighteenth century. The digital revivals used in this book are Double Pica for text with Great Primer for display, both originally commissioned by John Fell from Peter de Walpergen in the first half of the seventeenth century, based on contemporary Dutch models, and re-created by Igino Marini in digital form in the first decade of the twenty-first century.

Front Cover: *The Legend of Sleepy Hollow* by John A. Rice
Frontispiece: *October Moon* by John A. Rice

PROJECT EDITOR: Lauren Orthey
PROOFREADER: Jennifer Dixon
DESIGN: Misha Beletsky
PRODUCTION DIRECTOR: Louise Kurtz

 The text of this book was set in IM Fell Types. Printed in China.

First edition
10 9 8 7 6 5 4 3 2 1

ISBN 978-0-7892-1519-2

Library of Congress Cataloging-in-Publication Data available upon request

For bulk and premium sales and for text adoption procedures, write to Customer Service Manager, Abbeville Press, 655 Third Avenue, New York, NY 10017, or call 1-800-ARTBOOK.

Visit Abbeville Press online at www.abbeville.com.